Vam,

Supernaturally Yours Book One

S Lucas

To Emma

Thank you so much for your support.

S Lucas ♡

Vampire Kissed

(Supernaturally Yours Book One)

S Lucas

Copyright © 2022

S Lucas All rights reserved

This work of fiction is intended for mature audiences only.

The characters and events portrayed in this book are fictitious. Any similarity to real persons, living or dead are entirely coincidental.

S Lucas asserts the moral right to be identified as the author of this work.

No part of this book may be reproduced, or stored in a retrieval system, or transmitted in any form or by any means, electronic, mechanical, photocopying, recording, or otherwise, without express written permission of the author.

It is illegal to copy this book, post it to a website or distribute it any other means without permission.

Cover design: Blue Crescent Covers

Editor: BBB Publishings

Proofreader: Proofreading by Mich

slucasauthor@gmail.com

Preface

A lot happens in this story, and it's been a bit of a rollercoaster ride during the writing and editing process. After seeing a cover on a group, the characters all decided they were taking up permanent residence in my brain until I wrote their story. I had so many other things to be working on when NaNoWriMo started on November 1st, but these guys just took over and that was that.

Compared to my previous books, this one definitely touches on some much darker themes, so please make sure to read the content warning before proceeding.

Most of all I just really hope you enjoy the world and characters I have created, this won't be the last time this world is visited.

Content Warning

This is a paranormal reverse harem and has darker themes that may be triggering to some readers including:
- Sexual assault (including rape, not to the FMC)
- Strong violence
- Necrophilia

There is also M/M action between the men in the harem. Please keep these in mind before reading this story.

Prologue

Demi

The world has changed so much since my parents were children and not for the better. They used to tell me stories of how there was a time when humans ruled the world. But that's not the case anymore. Everything has changed. In fact, at this point, the world has gone to shit, or at least it has, in my opinion. When my parents were still kids, the world was normal. But then the supernaturals came out of the closet. The demons dragged themselves out of Hell in search of souls; the vampires came out of the shadows thirsting for blood, and the wolves crept out of the forest, taking women and dragging them back to their lairs. Or at least that's how the stories go.

Now they run the world, different supernaturals claiming their own territories. The United States has been split into factions, each taken over by a different type of supernatural. The vampires took the West, the wolves, the mountains and central, and the demons took the East. They make the rules now; what they say goes. Their takeover was slow at first, slipping into important roles and working their way to the top. There were some already hiding in plain sight we didn't know about. But once the others made themselves known, the rest followed suit until they were in charge.

There is now a Supernatural Council, with one member from each species, that runs their designated territories. The demons claim souls to take back to Hell, and once your time is up, you're all theirs. They can make all the deals they want and there is nothing anyone can do about it. The wolves have a ball each year to find their mate. All women of age must attend. In my area, the vampires are in charge. Each month, they require everyone over the age of eighteen to donate blood. If you don't donate and try to run from it, they hunt you down.

There are few who miss their monthly donation, and those that do are never seen again. For all I know, they kill you on sight. Or they could take you to harvest your blood, leaving you hooked up to machines to drain you at a slow enough rate so you keep replenishing it. Those in charge say they need the blood donations to keep the vampires fed, to keep them civilized, and to stop the risk of them draining people dry. But I'm not sure I believe that anymore. I've seen too much over the years.

My parents were born in Oregon. Even after they knew who was taking over, my grandparents didn't want to leave. They stayed, and here we are to this day, or at least this is where I still am. My brother Antonio left not long after my parents died. The cops filed their deaths as a home invasion gone wrong, but I never believed that, not after how I found them.

My mom had called me that fateful night. I still remember her screams as she told me a monster had killed my dad. Then the screams stopped, and the line went dead. I'd rushed straight over to their house, breaking every speed limit to get there. The door was ajar and I'll never forget what I saw when I opened it. There was blood everywhere. Odd you might think, for vampires. I found my dad in the living room, covered in claw marks, with his throat ripped out. I'd jumped into nurse mode and checked his pulse, but with the extent of his injuries, I already knew he was dead.

Walking carefully around the blood pool surrounding his body, I made my way along the hall to my parents' bedroom.

That's where I'd found my mom. Her eyes were looking straight at the door, her hand out to the side and the phone she'd called me from on the floor next to the bed. It was smashed to pieces as if someone had trodden on it. She was no longer clothed. Her legs were splayed open, and every inch of her skin was covered in blood.

I had crumpled to the floor next to the bed, holding her cold hand. That's where the cops I didn't remember calling had found me; my cell phone clutched in my fingers, tears streaming down my face. When they tried to move me, I started screaming, and they had to sedate me in the back of the ambulance. That's where my brother had found me after they'd called him. Curled up in a ball on a gurney, staring at the blood coating my skin.

Shaking my head, I pull myself away from the images flashing up in my mind. I know it wasn't a home invasion, it couldn't have been. There was too much blood, and after the cops had done their thing and left, I checked the house. Nothing had been taken, not even my mother's diamond necklace. Her words about the monster were cemented in my mind. She hadn't said 'intruder'; she'd said monster. But what kind?

A vampire would have drained their blood, not let it splatter all over the walls and floor. Blood is too precious a commodity to be wasted to vampires. I know there are other supernaturals in the area, however, they can only enter with special permission from those in charge. But what if there is something flying under the radar that they don't know about?

My brother asked me to leave with him, but I refused. My life was here. As soon as he thought I was okay, he hightailed it out of town and left me here to fend for myself. He still calls me once a month, but our calls are mundane. We tell each other about work. I never tell him I miss him, and he doesn't say it either. We never talk about what happened to our parents. It's a no-go subject. I tried to tell him what I saw straight after the attack, but he refused to listen and told me it was a home invasion.

Chapter 1

Demi

Looking down at my gloved hands, they are stained with blood. But it's not mine, just like it wasn't that night my parents died. Some days working in the emergency department are harder than others. You take the wins where you can find them because the losses are so hard. Having to tell families their loved one has died is one of the hardest things I have to do.

Taking off my gloves, I dump them into the trash can, sanitizing my hands as I leave. A multi-vehicle accident on the 205 left us needing all hands on deck. My patient, a young woman named Cindy Mitchell, had come in with crush injuries and internal damage. No matter what we did, there was no way to save her. It is her blood on my hands.

A hand on my shoulder startles me and I whirl my head around. Doctor Michael Scott, my friend and boss, is standing behind me. His face is solemn, and he looks as tired as I feel. It's been a hard shift, and the death of Cindy has taken its toll on both of us. Resting my hand on his, my shoulders droop as I let out a sigh.

"Your shift ended thirty minutes ago, Demi. Go get changed and head home. I'll speak to Miss Mitchell's family."

"Thanks, Doctor Scott." I would never think to call him by his first name in the ER, but we've been friends ever since I started at the hospital.

Michael gives my shoulder a squeeze before removing his hand and heading to the family room where Cindy's parents are waiting for news about their daughter. I watch as he walks away. I should go with him and offer my support, but I'm exhausted to the point where I just want to drop where I'm standing. All I need to do is get back to the locker room, get out of my scrubs, and head home.

Glancing at my watch, it's 6:32 am. My shift was meant to end at six, but with multiple casualties coming in, it wasn't like I could stop chest compressions and walk away. Leaving the ER, I head for the locker room. When I get inside, there is no one else around. I open my locker and grab my clothes, shoving them onto the bench behind me. Slipping off my crocs, I drop my pants and tug my shirt over my head. The blood on them still isn't quite dry.

Standing in just my underwear and socks, I grab my laundry bag and shove the dirty clothes and shoes inside. I have a pile of scrubs waiting at home to be washed. Slipping into my jeans, I tug them up my legs before throwing on a t-shirt and hoodie. The bench is hard beneath me as I pull on my sneakers and let out another sigh.

I still have to drive home, but the temptation to just call for an Uber and pick up my car over the weekend is real. Maybe I could even leave it here until my next shift on Saturday. Taking my hair out of my now messy ponytail, I pull the loose strands back from my face and throw it into a bun and gather up my things.

The locker room door opens, and Michael shuffles inside. His face is drawn, and there are dark circles under his brown eyes. His eyes drift to me and he smiles weakly.

"You okay?" He makes his way over to me, throwing an arm over my shoulder and pulling me close.

"I'll be fine. I just need to sleep. Though I'm not sure how much of that I'll get, Ginny's still dragging me out tonight." I shrug.

"Give her my love. Wish I could come out tonight, but my dad's not feeling too good. Promised my mom I'd head over for the weekend, take her to the store and stuff."

"You're a good son, Michael. I'm sure Momma Scott will appreciate it. Tell her I said hi." His mom is the sweetest woman I've met. Both his parents are amazing, just like him.

Leaning up, I give him a kiss on the cheek and smile. He squeezes me tighter. We've always had an easy friendship, even though he's my boss and meant to be totally off-limits. There was one night after one too many bottles of wine, but we realized it just would not work. We were better as friends than lovers.

"I'll see you on Sunday, Demi. Don't do anything I wouldn't do and try not to be too hung over for your shift on Saturday."

"So pretty much nothing, then?" I let out a giggle, and Michael joins me in my laughter.

Dropping his arm to his side, he kisses the top of my head and I leave the locker room. I walk past a few other nurses and doctors, nodding at them as I pass and head for the exit. The sun is barely up as I leave through the double doors. A few ambulances are pulling up, but I keep walking. My shift is over. It's someone else's problem now, as hard as that is for me to think.

As I move across the parking lot, a shiver races down my spine. I stop and look over my shoulder. It feels like someone is watching me, but I don't see anyone else. Hurrying along, I pull my keys out of my bag. When I reach my car, I open the door and jump inside, engaging the locks as soon as the door is closed.

Throwing both bags into the passenger seat, I scan the lot again, but it's still empty.

You're just tired, Demi. Stop freaking yourself out.

Jamming my key into the ignition, I start the car and head for home. I can rarely park directly outside my apartment, but there's a small lot at the end of the block. When I pull in, there are a few empty spaces available. Shifting my car into one of them, I grab my stuff and get out.

The walk to my apartment is slow. All I want right now is my bed. As I get closer to the apartment block door, I shiver again, but this time I ignore it. Opening the main door, I head inside and check my mailbox, just the usual bills and junk mail. They can wait for now. Moving down the hall, I reach my door and use the key to let myself in.

I kick off my shoes as I make my way across the living room, heading straight for my bedroom. It's pitch black in here, and I thank God for blackout curtains. Shoving the door shut, I don't even bother to turn on the light. I drop my laundry by the door and take my other bag to the bed. Plugging my phone in, I leave it on the side table.

One by one I shrug off my clothing, bar my t-shirt. I let them all drop to the floor along with my bra and crawl under the sheets. As soon as my eyes close, I'm dead to the world.

I'm running through a forest. My arms and legs are being whipped by twigs as I rush past them, but I can't stop. My heart is pounding out of my chest as I pump my arms. I can feel my calves cramping. My feet are bare, and every pound of them against the ground sends lightning pain through the soles of my feet as the debris littering the floor cuts them open.

A growl echoes around the forest. It's so close. When it comes again, it sounds like it's just behind me. Keep going, Demi. Just keep going. *I know I need to. I just don't know how much longer I can keep up this pace. I glance over my shoulder, but all I see are shadows. As I swing my head back around, I see it. A gnarled tree root in my path. I can't avoid it, and I don't have enough time to slow down.*

My left foot tangles underneath it and I go down hard. A solid blow to my knees as I land. My hands only just stop my face from smashing into the ground. Air rushes out of my lungs from the impact as I crawl across the leaf strewn dirt.

I need to get up, but my ankle is throbbing. I feel breath glance off the back of my neck, and I throw myself onto my back. Something jumps on top of me, and a scream escapes through my lips. Glowing eyes and fangs descend on me as I scream again, my hands raised above me to defend myself.

Sitting bolt upright in bed, my scream follows me from the dream world. My eyes cut around my darkened room. Scrambling for the lamp beside my bed, I click the switch and light floods the room, blotting out most of the darkness. Looking around again, there's no one in here but me. Resting my hand on my chest, I wait for my heart rate to return to normal. I've been having nightmares since the night my parents died, and they are always much worse after a bad night in the ER.

Pulling myself out of bed, I head for the shower and turn on the water. I have a few hours to get myself ready for tonight. Looking in the mirror, I'm going to need it. That and at least a bucket's worth of coffee. Stepping into the shower, I scrub my hair and body clean, washing away the grime from work.

Wrapped up in a towel, I head into the open plan lounge that leads into the kitchen and go straight to the coffee machine, clicking it on. The rich aroma floods the room as the liquid gold drips into the pot. Filling a cup, I dump in two sugars and creamer before taking a sip. With my towel still wrapped around me, I potter around my apartment for a while as I drink my coffee.

Looking out of the window, I can see the multiple shadows thrown across the grass in the yard behind my building as the sun disappears from the sky, I must have slept the day away. As I focus on the shadows, they seem to shift. Glowing eyes blink at me, and I take a step back from the window. What the hell is out there? When I look again, the eyes are gone. I mustn't be getting enough sleep at the moment. I'm seeing things and my nerves are fried.

I'm not sure if I want to go out tonight anymore, but I promised Ginny we'd go for belated drinks to celebrate her birthday. My shifts had fallen so that I couldn't make the original plan with the rest of our friends. I wanted to do something during the day; it's the safest time for us humans, but she wanted to go to this club that another of our friends had told her about and I don't want to disappoint her. We'd done nights out before and I'm not sure what is putting me off so much this time. Something in the back of my mind is making me wary, warning me about something. I don't trust the monsters. I haven't since that day, but this week it's been worse.

Most people live their lives normally, or as normal as they can when surrounded by vampires. They go out with friends, go to clubs, and drink the night away. Not me; I've always been cautious when I've gone out. We've usually gone out in a larger group, but this time it's just me and Ginny.

This is a bad idea.

Refilling my coffee cup, I move into the bedroom and grab the outfit I've already prepared off the hanger. Sliding the lace panties up my legs, I slip on the matching bra before I step into my dress and pull it up my body. I down my coffee and blow-dry my hair, styling it into soft curls that frame my face.

Checking myself in the mirror one last time, I fluff up my hair using my hands and smack my lips together before blowing a kiss at my reflection. Even if I say so myself, I look good tonight. My little black dress hugs my curves in all the right places, and my breasts look fantastic. Happy with how I look, I head back to the kitchen. Grabbing my cell phone and keys off the counter, I stuff them into my purse. I snatch my black leather moto jacket off the back of the couch as I walk through my living room and slip it over my shoulders.

I do one last check of my bag. Keys... check, cell phone... check, pepper spray... check, silver stake... check. Yep, I have a stake in my purse. I never leave home without it. I don't care that the Council says vampires aren't dangerous and are all law-abiding citizens. If I'm going out when they're in their element, I want some semblance of protection from them. They're faster than humans, stronger than us, too. Oh, and they like to drink blood.

The Council may tell everyone that vampires only drink donated blood that every citizen gives once a month, but I've seen some of the victims that come into the ER. All with their throats ripped out and their blood drained, even if *they* try to cover it up. There's no way I'm leaving the house without my trusty stake; tonight is no different.

Walking out of my apartment, I close the door and double-check that it's locked behind me before heading to the main door. A shiver runs down my spine as I head out into the cold night air. Looking out across the street, I don't see anyone around, but I feel tense, like someone might be watching me. Trying to shake off the feeling, I grab my cell out of my bag and request an Uber. The app tells me it'll be here in three minutes. I really should have done it whilst I was still in the warmth and safety of my apartment, but shit happens.

Standing on the steps outside my building, I lean against the stone pillar. My eyes continue to scan the street. Maybe I should head back inside to wait, but I'm already outside now and considering how close the Uber is, it would be silly. A movement to my right pulls my attention and I look down the street. I catch a figure cloaked in the shadows. Squinting, I try to see who's lurking, but I can't see a thing.

A horn honking has me almost jumping out of my skin as the Uber pulls up next to the curb. Clutching a hand to my chest, I take a deep breath to calm myself before walking down the steps and straight to the car. I climb into the backseat. The driver checks my destination, and we pull away from the curb. As we pass where I thought I saw the figure, I stare out into the darkness but there's nothing there.

Looking down at my cell, I open my messages.

On my way, meet you outside.

I shoot a message off to Ginny and it isn't long before three dots appear as she writes a response.

You better hurry up, biatch. I'm freezing my balls off out here. Shots are on you tonight!

A small laugh slips through my lips, and I shake my head. I love Ginny, but any time we go out she wants shots, and those are my worst enemy. Give me beer any day of the week and I can drink it for hours, but the minute I drink shots, I'm a lost cause. We both are. I'm often surprised we make it home afterward. The friends we usually go out with always make sure we do. At least I don't have to be at work until the early shift on Saturday.

That gives me tomorrow to recover.

Chapter 2

Demi

Looking out at the street, it's so quiet outside. It's almost eerie, but as we get closer to downtown, I see more and more people. Most of them are in clubwear, ready for a night out full of debauchery, among other things. The Uber slows and pulls up next to the busy curb. We're right outside the club, and there's a long line wrapping around the building already. Thanking the driver, I get out and adjust the hem of my dress. Hopefully, I didn't flash anyone my lacy panties as I got out.

Adding a tip and rating for my journey, I text Ginny to let her know I'm here. I look around, trying to spot her in the crowd of people, but I can't see her. There are just too many people. Someone passes by me, a hand slipping across my back as they pass. Another shiver races down my spine and I whip my head around. My hair falls in front of my face as I try to see who exactly caused the sensation, but they are lost in the crowd.

"Demi! Demi, over here!" A familiar voice shouts out to me. I turn in its direction and spot Ginny. She's waving frantically from within the line.

Rushing over to her, I throw my arms around her across the roped-off line. I'm enveloped by her familiar honeysuckle perfume, and I let out a deep breath, the goosebumps that erupted on my flesh slowly subsiding.

"What took you so long? I saved you a space." She unhooks the rope and drags me through before re-hooking it. There are a few grumbles from the people behind us in the line, but she just smiles at them as she wraps her hand around mine and pulls me close.

"I have no idea what you mean." Glancing at my phone, I check the time. "It only took me twenty minutes to get here."

"Exactly, that's twenty minutes of birthday drinking time." She lets out a laugh and I can't help but join in with her.

Now I'm closer to my friend, I feel safe. I don't know what is wrong with me tonight. Maybe working long hours is finally taking its toll and I'm getting jittery from the lack of sleep. Thinking about the night I found my parents hasn't helped in the slightest and I feel like I'm ready to jump out of my own skin at any moment.

The line slowly moves closer and closer to the door. There is a huge sign above it. 'Dark Desires' is written in red, and there's what looks like blood dripping down from below the first and last letters. *Interesting name.* I can feel the thump of the bass in the music through the soles of my feet. A couple of people ahead of us get turned away, but I can't work out why. The group looks ready to start a fight with the bouncer, but a quick flash of his fangs has them holding their hands up and retreating away from the door.

Shit, there's a vampire working the door. Where the hell has Ginny brought me?

I look over at my friend, but she doesn't seem phased by what just happened. She's bouncing on her feet, excited for the night ahead. I'm just not feeling it. My anxiety is shooting through the roof. First, the sense of being watched, then shadows on my street, and now the vampire bouncer is making it so much worse. I lean closer to Ginny.

"What the hell is this place, Gin? The bouncer is a freaking vampire." I glance back over at him, and he grins at me. *Shit, he heard me.* Of course he did. He's a vampire with enhanced hearing.

"Yep, I heard the club is owned by vampires, too. Come on, Demi. It'll be fun!" She wraps her arm around my shoulder and pulls me close.

Ginny knows my parents died, but like many others, she thinks it was a home invasion. I never told her I suspected it was something more. She probably wouldn't have believed me, anyway; she's pro supernatural. I blame all the romance books she's been reading about them over the years. The authors romanticize them and don't tell the truth about the blood-thirsty monsters they really are.

When we finally reach the front of the line, I'm ready to bolt, but Ginny keeps a firm grip on my hand and won't let go. The bouncer raises an eyebrow as he opens the door for us; I look back at him and he gives me a small nod. Another shiver runs down my spine, but this time it isn't fear. With Ginny still holding onto my hand, the door shuts and submerges us into utter darkness. The music is much louder now we're inside.

Another door opens a few feet ahead of us. The light which floods in temporarily blinds me. I throw my hand in front of my eyes, trying to blink away the spots now dancing in my vision. When we emerge through the door, we're inside the club. Strobe lights are flashing, and the temperature spikes, as we're instantly surrounded by dancing bodies.

Ginny drags me through the throng of people until we hit the bar. It's at least three people deep, everyone clamoring to get a drink. As soon as we are there, the crowd seems to close around us, and my heart rate spikes again. This is not what I class as fun at all. Considering the number of people, it doesn't take long before we are in front of the bar. I look up and down its length, spotting a sign to one side.

NO BLOOD FROM THE VEIN UNLESS PRIOR CONSENT IS GIVEN.
What the fuck?

I expected there to be vampires in a club they owned, but I wasn't expecting them to be allowed to drink from the source. The thought of it creeps me out. I really need to try and monitor my drinking tonight. I don't want to end up as a snack for someone of the fanged variety.

A bartender appears on the other side of the bar. His eyes are black orbs that stare at me as he waits for Ginny to give him our order. Ginny leans across the bar to tell him what we want, but the music is so loud I can't hear what she's saying. My focus isn't really on her though, it stays on the bartender. He's tall, probably over 6ft in height, with dark hair. I can't quite tell if it's black or dark brown in the dimly lit club, but it's short on the sides and long on top. His hair is styled perfectly into a bouffant, and I have the sudden urge to run my fingers through it to mess it up.

His black shirt is tight across the expanse of his chest, the top few buttons are undone, showing off golden skin and black swirling lines. His sleeves are rolled up to the elbows, and there is more black ink adorning his forearms. As he turns to get our drinks, I can see the tightness of his jeans across his ass, and my thighs clench together. He turns back with several shots in his hands, his eyes connect with mine, and his nostrils flare. A ring of red appears around the black orbs.

I swallow hard as it hits me that he's a vampire.

It's a vampire club, Demi. There's going to be more vampires working here than just the bouncer.

I roll my shoulders back and attempt to stand tall. Ginny turns to me and holds out her hand. I remember the fact she said that shots were on me. Reaching into my purse, I pull two twenties and hand them to her.

The bartender drops the shots on the counter and takes the money from her, his eyes only leaving mine as he turns his back to us again and moves to the cash register. He's back a few seconds later with the change, but instead of handing it to Ginny, he holds it out to me. Tentatively, I reach out my hand and he drops it into my open palm. His fingers trace across the skin of my hand as he does and a bolt of electricity runs up my arm, making me clench my thighs again.

I quickly snatch my hand back, shaking it out slightly to disperse the weird feeling. I put the change back in my purse and grab a shot from the counter, downing it in one before slamming the glass back down. Ginny grabs a few of the shots and I grab what's left. She tilts her head to one side, motioning for me to follow her. Staying behind her, I risk one last look over my shoulder at the bartender and he smiles, a hint of fang showing. It should creep me out, but instead, I'm finding it sexy.

For fuck's sake, Demi. Get your mind out of the gutter. You do not find vampires hot!

Weaving through the crowd, we finally make it to an area where there are fewer people and some empty booths. The dark red leather seats are half circles, with round tables in the middle. Sliding in, I shrug off my jacket as I deposit the shot glasses on the table and spot another sign on the wall.

PLEASE REFRAIN FROM DRAINING OTHER PATRONS, BODY DISPOSAL IS EXPENSIVE.

My mouth drops open as I take in the sign.

It has to be a joke, right?

"Demi, this is so amazing." Ginny all but shouts down my ear, wanting to be heard over the music.

She grabs a glass and downs it. I can only nod weakly in reply. Picking up another drink, I'm going to need all the Dutch courage I can muster to not bolt. I throw the shot back and wince as the alcohol burns down my throat. We've only been here twenty minutes and I already want to leave. We usually go to human-run bars, and this place is making me nervous. I don't want to think about how many vampires are in this bar right now.

There are still a few human-only places, or at least, places that vampires tend not to lurk. The hospital, for example. With their own abilities to heal, there is absolutely no need for them to be there. Whilst vampires may run the hospital at the very top, just like every other business, they still have humans running the everyday things.

Leaning back in my seat, I drink the last of my shots and line the glasses up on the table. The alcohol doesn't take long to work its way into my system and I'm finally loosening up. Ginny is bouncing to the music next to me, and I sway along with the beat. The anxiety that was wracking my body slowly dissipates. I nudge Ginny and point to the dance floor; she gives me a nod and we shuffle out of the booth, leaving our jackets on the seat.

Taking her hand in mine, we move back through the crowd till we reach the dance floor. The music changes to something with a faster tempo and I shake my hips to it. Running my fingers through my hair and down the sides of my body, Ginny dances with me, and I spin her around and pull her closer.

I feel sudden heat against my back as a body presses up against me. Their warmth engulfs me as I shimmy my body up and down theirs. Hands land on my hips and pull me closer until my back is to their front from head to toe. My alcohol-addled brain doesn't even seem to care whether they're human or vampire but being surrounded by so many witnesses helps ease my usual anxieties. Reaching back my hand, I run it up the side of their face, and tangle my fingers in their hair. From what I can feel, it runs past their ears with a slight wave. One of their hands creeps itself up the side of my body, around the outer curve of my breast, and up the inside of my bare arm, leaving a trail of goosebumps in their wake.

My ass brushes against their crotch, and I can feel their obvious arousal as they rub against me. I clench my thighs again. Turning, I close my eyes and wrap them around my dance partner's neck. Inhaling deeply, I can smell damp pine. The smell draws me in, and I lean in closer.

His nose brushes up against the column of my neck, and his lips brush just below it. I don't know what has come over me, but I can feel the dampness between my legs. His arousal now presses against my stomach, twitching against me as I let the music take over. His hands move down my back to the swell of my ass, pulling me hard against him. I lift my arms above my head and lace my fingers together as I sway within his arms.

The current song ends and the heat encasing me disappears. I open my eyes, but whoever I was dancing with is gone as quickly as he appeared. My eyes dart around, trying to spot where my dancing partner went, but the surrounding people are dancing with others and I don't feel like any of them are him. Turning back to Ginny, I see she's dancing away with her tongue thrust down some random guy's throat.

Shaking my head, I head back to the bar. I feel eyes burning into my back, but when I glance over my shoulder, I can't see anyone looking in my direction. My skin prickles for a few seconds before the sensation disappears just as fast.

Shrugging my shoulders, I continue my journey to the bar. It's another fight to get to the front, but once I'm there, I glance around to see if the vampire bartender from earlier is around. My shoulders slump when I realize he's no longer behind the bar.

Why are you even looking for him, Demi? He's a vampire.

A tall blonde comes over to serve me instead. She's wearing a corset that pushes her breasts up almost to her chin.

"What can I get you?" She shouts over the music, leaning over the bar as she does. Her cleavage nearly pops out of her top.

"Rum and Coke, no ice and a Peach Schnapps and lemonade." I've had enough shots at this point, and I'm not letting Ginny have any more either. I don't want to have to carry her home.

The blonde nods and turns her back to me to make the drinks. Once they're done, she places them down on the bar and I pass her a twenty. When she's back with my change, I throw a few ones into the tip jar and grab the drinks.

The table is still empty, and our jackets are still on the seats when I get back to it. Dropping down onto the spongy leather, I place the glasses on the table before taking a sip of my rum and Coke. I look out towards the dance floor to see if Ginny is still there, but I can't see her over the crowd of people between the seating and the dance floor.

My eyes move to the booth next to where I'm sitting. There's a guy with his back to me and a woman sitting on his lap, her head buried in his neck. I can't quite see her face through the curtain of hair covering it, but I can see her body gyrating to the music. Her head stays close to his neck and her hands run through his hair.

With a thump of the bass, she lifts her head and looks straight at me. Her eyes are ringed with red, and her lips are covered in blood. A small trickle runs down the side of her mouth and down her chin. As she watches me, she licks her lips. A finger raises to her chin and wipes up the trail. She opens her mouth, and I can see her blood-stained fangs, as she sucks her finger in and licks the blood away.

I swallow hard. I can't seem to pull my eyes away from the scene in front of me. Tilting the guy's head to the side, she licks up the column of his neck, keeping those red-rimmed eyes on mine. A shiver runs down my spine, and I grip the glass in my hand tighter, almost to the point I think I'm going to shatter the glass.

Finally, she pulls her eyes away from mine as she leans into the guy for a kiss. I'm still looking their way when someone obscures my view. Pulling my gaze away, I realize it's Ginny. Grabbing her glass, she mouths a thank you and downs it in one. I take a few more sips of my drink. I still can't believe we're in a vampire club and I thought the signs were a joke. After what I just witnessed, I guess not.

Chapter 3

Demi

Vampires really do make me uneasy. Yes, I may technically work for them, considering they run the city and the entirety of the West, but to see them feeding on someone out in the open, without a care in the world doesn't sit right with me. I knew there were clubs like this, I just never expected to end up in one. I'm really going to need to have a word with Ginny tomorrow after she's sobered up.

As I'm lost in my own thoughts, Ginny taps my hand and points off into the distance. I attempt to follow her finger, but I'm not sure where she's pointing. Looking back at her with questioning eyes, I shake my head and she leans forwards, dragging me closer to her.

"Bathroom." She shouts down my ear and I give her a nod.

She steps out from between the table and seats, and I notice the woman and the guy in the other booth have both disappeared to who knows where.

She's probably dragged him outside into a dark alley to drain him.

My thoughts run wild as I think of possible scenarios. Drinking the last of my beverage, I consider grabbing us both another while Ginny is in the bathroom.

A figure steps in front of me as I'm about to stand and I look up. I can't quite see the man's features with the light behind him, but he looks tall from where I'm sitting. Shifting across to sit in front of me, he drops down in the seating opposite me. My eyes follow his movements, causing me to raise an eyebrow as I look him up and down. He's wearing a dark t-shirt with a well-worn leather jacket over the top of it. His messy, dark blond hair looks greasy and is slicked back. *Ew, is grease the new hair gel?* His amber eyes never move from observing me.

"Sorry, that seat is taken. My friend is just in the restroom," I shout across to him, but he just shrugs at me. "Fine, if you want the booth, we'll move."

I grab mine and Ginny's jackets and slide to the edge of the seat. I'm about to stand again but another figure stops me, getting up in my space and the only thing I can do is move back. A hand on my shoulder shoves me back down on the seat.

"Going somewhere, princess?" The man who speaks looks just as greasy and disheveled as his companion.

"Like I just told your friend, if you want the booth, we can move." I try to rise, but he stops me.

The guy flops down into the booth next to me, his body close to mine, and I can't seem to keep my distance from him. I want to slide away, but his hand moves down to my bare leg. His fingers grasp my thigh, nails digging into my skin, and I let out a yelp at the sting of pain. My hand claws at the top of his, trying to pull his fingers off me, but he just holds on tighter.

"Where do you think you're going, princess?" His voice sends shivers through my entire body, setting my nerves on edge, and I want to run. I *need* to run.

"Please, I have to go. I need to find my friend."

"Awww, stay awhile, princess. We don't bite, not unless you ask nicely." He leans closer to me and I lean away, but he pulls me back toward him.

"Get off me." A laugh across the table has my eyes whipping over to his friend. He's smirking now, his eyes glowing as he licks his lips.

The guy next to me leans closer, his nose pushing into my neck as he holds me by my leg. His tongue darts out and licks my neck. Without thinking, I grab him by the hair and pull him away, slamming my fist into his groin. He lets out a grunt and loosens his grip on me. With all the strength I can muster, I shove him hard and he falls sideways off the seat.

Jumping up, I duck out of the booth, leaving both jackets on the seat. A hand wraps around my wrist and pulls me to an abrupt stop. I turn and see the guy from the other side holding tight to my arm. He pulls me close to him, his lips brushing against my ear, and I shiver with fear.

"Don't run too far, princess. This hunt must end." He lets go of my arm and I'm off.

Heading in the direction of the restroom, I shove through the people in my way. Some of them snarl at me, but I don't care right now. I need to find Ginny. Bursting into the bathroom, I startle a few of the occupants with my actions.

"Ginny! Ginny! Where are you?" I shout. It's quieter in the bathroom. If she's in here, she'll hear me.

"Demi?" Her voice calls back from inside the stall to the left.

I head in that direction and start banging on the door. When she opens it, she looks a little disheveled, but otherwise okay.

"We need to go, Ginny. We have to get out of here."

I grab her hand, not even giving her time to flush the toilet before I drag her out of the stall and toward the exit of the bathroom. Her hand slams against the door before I can get it open.

"Demi, stop! You need to calm down. What's going on?"

"Look, there were some really creepy guys out there. We just need to go, okay?" My voice is trembling as I speak.

I don't know exactly what it was about them, but my instincts are telling me I should get out of here. I need Ginny to come with me and stop asking me questions. We have to get going, and we need to get going now.

"Please, Ginny," I beg, "can we just go? I don't want to be here anymore." I squeeze her hand, my breathing coming out in harsh pants.

"Okay, Demi. I need you to breathe." She pulls my face up to look at her for a brief second before she looks down at my hands. "We can come back in the day for our jackets, okay?"

I'm shaking so hard now, I can't answer. My breathing is labored and I struggle to get it under control, and my chest feels like I have an elephant sitting on it. I give her a small nod, and she smiles at me. Opening the door, she pulls me into the corridor, but instead of heading for the main area, she drags me the other way toward the emergency exit sign.

When we reach the end, she pushes down on the panic bar and the door swings open. The cold air rushes through the opening, making us both shiver. As we get outside, she lets the door shut behind us. The weight on my chest lifts suddenly, and I feel so much better already.

Chapter 4

Demi

"This way." Ginny points to the exit of the alley and what I hope leads up back to the main road.

Ginny wraps her arm around me and pulls me close. It's freezing outside, and we hold each other close as we walk to share our body heat. A whole-body shiver runs through me.

"Tut, tut, tut. Where do you think you're going, princess?" The voice stops me in my tracks, and I pull Ginny to a sudden stop beside me.

I look up; the guy from across the table is staring straight at me with two men flanking him. There's something seriously wrong with all of them; they move like predators and I'm their prey. Their presence is telling everything in me to run away and not look back.

Ginny and I both spin on our heels and take off at a run down the alley. We're almost at the end when another figure steps out in front of us. I let out a yelp. It's the other guy from the table and he too has men flanking him.

"What the hell do you want from us?" Ginny screams at them.

"It's not you we want, little bitch." The guy in the middle calls out, taking a step toward us.

Ginny pulls me back to create some distance between us and them, but this just brings us closer to the three at the other end of the alley. It won't be long until they surround us, and there is nowhere else for us to go.

As they draw closer to us, a noise behind me pulls my attention to the other group. I spin round. One of the three is now naked, his eyes glowing brightly. The fact he has stripped should bother me, but it doesn't. It's the noise his body is making, like breaking bones - that's what bothers me. And from what I'm seeing, his bones are breaking in front of me, elongating in some places, shortening in others.

My stomach is churning. I have the sudden urge to throw up, but for some reason, I can't look away. He drops to all fours and hair sprouts across his naked skin, covering every inch of his body from head to toe. The last part that changes is his face. His jaw lengthens and his ears get longer and pointier.

In one blink, there is no longer a man standing in front of me, but a wolf. An enormous, snarling wolf. I let out a scream, and Ginny finally turns as well. Her mouth opens, ready to scream, but a hand wraps around her neck, cutting off the sound before she can make it.

I jump at the man holding her, punching and kicking at him, trying to loosen his grip on Ginny, but he won't let go. A hand grabs my shoulder and yanks me back so hard that I fly through the air straight into a dumpster in the alley. I let out a strangled cry as the air is pushed from my lungs on impact. I hear a crack, possibly a rib, and the pain is intense.

"Alaric, she's mine! Keep your hands to yourself." A different voice growls nearby.

A figure appears above me and crouches down on his haunches. He puts his fingers under my chin and lifts my head. It's none of the others I've seen so far. This is someone new.

"Now, now, little one. Don't fear me. I've put a lot of time into watching you. You wouldn't want to disappoint me, would you?"

"Who... who are you?" My voice trembles as I speak.

"Oh, you will know me soon. Every single part of me, my body, my cock... I'm going to sink into every one of your holes, and you're going to love every minute."

His words send tremors throughout my body. He's going to rape me, and I don't think there's anything I can do to stop him. My eyes flicker to Ginny. One of the other men is still gripping her by her neck. The enormous wolf circles them, watching one of the other men slice his claws down the front of her dress. They cut the skin there as he rips the tattered fabric from her body.

I can't move, I can't speak. I can only watch. The man in front of me drags me to my feet and pulls my back against his front. His erection pushes into my ass through his jeans, and he grunts. One hand comes across my mouth and the other works down the front of my dress. When he reaches the hem, it disappears beneath it, running up the inside of my thighs.

"Watch now, little one. I've given your friend to my men. I want you to watch as they enjoy her." The hand across my mouth forces me to look at Ginny. I want to close my eyes, but my body won't let me.

There's a resounding crack as one man lashes out and backhands Ginny across the mouth. A sob escapes her lips as she's shoved to the ground. She tries to move, but the wolf latches its mouth onto one arm, as another man grabs the other. She tries to scream, but she can only whimper. They must have broken her jaw with the force of the blow.

I pull against the man holding me, but his grip feels like steel and I can't break loose. His fingers brush against my panties and I squirm, but it only seems to excite him more. He pants down my ear as he rocks his hips against mine.

The man who shoved Ginny to the ground kneels behind her, his jeans undone and his erection already out. With a snap of fabric, he rips away her panties and throws them to one of the other men, who lifts them to his nose and sniffs. The man barks out a laugh as he pockets them.

I try to pull my face away, but a whimper from Ginny pulls my attention back. The man behind her is holding her tight by the hips, claws digging into her flesh and making her bleed as he thrusts inside her. Her eyes are on me, wide and full of terror as tears spill down her cheeks. My own tears drip down my face.

Another man drops his jeans, prying open Ginny's mouth. He shoves himself between her broken jaws. She tries to cry out, but chokes on his member. The man behind me rocks himself against me harder, his fingers now pushing under the lace of my panties and brushing against my core. My hips buck, attempting to get him off, but his grip is relentless.

"Oh, stop now, little one. You're just making me harder. I want to enjoy the show, but if you don't stop, I'll have to fuck you right here, right now."

I stop any movement. I'm hardly even breathing as I'm forced to watch the other men brutalize Ginny. They take it in turns to rape her. I think at some point she lost consciousness. I can only hope she did so she can't feel anything, as the men have their way with her. She's bleeding from one arm where the wolf bit down on her and there are various other wounds that now cover her body.

When the men have finished with her, she's limp, her body splayed out on the floor. The man behind me has been whispering the things he is going to do to me throughout the entire ordeal, but now I just feel numb. I don't know at what point I stopped listening, but his fingers are still buried deep inside me, thrusting even though I'm mostly dry.

"Alaric, come get my little one. I need my turn." He shoves me toward the one called Alaric.

A muscular arm wraps around my front from behind, holding my arms down. This is the one I dick punched in the club. His other hand goes over my mouth to keep me quiet, but I don't have the energy to cry out anymore. The one in wolf form moves closer, sniffing me before sitting down on his haunches next to me. The man who seems to be the leader, the one who calls me 'little one', approaches Ginny's prone form.

His pants are undone, and his hard cock is already out. Pulling Ginny back up to her knees, he holds her there. He dips his fingers into the blood that coats her thighs from where one of the others with claws rip open her flesh and slicks it over his cock. He lines himself up with her back entrance and shoves himself inside with one thrust.

He doesn't relent his thrusts, his passage made slicker by the blood that seems to come from Ginny's body. His moans and grunts make me want to puke. Pulling her lifeless body up against his, he runs his hands over her naked flesh. His claws dig into her skin, blood pooling around them both, but he doesn't seem to care.

I see Ginny's eyes flicker slightly, and my heart all but stops. As her eyes focus on me again, I can see the pain there, the terror. She tries to struggle, but the leader holds her tighter. A hand holding her by the throat.

"Don't struggle, little bitch. I prefer my women when they are compliant." He looks over at me. "Just like my little one over there, she didn't struggle."

Ginny doesn't stop moving, though. She must be in so much pain. They have almost cut her body to shreds, and she's bleeding from everywhere.

"Fine, have it your way!" He bellows.

The hand on her throat tightens, and his fingers dig in. The claws on the tips of his fingers slice into her throat. Blood spills from her mouth as they push through her flesh. He continues to rut into her as he rips her throat out. Blood pours down her neck and her head drops to her chest, her body slumping in his grasp. Even so, he doesn't stop until he groans as he comes.

Pulling his blood and cum covered cock from her body, he lets her drop to the floor to lie in a pool of her own blood. Her eyes are staring into nothing, her legs open and her hand falls to one side. I draw in a sudden breath. I've seen this before, or as near as. My mother's dead body flashes in my mind.

My mind whirls as I look at the scene before me, remembering that horrific night. The markings on Ginny are almost the same as those I found on my mother and father. My eyes connect with the leader of the group as he wipes his bloody hands on his jeans and rises slowly.

His amber eyes glow as he watches me. I know I need to get away. If I don't... I don't even want to think about what will happen to me. But I *know* it will probably end in my death. Without thinking, I grab my captor's hand and try to pull it from my face. It barely moves, but it's enough for me to sink my teeth into his hand. With a howl, he lets go of me and I take off down the alley.

One of the other wolves tries to grab me, but I move my arm at the last second and his claws rake across my side, gouging into my skin. The pain from my ribs and this new wound flares. I place my hand against it and carry on running. I get a little further before an enormous weight lands on my back and takes me to the ground.

My hands and knees scrape on the floor, and my skin tears open. Pain ignites through my shoulder as teeth sink into the soft flesh next to my neck. I feel claws dig into my back and sense the blood pouring from my wounds.

The teeth drag me across the ground until I'm level with Ginny's body. I can see her out of the corner of my eye, her dead eyes staring straight at me.

"Adam, get off her!" The leader's voice bellows. I can hear the anger in his words.

The wolf attached to my neck is ripped away, taking a chunk of my flesh with it. I let out a scream, and a whine sounds off to one side. Hands grab me and roll me over. The leader stares down at me, his eyes wide.

"Goddammit, I told you all no harm was to come to her. What the fuck did you think you were doing?"

My head turns to the side. The wolf is standing close by, one paw raised up off the ground. He's becoming fuzzier as I try to focus on him. I'm exhausted, and the pain is just too much. I want to close my eyes and die. A hand grabs my chin and turns my face back to the leader, but he's just a blur now.

"You don't want to die, little one. I need you alive to bear my pups." His fingers stroke my cheek. "I've been watching you from the shadows for a long time. I've kept you protected. I'd like my investment to stay very much alive."

I try to keep my eyes open, but I'm struggling. The hand holding my chin tilts my head, and lips press against mine. His tongue pushes between my lips, but I don't even react. My body feels heavy. I can feel the life draining out of me. Breaking the kiss, he wrenches my head to the side, inhaling deeply as his nose presses to my neck.

"You smell divine, little one. Fear is so intoxicating. I should take you right now, but that would be a waste considering what I have planned for you."

He lets go of me and my eyes slip shut; the darkness trying to consume me.

"Heal now, little one. I'm sure a fanger will find you soon. The real hunt has only just begun. Run all you like. I have your scent now. No matter where you go, I'll always find you."

I hear footsteps walking further and further away until I can't hear anything anymore. It's silent around me. All I can hear is my labored breathing as I attempt to inhale the oxygen my body craves. As I lay in a pool of mine and Ginny's blood, I reach out my hand, feeling for her. My fingers brush against hers and I weave my fingers between her cool ones. Darkness finally claims me.

Chapter 5

Diego

As soon as I met the raven-haired beauty at the bar, my cock was instantly hard. Her scent was intoxicating, and I wanted to claim her. My gums ached as my fangs throbbed, needing to descend and taste her blood. Would she taste as good as she smelled? After watching Jax with her on the dance floor, I'd seen enough. I needed to get away and relieve the pressure in my cock. If I didn't, I was going to risk coming right where I stood. And that would be embarrassing.

I signal for Harley to cover me on the bar while I go on a break. Thursday is one of our busier nights and tonight is no exception, but I know she has it covered. Making my way to the back room, I close the door behind me and thread through the stacked boxes until I come to the darkened corner. No one should disturb me, the bar is fully stocked already. I made sure of it. Unzipping my jeans, I pull out my throbbing cock and wrap my hand around it.

Rubbing my fist up and down my length, I think of her. Everything about her is so perfect: her scent, her body in that tiny black dress, and the way she reacted not only to me but to Jax as well. I picture her hand running up and down my steely length. My hips jerk as I speed up the motion on my cock.

How would she feel as I sink inside her? Would her walls grip me tight as I thrust into her? Would she let me bite her and drink her blood, heightening both her orgasm and mine as I fuck her senseless? What would my name sound like, ripping from her lips as I push her over the edge?

Leaning my head against the wall in front of me, I try to cool my overheating skin. It's one thing humans seem to believe about vampires - that we are cold-skinned, but it's far from the truth. If we drink blood frequently enough, it keeps our bodies at almost the same temperature as a human.

My balls tighten and draw up. A groan escapes me as I come. Thoughts of taking her whirl through my mind as I explode. Grabbing a roll of tissue, I wipe up the mess I have made and tuck my softening cock back into my jeans; the material catching against my overly sensitive skin.

Placing the roll back on the shelf, I make my way out of the back room, throwing the wad of tissue in the trash as I pass. Opening the door, I run straight into Bane. It's like hitting a brick wall. Bane isn't his real name, but he reminds most people of the character from Batman and as soon as he started working at the club, the nickname just stuck.

Jax and I had known him for years before we ended up here. We never used a nickname before, but now it's all we ever call him. It suits him better than his real one. At well over 6ft 4in, he's built like a brick shit house, all muscle and not a scrap of fat on him. The black t-shirt he's wearing stretches over his muscles, leaving nothing to the imagination.

"On a break?" I comment nonchalantly.

He grunts and nods at me, but adds nothing else to the conversation. We have a small fridge in the back room filled with blood sachets. Employees are allowed up to three during shifts. It's not that we need them. A vampire can go for up to a week on as little as a pint of blood, but the fact that Jax allows drinking from the vein in the club means the extra keeps our bloodlust under control.

Brushing past me, Bane makes his way through the door I just came out of as I head into the main club. When I get back, I check the bar. Harley is still there, serving, and I glance around to see if I can see the dark-haired temptress again. I shouldn't be wanting to find her again, but my body is telling me I need to.

I make my way to a spot where her scent is the strongest. It's an empty booth, but two jackets lie on the seat. Lifting the jacket I know is hers to my nose, I inhale deeply.

Wrong move.

My cock twitches in the tight confines of my jeans. Pulling the jacket away from my nose again, I look out at the dance floor. It's the only place I can think she would be if she left her jacket here.

As I'm about to head for the dance floor, I catch a whiff of something else mingled with her scent. *Fear.* My instincts are suddenly on high alert. I widen my senses, following the fear-laced trail to the women's bathroom. I don't stop to think as I walk inside. A few startled screams don't even get my attention as I survey the room, but she's not here anymore. She was. But she's gone now.

Turning, I follow her scent back outside. Looking down the hallway, I notice the emergency exit door is ajar. Odd. No one should use that door unless there's an emergency. As I get closer to the door, another smell hits me. *Blood.* Blood that mingles with her scent and another's. Using my speed, I burst out of the door into the alley. It crashes against the wall.

I snarl at the scene before me. There is blood everywhere. Inhaling, my nostrils flare and my fangs ache to descend. I clench my fists as I attempt to get control of my blood lust. It's trying to drag me under, to make me drink. I glance down to the left of the alley where two prone forms lay.

Speeding over to them, I drop straight to my knees, their blood soaks into my clothes. It's the women from the bar, my dark-haired temptress and her friend. Sensing my female still has a heartbeat, albeit it slow, I turn my attention to the other woman. She's naked and covered in deep cuts - obviously dead. There is no color to her now pale skin, and there's no heat coming from her.

I check her pulse, just in case, but I can't hear a heartbeat. The lack of a pulse confirms what I already know. Moving to my female, I can hear the slow beat of her heart, but it's struggling. Her shoulder is ripped open, and like her friend, she is covered in slash marks, which are all bleeding. She's still clothed, but her dress is ruined. Her blood is pulling me in, and I lean closer to her. I want to taste her, even if it's just a drop.

A hand grabs my shoulder, pulling me back, and I snarl. I turn on the person. It's Bane.

"No." His one word is firm, and he doesn't let go of my shoulder. "Call Jax."

Shoving me away from my woman, he crouches down next to her. Brushing her hair back from her face, it's the gentlest I've ever seen him. He gathers her up in his arms and lifts her like she weighs nothing. She looks so small in his arms. He holds her close as I pull my cell phone out of my pocket and dial Jax's number. It doesn't take him long to answer.

"Diego?"

"Back alley. Now." I hang up and pocket the phone.

I look back over at Bane. He's cradling my woman in his arms. I take a step closer, wanting to pull her from him, but his head whips up and he snarls at me. His long fangs are showing, and his eyes are rimmed with red. I'm not sure if it's his bloodlust or the fact he can sense I want to take her from him.

Holding my hands up in defeat, I take a step back. My fangs are cutting into my lip, blood dripping from the tiny holes. I look down at the body on the floor. Sniffing the air, I can smell them now. The smell of wet dogs. Wolves; on *our* territory. I clench my fists. I will find them and I *will* kill them. They touched what's mine, and they deserve to be ripped apart.

A disturbance in the air makes me turn. Jax is standing in front of me. His nostrils are also flaring, but he has more control than me. His fangs have yet to descend as he surveys the scene before him.

"What the fuck happened?" He glares at me.

"Don't look at me! I found them like this. She's dying." I point to my female and he follows my finger to where she lies within Bane's arms.

"Get her upstairs. NOW! If someone in the club smells her, they will attack."

Bane is off before Jax even finishes his sentence. He heads down the alley and cuts to the left. There's a set of stairs there that leads up to Jax's apartment above the club. Myself, Jax, and Bane are the only ones who know the codes for the doors at the top and bottom. They lead up to a heavy security door that even the strongest creatures couldn't break down.

"And what about her?" I tilt my head towards the dead friend.

"We can't leave her out here. We don't know what sort of things the blood will attract. I'll take her inside, find somewhere to put her until clean up arrives."

Taking out his phone, his fingers fly across the screen before shoving it back into his pocket and moving over to the dead girl. He shrugs off his suit jacket and lays it over her body before gathering her up in his arms and heading the same way as Bane. I collect her bag and discarded dress and follow him. We head down to the basement and I throw the clothes in the incinerator, leaving Jax to deal with the body before I head up to the apartment.

The last time I saw both women, they were on the dance floor. The dark-haired temptress was dancing with Jax, and her friend was close by. After that, I left for the back room, needing release. How did so much happen between me leaving and now? With the amount of blood, I'm surprised no one else found the bodies first. There was enough to draw even the oldest vampire into bloodlust.

In that short space of time, it looks like they were attacked. Her friend was mutilated, raped, and murdered; I could smell the individual scents of many men. But I didn't smell semen on my woman, only the smell of wet dog. Did she see everything that happened to her friend, or was she already unconscious at that point? I can't begin to imagine what she has been through, or how she will react when she wakes up. *If* she wakes up.

When I get inside, Bane has cleared off the dining table. He has laid the raven-haired woman on top of it, her blood soaking into the wood. Bane's huge hands cover her body, trying to stem the flow, but he can't reach every wound. The one on her neck is bleeding profusely.

I approach slowly, stopping myself from breathing. As a vampire, I don't need to, but old habits die hard. When I feel I can get close enough without being triggered by her blood, I place a hand over the gaping wound on her shoulder. The liquid coats my hand and streams steadily between my fingers.

Lifting my head, I look at Bane. His eyes bore into mine. The red rings are still prominent around his irises, his fangs still out, but he doesn't move closer to her. He's touching her like she is glass about to shatter.

Jax appears between us. With no warning, he bites into his wrist, letting his blood flow down to his cupped hand.

"Move." He speaks in my direction, and I pull my hand away from her neck.

With the blood that's in his hand, he smears it over the gaping wound. The best way to heal someone is to get them to drink our blood, but adding it to the wounds, for now, should be enough to stop her bleeding out before I can get her to drink my blood.

Wait, why my blood? It doesn't matter whose blood she drinks, but for some reason, I want it to be mine. Just like

I've been calling her mine, I want to be hers as well. Movement draws me back to the present as Jax finishes applying his blood to her other wounds. The flow of blood is slower now, but she's still so pale.

"Tell me what you know, Diego."

"They came to the bar and ordered drinks. Not long after I saw her," I look down at the woman on the table, "dancing with you. I went on a break." I don't feel the need to voice the fact that I was so turned on I needed to get away and find release.

"When I came back, I was drawn to her scent. I found the booth they had been sitting at, but only their jackets were there. Then I smelled her fear, so I followed it." I recount, wincing as I remember what happened next, "I was near the bathroom, close to the emergency exit, and I caught the smell of blood. When I got outside, I found them. I checked them both, the friend was already dead. Bane arrived, and I called you. You know the rest."

My eyes cut to Bane, wondering if he will voice the fact I was ready to sink my fangs into her neck, despite how much blood she had already lost. But he just looks at me and tilts his head to the side, his silent way of telling me he won't say anything.

Jax looks down at the woman. His hand reaches out, and he runs his fingers through her hair. Part of me wants to snap at him, to pull him away and demand he doesn't touch her again, but another small part of me tells me she's not just mine. But his too, all of ours. Fighting with each other will get us nowhere.

"I'll take her to my bedroom. One of us needs to stay with her. If she comes to, you need to give her your blood. It'll help to heal her." Jax orders.

Lifting her carefully, he moves down the hallway towards his bedroom. Kicking open the door, he disappears inside. I look back over at Bane. He's standing perfectly still next to the table, like he's scared to move. His fangs have retracted, and his pupils are fully blue again.

"Why?" I whisper, quiet enough that Jax shouldn't hear me.

"She's ours. And I'll protect her, even from you."

Without another word, he takes off after Jax. I'm guessing he's decided he's going to be the one to watch over her first. I want to be the one that is there when she wakes up, but until her wounds have healed a little more, I don't think I can trust myself to be too close to her. Not without wanting to taste her.

Chapter 6

Demi

Consciousness slowly drifts back to me. *Where am I?* I must have died and gone to heaven because where I'm lying now no longer feels like the cold, damp tarmac in the alley behind the club. My heart breaks when I remember Ginny's whimpers as the wolves ravaged her body, doing with it what they wanted. The look of horror on Ginny's face as the wolf's leader ripped out her throat and continued to rut into her as her blood ran down her torn skin would haunt me for the rest of my days.

Tears prickle the corners of my eyes. That could have been me. I could be the one left in the alley, my corpse cold and covered in blood, my dignity ripped away from me. It was bad enough that they violated me whilst they forced me to watch, but Ginny is dead. Her life ended for some sick game.

Why doesn't my body hurt anymore?

A wolf attacked me and bit down hard into my shoulder, bone crunching under his powerful jaw. Then, there was a ripping sound as he was pulled away from me, taking a chunk of skin with it. My shoulder still hurts, but nowhere near as much as it did in the alley - nowhere near as much as it should. How long have I been laying here? There is only a dull ache in my shoulder now, no more fire traveling through my nerves.

Testing my limbs, I can move them all, but they feel heavy. Like I've got weights attached to them. Panic takes over. Am I tied down? Did the wolves come back for me and take me to God knows where? I try to open my eyes, but they feel heavy too. My mouth feels dry, but there is a lingering metallic taste and undertones of sweetness, like honey. I run my tongue over my dry lips. Whatever liquid is still on them, I can taste it more as my tongue dances across my lips. I want more of it.

I try to open my eyes again, but they still don't want to open. That feeling alone is enough to make me panic a little. Testing my hands again, I lift one of them slightly. Expecting restraints to be holding me down, I'm surprised it moves freely, if not a little stiff. Reaching one hand to my face, I rub my eyelids. The tears I cried have solidified like the strongest glue and make my eyes impossible to open, at least until I wipe the residue clear. At last, I can open them, but only a little. Just enough for the soft light around me to penetrate my eyeballs.

The room is dimly lit. But there is enough light to see the shape of the fitting above my head. All at once, my fear is shoved to the forefront as the wolf leader's words penetrate my mind. They must have come back for me. He must have changed his mind. If I'm not dead, then that's the only place I can be, 'cause wherever I am it's definitely not a hospital. He's taken me to his lair so he can torture and rape me like he did Ginny.

Oh god, Ginny!

I squeeze my eyes shut and images of what they forced me to watch flash behind my closed lids.

Sitting bolt upright, my eyes open fully. I look around, taking in a bedroom. The walls are a dark red, and the furniture is all mahogany. Did he bring me to his red room of pain? I still don't understand why I don't hurt anymore? He left me for dead, but other than the dull ache, I'm no longer bleeding out.

Looking down at myself, I'm still in my dress. The wounds from the wolf's claws are closed, but I can still see the pink puckered skin like they are in the last stages of healing. So he didn't rape me whilst I was out, but he said he enjoyed the thrill of my fear. He probably wants me awake to feel everything. My heart is pounding behind my ribcage now, threatening to break out of my chest. My breathing comes in hard pants.

I swivel my head further round. There's a figure sitting on a chair in the corner. Scrambling off the bed, I fall off the side as I try to stand. I need to get out of here; I need to get away before he wakes up. Running for the door, I reach out my hand for the door handle. A blurred arm shoots past my shoulder and slams into the door before I can open it, holding it shut.

I'm cloaked entirely in shadow now, the enormous figure looming over me. I don't know if I should move or if I should face my attacker. Spinning on my heel, I lash out with my hands. My fists smack into a solid chest, and pain ricochets up my arms. Lifting my eyes slowly, I follow the dark t-shirt up over a wide torso and broad shoulders until they reach his face.

It's not the wolf. This man is too tall. He's well over 6ft 4in, the wolf wasn't even 6ft. His other arm comes out to cage me against the door. Where the hell am I? And who the hell is this guy? I can't see his features in the light. He's an unknown entity, but I'm still in flight mode and I need to get away.

Ducking under his arm, I take off across the bedroom, aiming for the closed door on the other side, but he's in front of me before I can even take three steps. His hands grab my arms, holding me in place. But they aren't tight. His grip doesn't hurt, almost like he's being gentle with me.

When I look at his face this time, I recognize him. His blue eyes gaze down at me, and the longer, dark blond hair on top of his head flops down into them. Thick scruff covers his jaw and chin. It's the vampire bouncer from the club.

"Who are you?" I whisper, my voice trembling.

"Bane." His voice is rough but quiet. Like he's keeping it low for my benefit.

"Why am I here?" I wriggle in his grip, but he doesn't let go. His thumbs rub gently across my skin.

My eyes trail to his hands. They are covered in dried blood, just like most of my arms. Is it my blood, or is it someone else's? Is it Ginny's? Did he drink what little blood was left in her?

"You were injured. We saved you."

My eyes cut back to his. "What do you mean? Where am I? How did you save me?"

His grip finally loosens on my arms as he lets me go. I'm still ready to bolt. I look back over at the door behind me. Skirting around my tensed frame, he walks towards the door.

"Come." It's a demand, not a request, but his voice is still low.

Opening the door, he walks out into the dark hallway. I need to get away from here, and I'm guessing my best bet for escape is somewhere outside this room. I turn and follow him, and when I reach the hallway, I look each way. There are more doors to my left, but I think they're more rooms, not an exit. Taking a right, I follow behind his hulking form to the light at the end of the hallway.

We exit into a huge open-plan living room. To my left, there is a dining table. It looks like someone has spilled wine on the beautiful wood. Only it's dry, not wet.

Wait, is that blood?

A shudder races through my body.

My eyes continue to take in the room. There's an L-shaped slate gray sofa with a small coffee table in front of it and beyond that is a huge TV which takes up most of the wall. Continuing around, my eyes fall on the kitchen, all black marble, with white cabinets. There is another hallway next to the kitchen. Maybe that's the exit. I take a tentative step toward it, when I see movement out of the corner of my eye.

My gaze drifts that way. There are two other figures standing on the other side of the breakfast bar. One is the bartender from the club. Another vampire. The other man I don't know. He's dressed in slacks, and what I can only assume was a white shirt. There are now red stains covering most of it, the top few buttons are undone and the blood marks the skin there.

"She's awake?" The bartender asks. I can see him better in this light. His hair is black with highlights of blue, and those black orbs are still just as dark as when I first saw them as he watches me as well. He goes to take a step toward me, but the other man stops him dead in his tracks with a hand to his chest.

"How long have I been here?" I spot the clock over his shoulder. 8:19 pm, I left to meet Ginny at 9 pm.

That can't be right.

"It's been the best part of a day since we brought you here." Slacks guy answers.

Looking closely at the man, my gaze snaps to the greenest eyes I've ever seen. They're watching my every move, not that there is much to watch. Lifting a hand, he brushes his wavy, golden blond hair away from his eyes as he looks me up and down.

The man I don't know takes a step towards me, his hands held up in front of him to show he meant no harm. I take a step back, but I collide with Bane instead. His imposing body stops me in my tracks and he brings a hand up to rest against my shoulder. His touch should scare me. Just being in his presence should terrify me. He's a vampire. But instead, warmth floods through my body. His touch is comforting and I feel my shoulders begin to droop as I relax into his touch.

The man takes another step forward, and I cower away from him this time. I hear a snarl before Bane steps around me and stands defensively in front of me. I cower behind him. I shouldn't be thinking of him as my protector, but he said he saved me, and so far, he's been nothing but gentle with me. It could be an act, but he scares me less than the other man.

"Calm it, Bane!" The man orders. "I'm not going to hurt her."

I peek around Bane's arm, my hand resting on his forearm. I don't know why I feel the need to touch him, but he makes me feel safe. The warmth that spreads through my body is calming. The need to run subsides the longer I keep my skin against his. He looks down at me and shrugs a little, stepping to the side but letting me keep my connection with him.

The man whose name, like the bartender, I still don't know, takes another step forward. This time, I don't flinch away from him. I know in my heart that if he tries anything, Bane will stop him.

"My name is Jax. You're still at the club, sort of. This is my apartment. It's above the club." I remember when I approached the building there were more levels above, but I never realized it was living space. "We found you outside. You were bleeding out. What happened?"

"I... I don't..." I whisper. "Where's Ginny?"

"Was that the girl you were with?"

"Yes. She is... was my friend."

"She's gone." I flinch at his words. "She was already dead when we found you." I know what he says is true. Her body was cooling, even before I lost consciousness. Tears form in the corners of my eyes. I knew she was dead but having someone else confirm it makes it so much more real.

"But where is she?"

"We had to move her body. We couldn't leave her outside. Her blood would attract too many creatures. She's here for now until someone can come and pick up her body."

I ponder on what he means by creatures. There are only meant to be vampires, wolves, and demons. But the way he says it implies there is more than that.

"I want... no, I *need* to see her."

"I don't think you're in any fit state for that, *tesoro*." This time it's the bartender who speaks. He still hasn't moved from his place by the breakfast bar.

"And who the hell are you to tell me what state I'm in?" My anger flares as I glare at him.

"I'm sorry about him. That's Diego. Now you know who we are, why not tell us your name?" Jax asks.

"Demetria... Demi. Can I leave? Or are you my captors now?"

"We'd never think to keep you here against your will, Demi. But we need to know more about what happened out there. We can't let what happened to you and your friend happen again."

It's all too much to think about. They want me to tell them what happened, to relive the worst moments of my life. I don't know if I can. It's still too fresh, Ginny's tear-streaked face flashes up in my mind, and I can feel my breath quickening.

"She's having a panic attack." I hear the words, but they seem so far away.

Then he's in front of me, Diego. His hands rest on my shoulders. Warmth spreads through my body again from where his hands connect with my skin. He bends a little, so he is at eye level with me. Warmth covers my back as another body presses up behind me. More hands gently resting on my hips, keeping me upright.

My heart is beating so hard, it feels like it will crack my rib cage and burst from my chest. I squeeze my eyes shut, willing it to stop.

"I need you to breathe, *tesoro*. Look at me and copy what I do."

My eyes crack open a little, and those jet-black eyes look straight into my soul. He takes a deep breath in through his nose and lets it rush back out of his mouth after a few seconds. I try to do the same, but I can't seem to slow my own intake of breath. I'm panting now.

The hands on my hips begin to rub small circles through the fabric of my dress. Diego's hands move from my shoulders to cup my face, keeping my face level with his.

"Come on, you can do it." His words are soft but still muffled. I try again, but as I inhale, my breathing shudders.

"This isn't working, get out of the way." Diego is pulled away from me, and Jax is in front of me.

He places his hands on my cheeks and brings his face close to mine. Those green eyes feel like they are hypnotizing me. Before I have a second to even think about what is happening, he drags my lips to his. As they collide with mine, I stop breathing. I melt into the kiss. His tongue runs across the seam of my lips and as I inhale, I smell damp pine. Spotting a moment of opportunity, he thrusts his tongue into my mouth.

With my senses returning, I can't believe what he's doing. I feel violated all over again. Ripping my lips away from his, I whip my hand up and smack him hard across the cheek. His face is like hitting marble and my hand stings.

"Don't fucking touch me!"

I shove against his shoulders, pushing him back, and he lets me. Red is ringing his emerald pupils, and his nostrils are flaring. A snarl sounds behind me again. Bane is warning him off. It's only then that I realize my breathing has returned to normal, but my anger is ready to burst from within. How dare he touch me without my permission? He's just like the wolves, taking what isn't his. But this time I'm ready.

Chapter 7

Jax

The crack across my face stuns me. I had a feeling this one might be feisty, but I wasn't expecting her anger to come forward so soon. When she shoves me back, I let her. She needs to feel like she's in control. Having had so much ripped away from her already, it's the least I can do for her.

The snarl coming from Bane has my eyes cutting to his. The red ring around his pupils is slowly taking over. If he loses it right now, he could easily rip me apart. Bane wraps an arm around Demetria, pulling her against his body. She's shivering in his arms, but I'm not sure if it's from fear or anger.

"I apologize, Demetria. I needed you to calm down, and it worked, didn't it?" She continues to glare at me. "I meant nothing by it."

"I don't want you touching me. I don't trust you. You're a vampire. And it's Demi!" She snaps, scowling at me as she repeats the shortened version of her name, but I much prefer Demetria. I'm old fashioned, and Demetria is such a pretty name, a reminder of bygone days.

"You seem to be fine letting him hold you though." I nod my head toward Bane.

"He feels safe." A pleased rumble comes from Bane's chest at her words.

"I wouldn't be so sure." Diego snarks from behind me, letting out a low chuckle.

I take a step back; I don't want her to fear me, or any of us. There is a chance the wolves that attacked her and her friend last night will be back. They really do enjoy the hunt, and now they know the scent of her blood, they'll come for her. Even when she leaves, I'll be making sure one of us is monitoring her at all times.

I'm not sure why I'm thinking of doing this for her. I wouldn't do it for anyone else. Humans are our food, and my mother always told me not to play with my food. Though by the way my cock is twitching, it clearly hasn't gotten the memo. There's only been one other human I have cared about since I was turned. I've had sex with multiple humans and vampires alike, but that was to scratch an itch and nothing else. But there's something odd about this one, the scent of her blood calls to me.

Casting a glance at Bane, I see he still hasn't loosened his grip on her. She seems calm enough, leaning back against him. The whole situation seems bizarre.

"I know you've been through a lot, Demetria. But you are still covered in blood. Can I suggest a shower? Then after that, maybe we can talk."

At that comment, she looks down at herself, only just realizing she's covered in blood. It's everywhere. The wounds inflicted on her bled for a while before Diego found her. She nods weakly, looking utterly defeated.

"Bane, could you please escort our guest to the bedroom at the end of the hall on the left? I'll grab you some towels and something to change into."

Bane slides around to her front. She looks up at him and steps back a little. He guides her down the hall. She doesn't let him get ahead of her but instead quickens her steps and places her hand on his arm. For someone who doesn't seem to like vampires, she sure has taken a liking to Bane.

"We really need to find out what happened, Jax." Diego throws my way. "I need to know who to kill for her."

"You're going to kill someone for a human, Diego? I understand wanting to end them for being on our territory, but to kill them because they touched her? It's very unlike you."

"Shut the hell up, Jax. Just because you have no feelings doesn't mean I don't. That poor girl has been through hell. Whoever it was raped her friend, more than one person from the scents on her body, then murdered her. I'm surprised she isn't catatonic."

A growl rumbles through his chest as he speaks, before he moves to the fridge and pulls out a sachet of blood. He rips his fangs into the bag and gulps it down cold. Even though we all let her drink from us, Diego insisted on giving her the most when she was conscious enough, to help heal her wounds. Not that she seems to remember those moments. The lack of blood must be getting to him, maybe that's why he's acting so strange.

"What's going on with Bane? He's usually all grrr." Diego lifts his hands up, hooking his fingers into claws, doing an impression of a bear. "And other than the fact he wanted to rip your head off, he's being... gentle? With her at least."

Diego's behavior is odd, but Bane's is even more so and I'm glad I'm not the only one who has noticed it. He's the muscle around here, not the careful, gentle type. Usually, he's more of a bash skulls in first, ask questions later, except you can't 'cause they're already dead type.

I shrug. The only way we'll find out what is happening with Bane is if he decides he wants us to know. Chances are we won't get much out of him. For now, I need to know everything Demetria knows. If she knows the wolves that attacked her, or if she can at least describe them to us.

We will be able to smell them again if they are close, but unlike wolves, we can't track by scent alone. By the time we know they're here, it might already be too late. Leaving

Diego to drink his blood, I make my way back to my bedroom. It's the room she woke up in and her scent still lingers in the air.

Moving into the bathroom, I grab two of the plushest towels I can find before heading back into my room. Opening the drawers, I grab some boxers, sweatpants, and a t-shirt. They'll probably drown her, but it's better than nothing.

Heading to the end of the hall, Bane is standing outside the door. His thick arms are tight across his chest. He's protecting her like he protects the club. As I get closer, he looks me up and down before stepping to the side. I knock on the door gently, but I can already hear the shower running.

Opening the door, I walk inside. The bloody dress she was wearing is thrown haphazardly on the floor outside the door to the en-suite. Leaving the clothing on the bed, I move to the bathroom door. My hand poised to knock, I pause a few inches away from it.

I pick up on muffled sobs beneath the sound of running water. I'm surprised it took this long for her to break down, but I don't want to interrupt her. She needs to get it out, all the pain and the anger that is brewing just below the surface of her skin.

I place the towels on the set of drawers to the side of the en-suite. They should be easy for her to reach without having to leave the bathroom. Turning to step away, I pause briefly. A strange part of me wants to go in there and comfort her, but I don't think she will appreciate my intrusion. She needs to feel safe. By entering the bathroom, I'd be taking that safety away.

I start walking again, grabbing her discarded and ruined clothing from the floor on the way past. The best thing to do is to dispose of what she was wearing. I'm sure she won't want to see it again. Leaving the bedroom, I close the door quietly behind me. I look up at Bane as he takes his position back in front of it.

"What's going on with you, Bane?"

"She needs protecting. I'll keep her safe."

"You know she's safe here. No one will harm her whilst she's within these walls." He nods, and I guess that's the end of the conversation.

Heading back into the kitchen, Diego is nowhere to be found. Throwing her bloody clothing in the trash, I think back to my dance with Demetria. I couldn't resist approaching her. Something drew me towards her. I've not felt a connection like that with anyone since I died, apart from Bane and Diego.

When I was first turned, I stayed with the nest my sire had built, but after two centuries together, they became dull. Throwing lavish parties night after night and tormenting humans as they drained their blood became repetitive. I grew bored.

This was long before the supernaturals took over. There was no Council back then to stop them. When I contemplated leaving, my sire gifted me with a human lover, but I didn't feel the connection I feel to Demetria. My lover had asked me to turn her. I didn't want to be alone, so I approached my sire to ask for his permission.

We planned to leave together and start our own nest. I may not have loved her, but she was my companion and certainly kept my bed warm. But asking was where I went wrong. I shouldn't have asked and just done it instead.

When I returned to my room that night, I found her dead on my bed. Her naked body was covered in bite marks and her blood had been drained. He'd given her to me, expecting her to keep me with him, but as soon as he found out we planned to leave, he murdered her. I stayed for a little while after, but really I was plotting his demise.

I joined him for an orgy one evening with his blood slaves, and as one girl rode him, I slit his throat. I smiled as his blood soaked into the bedsheets. In the chaos caused by his death, I slipped out of the mansion and never looked back. I ended up leaving Louisiana and heading for California instead.

I was alone for a long time before they appeared in my life. After being turned in the early sixties, Diego moved up from Mexico to California. His sire had abandoned him, and at this point, the vampires already ruled here. He figured his best plan was to leave and go to where his own kind lived. Bane had appeared sometime in the eighties.

Since then we've stuck together. It wasn't until the early nineties we felt compelled to move North. Now here we are, in Portland, Oregon. After drifting for a while, we opened Dark Desires, a place where humans could feel safe, and where vampires could mingle with them without being brought up before the Council for drinking from the vein. We may not be the first here, but we plan to be the best.

We've put a lot of time and effort into getting this place started. Making rules we expect all patrons to follow, whether human or vampire. If they don't, the police arrest the humans and the vampires... well, we take care of them ourselves. Usually with a visit to the basement where Bane relieves them of their fangs.

Chapter 8

Demi

Bane shows me to the bedroom at the end of the hall. It's a fairly decent-sized room, with a large double bed against one wall and bedside cabinets on either side. There are two doors opposite the bed. I'm hoping one is an en-suite, and my guess is that the other is a closet. There's a set of drawers between the frames made of mahogany.

What is it with mahogany?

The hulking vampire stops just inside the door, my hand still touching his arm. He looks down at it, but doesn't say a word as his eyes flicker to mine. I swallow hard. There is something drawing me to him, but I can't put my finger on it. A part of me wants to get closer to him, but another part tells me to run away. He is a vampire, after all.

From what I've seen of vampires so far, they just take what they want. I've seen too many people with throats ripped out and drained of blood in the ER, but Bane makes me feel safe. He has defended me, snarled at his friends, and made sure he has stepped between us. He comforted me and held me close to his huge body.

I spot my bag on the end of the bed, and I rush toward it. Opening it, I find my silver stake inside. Pulling it out, I hold it close to my chest as I turn back to Bane. His eyebrow raises as he looks from the stake clutched in my hand and back up to my eyes before giving me an understanding nod.

"Thank you," I murmur.

He grunts at me as he walks out of the room and closes the door behind him. The one called Jax said he'd bring me towels and fresh clothing. I look down at my ruined dress. It's sticky with blood and I want nothing more than to remove it from my body. Pulling down the zip, I let it drop to the floor. My bra is in tatters, and my panties don't look much better.

It was my favorite dress, but now I want to burn it. I never want to see it again. Checking the first door, it reveals a bathroom, just like I hoped. As soon as I'm through the door, I close it and engage the lock. I'm sure it won't stop anyone, but I need some sort of deterrent, something to make me feel a little safer. There is an enormous bath that looks big enough for more than one person, and a huge waterfall shower along one wall. I catch a glimpse of myself in the large mirror that sits behind the sink unit. I place the silver stake on the edge of the unit, so it's close to hand.

Blood covers me and I'm not sure it's all mine either - I shudder at the thought. I told them I wanted to see Ginny, but for now, the one called Jax has refused my request. Refusing to back down, I let the need to see her, to apologize to her burn in my soul. I remember the words of the wolves; they came for me, not for her. They used her like she was a toy they could throw away and now, because of me, she's dead.

A sniffle catches in my throat, and tears burn the back of my eyes. Moving to the shower, I turn it on as quickly as I can to muffle the sounds of my crying. Once the water is warm enough, I step under it. The water pooling at my feet is tinged red. Grabbing the soap, I scrub at my body as tears fall down my cheeks. I rub until my skin is raw, and then I scrub a little more.

Shoving my head under the cascade, I attempt to wash the tears away, but they keep coming. Even as I wash the blood from my hair, I can't stop the whimpers. When I close my eyes to wash the shampoo off, I'm assaulted by a replay of what happened. It's enough to take me to my knees and curl into the fetal position as the water continues to rain down on me.

I'm shaking as the tears and anguish take over. I let her die. This is all my fault. We should have stayed in the club and approached security.

They're vampires though, Demi. For all you know, they would have just thrown you to the wolves. Literally.

But they wouldn't have, would they? There are three of them here now. And not one of them has shown any sign they are going to hurt me, even if I don't know what they want with me.

I lie on the floor of the shower, letting the pain wrack through my body, staring at the tiled wall next to me. I don't want to close my eyes again. If I do, I know all I'll see is Ginny, assaulted and murdered in front of me on an endless loop.

I'm not sure how long I lie there for, but the water is no longer as warm as it was when I first got in. I've cried until I can't cry any longer; my tears have all dried up. Picking myself up off the floor on shaky limbs, I cut off the shower and step onto the mat.

Edging towards the closed door, water drips from my wet body and hair, leaving a trail behind me. When I reach it, I twist the lock. I'm hoping none of the vampires are waiting in the bedroom. I'm not dressed, and I'm in no state to want to see any of them just yet.

As I open the door slowly, I spot two fluffy white towels on the drawers just outside. Slipping an arm through the gap, I snatch them up and pull them back inside the bathroom before slamming the door closed and locking it again.

Throwing one towel onto the sink unit, I wrap the larger of the two around my body. I grab the other and wrap my hair up inside it before turning to face the mirror. My skin is still red, protesting from its thorough scrubbing, but at least I'm not covered in blood anymore.

My eyes look hollow and slightly sunken, and my already light skin is paler than normal. Where the wolves ripped through me there are puckered red marks, but they aren't painful. I can't believe how much they've healed already.

I really need to ask one of the vampires what the hell happened. I'm only human. From experience as a nurse I know how deep some of them were, so there is no way they healed of their own accord. I shudder at what they might have done to heal my wounds. After I finish inspecting myself, I grab up the stake again; I feel prepared enough to venture into the bedroom once more.

Unlocking the door again, I open it slowly. It's empty, but there is a set of clothes on the bed. Hurrying over to them, I survey what's been left for me. Sweatpants, boxers, and a t-shirt, whose I'm not sure. They certainly aren't Bane's. His clothing would probably drown me.

Pulling the clothing up my legs, the pants feel too long and loose, but I cinch the waist using the drawstring and roll them up at the waist and ankles. They'll have to do. It's not like I'm going to put my blood stained dress on again.

I look to where I dropped my dress and underwear, but I find them missing. It must have been Jax. The underwear was in no fit state to be worn and I'm glad he took them. I'm not sure I could have looked at them again. I don't want to keep reliving what happened.

Picking up the t-shirt, I throw it over my head and shove my arms through the holes. It reaches well past my ass. Now I'm finally clothed, I feel a little better, a little more human.

Sitting on the bed, I sink down into the mattress. It's as comfy as the bed I woke up in. Whose bed was that? The thought suddenly pops into my mind. I lift the fabric and sniff it. All I can smell is whatever detergent was used.

My shoulders slump. I'm exhausted. Between the trauma of what happened, and spending God only knows how long crying in the bathroom, I'm bone tired. Dragging myself from the bed, I move to the door that leads to the hall, looking to see if it will lock. Thankfully, there is one and I engage it straight away.

Shuffling back to the bed, I place the stake on the bedside table, pull back the covers, and slip beneath them. I'll just close my eyes for a few minutes. That's all I need. As soon as my head hits the pillow, I'm out like a light.

Chapter 9

Bane

I can hear her crying in the bathroom, the sound of the water pounding against the tiles doing nothing to hide it from my sensitive ears. I want to go to her, but I know she won't appreciate me barging in where I'm not welcome. Instead, I stay standing outside the door. I want to make sure no one can go in there without her permission.

After Jax took her the towels and clothes, I think back to his words. I really don't know what is going on with me. All I know is that I need to keep her safe. I *will* keep her safe, and I'll kill anyone who tries to harm her.

When the water cuts out, I can hear her moving around inside. She shifts to the bathroom door, unlocking it before opening, closing, and locking it again. I hear when she finally leaves the bathroom, too. Even from here, she smells clean, the lingering smell of her blood, and that of her friend, has long since been washed down the drain.

As soon as I hear her footsteps approaching the bedroom door, I step away so as not to startle her. But the door never opens. Instead, I hear the lock on the door being engaged before she moves back towards what I assume is the bed.

Listening closely to her breathing, I hear when it evens out, and she drifts off to sleep. I'm compelled to check on her, to make sure she is okay, but with the door locked, the only way in is to break it down. I growl under my breath as I move back towards the door.

Placing my palm against the wood, I have to stop myself from smashing it to get to her. It's not something I can do. After what she has been through, she will think I'm trying to attack her. Dropping my hand, I shift away from the door and head back to the living room. Jax and Diego are nowhere to be found.

I move to the fridge and grab a sachet of blood from inside it. There has been a lot of it spilled, and I'm actively fighting my bloodlust every step of the way. It's something I've always had a problem with and part of the reason Jax keeps me on the door instead of working in the club.

The humans there only pass me briefly, not long enough for me to smell them and want to sink my fangs into their neck. But tonight was different. I caught Demi's scent as she entered the club and it sang to me; I wanted to leave my position and go to her, to drown in her intoxicating scent. I wanted *her*.

It had waned as she entered and left me outside in the cold. I spent a few hours wondering if I should seek her out, but I did my job. A few fights broke out at the entrance when I refused to let some humans in, but they soon cleared off as soon as I bared my fangs at them.

It wasn't until I went inside for a blood packet on my break and came back into the hallway that I realized something was wrong. My bloodlust shot to the forefront of my mind, and the girl's scent pounded into my nostrils.

When I got outside, I found Diego kneeling over her. His fangs were down, and his heart rate was increased. The scent of her blood was overpowering, and I knew if I didn't stop him, there was a chance he would bite her and drain what little blood she had left. We'd have been removing two dead bodies, not just one.

I gathered her up and brought her to Jax's apartment above the club. Though, at this point, it's more like our apartment.

We spend more time here than we do at our own places; it's easier after a long shift to come upstairs and crash than traipse across town to our own places.

Thankfully, Jax's place has enough rooms to accommodate both me and Diego, and now our new guest. I even keep a few sets of clothes here to get by. After finishing my sachet of blood, I throw it in the trash, spotting her trashed clothing inside. I grab one of the dining room chairs, carrying it back down the hall.

Setting it up outside her room, I take my place on the hard wooden seat. I cross my legs at the ankles and lean back, letting my eyes slip shut as I listen to the sound of her sleeping.

I can hear Jax and Diego showering in their respective rooms, presumably to clean the blood from themselves. After we took Demi to Jax's room, none of us left her side until all her wounds were closed. The blood on our clothes doesn't bother us and as we didn't want to leave her, we hadn't taken the time to clean up. I'm still sitting here in my blood-drenched clothes, not wanting to leave her for even a moment in case she needs me.

My mind flashes again to what I found in the alley. Both women lay in a pool of blood, one completely naked and the other with her clothes in tatters. I wanted to rage, to punch and break things. To rip apart the ones who had hurt her - I wanted revenge.

When I find those wolves, I will make them wish they had never set foot in vampire territory. I will become their worst nightmare. I'll make their deaths slow, and they will beg me for death before the end. I'm sure Diego will be right there with me. Jax, I'm not so sure about. He seems to want to know who hurt her and killed her friend, but I'm not sure for what reason.

I'm stationed in front of her door for quite some time before the whimpers begin. I can hear her thrashing around on the bed and the compulsion to go to her grows again.

Standing suddenly, the chair scrapes back across the wood flooring, the sound echoing down the empty hallway.

I rush to the door and turn the handle, but it won't budge. She locked it earlier before she crawled into bed and now it's stopping me from getting to her.

"Ginny... no." I hear her cry. Her heart is pounding within her chest, I can hear it effortlessly through the door.

Pushing on the wood, I feel the surface straining under my hands. Her cries of anguish grow louder and the need to get to her intensifies. Gripping the handle, I yank it back. It breaks off in my hands, and the door cracks open.

Jax is going to be pissed. I scold myself, but I can't bring myself to care.

Nudging the door open, I can see her sprawled out on the bed in the dim light. The sheet is tangled around her limbs as she thrashes around like she is fighting off an invisible attacker. The stake she had earlier is still on the bedside table.

"Don't... please, don't." She cries out again.

I'm by the bedside in less time than it takes to blink, but I'm not sure what to do. My hands clench into fists, wanting to reach out to her, to calm her, to try to take away her pain. Toeing off my boots and dropping my bloody t-shirt to the floor, I'm left in just my black tank top. I do the only thing I can think of and get onto the bed beside her. Keeping myself above the covers, I pull her into my arms, spotting the tears falling down her cheeks as I rest her head under my chin.

Turning so she is facing me, her fingers grip the material of my tank. She pushes against my huge body, but I don't move. I rub my hand up and down her arm, attempting to soothe her. Slowly, her breathing evens out and she rests her cheek against my chest.

I can feel her tears soaking through the material of my top as her fists unclench. One rests above my beating heart and the other moves down to my side. Her skin connects with mine where my tank has lifted on the side and my whole body shudders.

Holding her close to me, my hand moves down her back, rubbing small circles over the top of the material. Other than that, I daren't move. Instead, I close my eyes so I can rest. Vampires can get away with much lower amounts of sleep, but it's been a taxing time for us all. With her gathered in my arms, at least I'm here, ready to protect her.

I hear movement by the door, my senses on alert. But I know it's a friend, not a foe. I'd know Jax's damp pine scent anywhere.

"Fuck." I hear him whisper, probably surveying the damage I caused to the door.

He pulls the wood to the frame as best he can before his footsteps drift away down the hall to his bedroom, muttering under his breath as he goes.

Chapter 10

Demi

The nightmares plague me for what feels like forever. I watch as the wolves take Ginny repeatedly. It's not long before the nightmares shift, and instead, it's me on the ground. The gravel bites into my palms and knees, their claws slice through my flesh. Blood pools beneath me as they take what isn't theirs. The lead wolf lifts my body against him, his hand wrapping around my neck.

"You'll always be mine, little one. Don't try to run." He whispers against my ear as he continues to pound into my broken body.

His claws slice into my throat like butter and wrap around my windpipe before he yanks. Everything goes black before it starts all over again. Each time he whispers the same words to me. Sometimes I'm in my own body, and I can feel everything. Other times it's like I'm on the outside, watching as everything happens. But those words always echo through my head.

I always thought it was the vampires who were the monsters, but maybe I was wrong all along. Maybe there has always been a different type of monster lurking in the shadows. And now they've found me.

The nightmares eventually fade away, a warmth cocoons me, wrapping me up tight and pushing the nightmares away.

I'm so warm when I wake; there's something hard under part of me, as well as something heavy across my back. Flexing my fingers, I feel material under them and my eyes snap open. Looking up, I take in Bane's face. He looks so peaceful with his eyes closed.

How did he get in here, and why am I sprawled across him?

My leg is tangled with his, my hand is on his chest and my head is leaning on his arm as the other holds me against him. Moving my hand from his chest, I reach up for his face, tracing my fingers over his relaxed features. His nostrils flare and his eyes jump open, but he doesn't move as he lets me continue touching him. There's a need within me, craving him, wanting him. A need I can't explain but need to quench.

My fingers move across his lips, the coarse hair of his beard tickling the undersides of them. They are so soft. I wonder what they would feel like if I pressed my own against them?

Fuck Demi, you're so messed up.

I can't stop touching him though. After what happened, I should be jumping away from him. Even without his arm holding me against him, I should bolt for the other side of the room. But there's something deep inside pulling me towards him.

A groan escapes his mouth and I pull my hand away when I spot his fangs peeking out from between his lips. His breathing has quickened slightly, and that ring of red has appeared around his irises. I can feel my own pulse increasing, and my temperature is rising.

Moving my leg slightly, it brushes against his arousal, and the arm around me tightens. He's hard for me, and that thought alone sends a thrill through me. What is it about this man that makes me want to climb him like a spider monkey and feel his hardness between my legs? I hardly even know him, and so much has happened, but something is pulling me toward him.

Without a second thought, I push up onto my knees and trace my hands up and down his top, his steel-blue and red eyes observing me curiously as I touch him. I note the fact he's still wearing the same jeans he had on earlier but he's ditched the bloody t-shirt for a black tank top. When I reach the hem of his top, I push my hands under it. As soon as they connect with his skin, a shiver runs through his body and a moan rushes through his lips. It's like music to my ears.

My fingers move over the dips of his abdominals as they reach higher. I can feel the light spattering of hair on his chest beneath my fingertips. His pectorals flex and tremble as I ghost my fingers over them. I was expecting his skin to be silky smooth, but instead, I can feel bumps and ridges all over his torso.

Lifting his top, he raises his back slightly so I can pull up the fabric till it bunches under his arms. I thought vampires healed and didn't scar, but he's covered in them. There is a mixture of everything from what looks like burn marks to stab wounds. I trace my fingers over each mark in turn, cataloging every one of them.

I'm wondering if he has scars anywhere else. Maybe he will let me strip him down and check every inch of him. I'd love to lick them all. *Jeez, Demi! What is wrong with you?* I continue my exploration up his chest, and over the bunched up material. His neck is corded with thick muscle, and I can feel him swallow hard as my fingers move over him.

My eyes dart to his face and spot his fangs still peeking out. Continuing my inspection of him, I sweep a finger over his lips, catching the tip of one of his fangs. As my index finger touches it, he shudders again, the sharp tip glancing off the end of my finger and causing it to bleed.

I go to move my hand away, but his hand shoots out and grabs my wrist, startling me slightly. His tongue darts out and licks the bead of blood welling on the end. A shudder runs through me as his tongue laps at my finger before drawing it inside my mouth. He sucks gently on it, his tongue still running over the tip.

"Bane..." My voice trembles as I whisper his name and my core clenches. His simple action drives me wild.

My other hand reaches out, cupping his cheek. Pulling my finger from his mouth, I notice his blue eyes are almost entirely red now. Running his hands up my arms, he pulls me forwards. My own land on either side of his head, my face only inches from his. But now he stops, not moving those last few inches, so his lips will connect with mine.

My breathing is harsh, and my heart is pounding as I stare into those red eyes. Closing the gap between us, our lips connect and it's like fireworks. His tongue darts out, brushing against the seam of my mouth, and I open for him.

Bane thrusts his tongue inside my mouth, his fingers tangle in my hair, and he holds his mouth against mine. Our tongues battle it out, I should be repulsed, but instead, I'm growing hornier. I rub myself against him, a moan escaping me, which he swallows as he kisses me harder.

His heat is all over me, but I want to get closer to him, to feel his skin on mine as his hard length thrusts inside me. It's like I won't be complete until we're joined as one. I rock myself over him. If I can keep rubbing like this against him, I'm sure it will be enough to push me over the edge, to quench the thirst inside me.

I hear a knock on the door, but I ignore it as I thrash against him. My need for release is building.

"Bane? Demi?" Diego's voice calls from the other side of the door.

Bane tugs on my hair, pulling my lips away from his, and I'm left panting. My body is still rubbing against his, fighting for release, and my lips feel bruised. I can see the lust in Bane's eyes as he holds me away from him. A knock comes from the door again, and I quickly scoot away from Bane. His red eyes follow my movements.

The kiss has left me damp between my legs. I'm still horny as hell and I want to strip both Bane and me naked and sink down onto his cock - to feel him fill me. Maybe then he can fill the emptiness inside and the ache in my groin will finally go away.

Instead, he shifts on the bed. Readjusting his hardened cock and shoving the stake into my hands before striding to the door. Slamming it open, it's only now that I notice the missing handle on the other side of the door. He must have broken it down to get to me.

"What?" He barks in Diego's face.

"Jax wants to speak to Demi. He heard you were both awake, figured now was the best time." A growl erupts from Bane, and his fists clench at his sides. "Hey man, don't shoot the messenger, okay?"

Bane shoves past Diego, and out of the door, but Diego lingers. His eyes shift to mine. There is the telltale red ring around his black irises, and his nostrils flare. We learned at school that vampires have excellent hearing and sense of smell, among other things. Can he really smell my arousal? Is that what happened in the club, too?

"You coming?" He steps back from the door, leaving me just enough space to get past him.

I hurry to the opening and brush past him. As I do, he inhales deeply, a contented rumble sounding in his chest.

Chapter 11

Diego

I knew exactly what Bane and Demi were doing before I even approached the room. It's the reason Jax sent me. He figured if she was recovered enough to be trying to fuck Bane, then she was awake enough to tell us what had happened to her. I feel bad for her; she went through a traumatic experience and now he wants to force her to relive it. I get it though. We need answers, and Jax needs to know exactly what happened so he can protect our territory.

Bane doesn't look happy as he shoves past me. His eyes are fully red, and I catch sight of the bulge in his pants. Just how close was he to fucking her? She's all I've been thinking about since I first saw her in the club. I've come twice with images of her in my mind, once in the back room in the club and again in the shower, knowing she was naked just down the hall.

I should be jealous of Bane for getting close enough to her to leave her lips bruised, to get to taste her, but there isn't a single twinge of it. It wouldn't be the first time Bane and I have shared a woman, but things would be different with Demi.

I spot the flash of silver in her hand as she passes me at the door, but I don't see exactly what it is. I can't resist inhaling her scent again. Her arousal is at the forefront, and my cock twitches, thinking about how wet she is. Every single one of us will be able to smell it.

I follow her down the hall. As we reach the main room, I catch Jax's nostrils flare before his face is impassive again, like her scent doesn't affect him.

"You wanted to talk?" Demi's sweet as honey voice slips between her lips. She's standing close to Bane, but she isn't touching him this time.

"Please sit, Demetria." Jax signals to one of the bar stools at the breakfast bar.

She's unsure at first. Demi looks to the seat before looking up at Bane. He gives her a small nod, and she makes her way over to it before sitting down, placing a silver stake on the table in front of her. So, that's what she had in her hand. Jax moves to the other side of the breakfast bar, resting his hands on the marble top.

"I'm sorry for what you went through, and for the loss of your friend." He keeps his voice calm, not wanting to cause her any alarm. "But I need to know what happened, and why those wolves were in our territory."

Demi's breath huffs out. I was right. She doesn't want to relive what she went through. I see the tension in her shoulders as she lets out a sigh.

"I'll tell you. But first I have questions for you." She's demanding, I like it.

"Of course. We will answer what we can." He looks from me to Bane, and we both nod.

"First, how the hell did I get here?"

"I found you." I find my voice, and her head whips round to me. "I went on a break, and when I came back to the bar, I couldn't see you. I found where you'd been sitting, you'd left your jackets. Then I smelled fear, so I went looking for you and found you outside."

"I don't understand. Why were you even looking for me to start with?"

"Because..." I try to find the words I want, one that won't scare her.

"He's drawn to you." Jax cuts in. "The same way Bane is. You're like a honey trap to them." I throw a glare at him. He doesn't mention that he is also drawn to her, but I can see it in the way he watches Demi. He can try to deny it all he wants. She might not notice it, but I do and I'm pretty sure Bane does too.

"Then what?"

"As I said, I found you outside." I remember the scent of her blood, the fact it was drawing me in, and I almost drained her dry. "The wolves that attacked you were already gone. We brought you upstairs."

"My wounds, though, shouldn't I be dead?" Her hand raises and touches the pink mark on her neck. It looks much better, but she will still need more blood before it fully heals, otherwise, it will take weeks and leave a scar. With a vampire's blood, it will heal like it never even happened.

"But you aren't." There's Jax again, so blunt.

"The wolf, he told me to heal." Her voice shakes as she talks. "But my throat, they almost ripped it out. I should be dead. He thought someone would find me and heal me." I can hear the increased tempo of her heart, and I go to take a step forward, but Bane beats me to it. He rests a hand on her shoulder.

As soon as his skin comes into contact with her, she seems to relax a little. I wish more than anything that it was my touch giving her solace from the nightmare she must have endured at the hands of the wolves. Just the thought of it has my fists clenching and my fangs wanting to burst free so I can rip their throats out.

"We healed you, Demetria. We gave you our blood." Jax sounds so matter of fact, and I want to punch him in the face.

The sound of a chair screeching back echoes through the apartment as Demi pushes back on her chair. Dislodging Bane's hand from her shoulder.

"You fucking did what?" She shouts at him, not happy with his response.

"It was the only way to save you. You would have bled out before we could have got you human help. I bathed your wounds with my blood until you were strong enough to drink from us. We all fed you, but Diego gave the most."

The thoughts of her lips wrapped around my wrist as she drank my blood has my cock jumping. I'm not ashamed to admit that I was hard the entire time she drank from me. The thought of her drinking from me as I sank into her wet heat almost had me coming in my pants.

"You had no right! You should have left me to die. I don't want to be like you." Her eyes move to mine and she glares at me. "You... you fucking bastard!" She stalks towards me, her finger pointing into my chest as she attempts to push me back, but I stand my ground.

"It was the only way, Demi. Jax is right. Without our blood, you would have died."

"I can't believe you... any of you." She drops her finger from my chest and spins around, glaring at Bane and Jax as she does. "You took my choice away, just like those wolves." Her glare falls on Bane. "And you… you said you'd protect me. Being one of you is going to kill me."

"Demetria!" Jax barks. "You will not become one of us." He makes the comment nonchalantly. "To be one of us, we must bite you first, release our venom into your bloodstream, and then let you drink from us." The way he speaks is to the point, but I can see her eyes narrowing as her anger rises.

"I don't care. You did something to me that I didn't agree to! I hate you, I hate all of you!" She spins on her heel, grabbing her stake off the table as she passes and takes off down the hallway. When she reaches the room Jax designated as hers, the door slams behind her. I turn back on Jax.

"You couldn't have been just a little more careful with how you worded it, could you? Instead of dropping her in at the deep end." I shake my head at him.

"She asked questions, and I answered. Yet still, she hasn't answered mine." Jax snaps at me.

"You're a fucking asshole sometimes, Jackson. You know that?" I only ever call him by his full name when I'm angry with him.

Bane growls in agreement with my statement before stomping off to his room. He slams the door behind him. I can hear him moving across the floor and into the en-suite bathroom before the shower turns on. It's about time he cleaned up. He's still wearing the same clothes he had on when he came across me and Demi outside two nights ago.

Frustration builds within me. Demi, for reasons unknown to us, hates vampires and the longer she is here, the more her hatred for our kind is growing. Jax is not the best person to be talking to her, and he's only making it worse. Stalking away, I leave Jax in the kitchen and head towards Demi's room.

When I'm outside the door, I spot it's partly open. With Bane having busted the door open earlier, there's no way for her to shut it completely. Through the crack, I can see her pacing back and forth, muttering to herself.

"Stupid fucking vampires... coming in here with their hotness, sexy tattoos, and muscles. Nope, they're vampires, Demi. You still hate them!" Most of her words brush over me, but my ears perk up when I hear my name.

She thinks my tattoos are sexy. She could hardly even see them with the shirt I was wearing in the club. But if she wants to see more, I'll gladly show her every single one of them. Raising my fist, I knock gently, her pacing comes to a stop as she swivels around to the door.

"Fuck off!" She rasps.

"Demi, please. I just want to talk." I want to push the door open further, but I resist the urge.

"Just leave me alone! I've had enough of you vamps for one day."

She rushes to the door and slams it in my face; I hear a chair being scraped across the floor and pushed against it. Fuck, I just need to talk to her. To try to calm her racing heart. But I won't barge in there when she doesn't want company.

Spotting the chair Bane must have put outside her door, I sink down onto it. I'll just wait for her to come out. She's going to want food at some point, right?

Chapter 12

Demi

Fucking vampires, and their stupid blood.
That must have been what I licked off my lips when I first woke up here. Even though there was a metallic tang to it, it was still the best thing I've ever tasted and a part of me craves more. Rubbing my hands against my forehead, my thoughts are racing. I'm disgusted by the fact they gave me their blood but relieved it won't turn me into one of them.

But what kind of life do I have right now? I have a psychotic wolf who is clearly going to come back for me at some point, and three vampires, one of whom I've kissed, protecting me. Well, maybe not Jax. He's an asshole. He has absolutely no concept of human feelings, and the shit show he dumped on me with his bucket load of information.

My head is throbbing a little, a headache forming. I'm back to pacing the room again. If I carry on at this rate, I'll wear a hole in the floor in no time. Making my way into the bathroom, I turn on the tap, waiting for the water to warm a little before splashing the liquid over my face. Glancing in the mirror, I look gaunt, dark circles visible under my eyes.

How long has it been since I last ate? I remember eating before heading to the club to meet Ginny.

Ginny.

The thought of her name makes the loss of my friend break my heart all over again. Do her parents know? Has anyone thought to tell them? And if they have, what have they been told? That a group of wolves savagely raped and murdered her? I'm guessing not. The Council wouldn't want that getting out in the open.

Every case we have like this in the ER is never marked as a vampire draining someone's blood. It's always heart failure, or a wild animal attack depending on if their throat was ripped out or not. The family never gets to know that their relative was murdered. There have been so many times I've wanted to tell someone, anyone. But an NDA makes that impossible.

The hospital would happily fire me if they found out it was me, and even then, who would I tell? Vampires run this sector; the news, the radio, even the travel in and out of the area. If I came forward, I'd probably disappear like those that try to run from the monthly blood donations. No, instead I'll have to keep my trap shut and try to save the people I can.

My brain is going a mile a second, and I can barely even think of one thing before it shifts to something else.

Will I be safe if I go back to my apartment? Should I stay here? Will they let me?

I know the wolves will come for me, I just don't know when. The one in charge wants to take me as his own, but I have no idea why.

I thought they had balls in the wolves' sector, where they found a human to mate with. I don't know how it works exactly, but I'm sure it's not their choice. If it isn't, why haven't any of those wolves taken a woman there, rather than coming here and wanting me? What the hell makes me so special?

Nothing, as far as I know. I grew up in a loving family with my parents and Antonio. I started training to be a nurse and got a job at the local emergency department. Other than my parents being murdered, there really isn't anything significant about me.

The headache is getting stronger, and my temples are throbbing. I'm still standing in the bathroom, not sure what to do with myself. Opening the drawers, I search for some Tylenol, or any type of pain med. As long as it makes this throbbing go away, I don't care at this point.

I find nothing of use in them, they're empty. I'm guessing this room isn't used much, considering there weren't even any towels in here. Slamming the drawers shut, the sound seems to reverberate through my head. I rub my temples again.

Do the vampires have any pain meds? Is that something they even need?

Before I ask them for help, I plan on searching the rest of the room, just on the off chance there's something in here, although I'm already doubting it. Making my way back into the bedroom, I head for the other door. Opening it, I find an empty walk-in closet. I make my way back out and check all the drawers in the room, but like the ones in the bathroom, they're all empty.

I stormed off to the bedroom, not wanting to talk to the vampires anymore, but it looks like I'm going to have to suck it up if I want something for my head. Moving to the door, I pull the chair from under the handle. I'm going to have to see if one of them will fix it, if they let me stay here for now. Maybe I can ask Bane, seeing as he's the one who damaged it.

Cracking the door open, there is someone sitting outside on a chair I hadn't noticed before. The hallway is so dark, I can't see who it is. By the size of them, it's definitely not Bane, so that leaves Jax or Diego. God, I hope it's Diego. I really don't want any more of Jax's shit. The guy is a grade-A douchebag.

The figure's head whips around, and he stands suddenly, stepping into the light coming from the bedroom. I let out a sigh. Thank God, it's Diego. I take him in just like I did at the bar. He really is gorgeous. He's all muscle and tattooed skin. I still can't see his tattoos in their entirety, but I want to divest him of his clothes and explore where the ink goes.

Demi, stop. You've kissed Bane. You can't be thinking of getting down and dirty with Diego, too.

"Hi." I squeak out. His lips quirk up on one side as he gives me the most beautiful smile.

"Demi." It's only now that I'm noticing his voice. Even in that one word; it's like honey that reaches straight to my core.

"I have a headache and I need some Tylenol. I have no idea if you guys need them. I mean, you're a vampire, of course you wouldn't. You probably only need blood. But for us humans, we need a little more than that." I rush out, unable to stop my verbal diarrhea.

Diego's eyes widen at the mass of words I just threw at him, a smile still gracing his lips. His lips look as soft as pillows, and I want to feel them on mine.

"I'm sure we can sort something out. There is a twenty-four-hour store a block down. One of us can go get them for you."

"I can always go by myself." I don't want to be reliant on anyone, and definitely not vampires.

"No!" The force of that single word has me taking a step back. Diego holds his hands up in a peaceful gesture. "I'm sorry, Demi. We're just worried the wolves could still be out there waiting for you."

A shudder races through my body at the thought of that psycho and his pack getting their hands on me after what they did to Ginny. I'm panicking again. I didn't even think before suggesting I could go myself. Diego takes a cautious step forward, his arms wrap around me as he pulls me into his chest.

My head rests on him, and I can hear his steady heartbeat. The sound is soothing. Placing my hand on his chest, I can feel the heat from his body. His hands rub circles on my back, and I almost melt into him.

"I'll go to the store for you. Don't worry, Demi. I won't let the wolves get you." He murmurs in my ear.

Leaning back slightly, I lift my head to peek at him. His pupils are dilated as he looks into mine. As my gaze stays on him, I start to calm again. I'm not sure what it is about these men that eases the fear rushing through my body, but Diego and Bane both make me feel safe. Is it because they fed me their blood? Is that what is making me a horny mess? My reactions don't make sense.

As I stare into his eyes, he leans his head down towards mine and I raise up on my tiptoes. His lips are so close I can feel his breath feathering over mine and I clench my thighs together again.

What am I even doing? Why am I so drawn to these men?

Our lips touch, and I gasp as my body tingles all over. I was right, his lips are the softest I've ever felt. Moving my hands around his neck, I hold him against me. He nips at my lips with blunt teeth till I open them for him. As soon as I do, our tongues tangle, and he tastes divine. His hands move to my ass, and he squeezes it.

I feel something sharp against my tongue and it takes a second to realize it's his fangs. I should pull away, but I don't. Sweeping my tongue against each one, he lets out a groan. With his hands spanned over my behind, he pulls me closer to him. Our groins rub together and I can feel his arousal.

As our tongues battle, I feel a sting as one of his fangs cuts my flesh. He releases another groan as he sucks on my tongue, taking small tugs of the blood coming from the wound. His hands grip my ass as he lifts me, and my legs wrap around his waist instinctively.

Suddenly, we move, and my back is slammed into a wall. His erection is in just the right place, pushing the seam of the sweatpants against my clit. With my legs locked around his middle, he moves a hand down to the waistline of my pants.

Breaking the kiss, he pulls back. My blood is smeared across his lips and his eyes are blazing red.

Should it terrify me? Probably. But I can't deny how horny I am. Diego's touch is nothing like the wolves'. Theirs repulsed me, but with him, I want more. His fingers brush along the top of the borrowed sweatpants as he looks into my eyes, asking for permission.

I give him a small nod, and he pushes his hand under the layers of fabric. His rough finger brushes across my clit and I groan. I'm so wet already, and he uses it to his advantage. Slicking his fingers with my natural lubricant, he pushes two of them inside my tight heat. Another groan escapes me.

His lips connect with mine again as his fingers thrust in and out of me. I can feel his erection pushing against my thigh as he rubs against me. Between his fingers, his lips, and his thumb now rubbing my clit, my senses are overwhelmed. I'm getting so close to the release I was denied earlier.

His lips trail away from mine and brush down the side of my neck. He pushes a third finger inside me as I ride his hand. I'd prefer his cock inside me, but this will do for now. His fingers brush against my g-spot and another moan rushes from my lips.

I let my head fall back against the wall behind me, dropping to the side slightly. Looking down the hallway, I see Bane standing at the end, watching us. I can see the clear outline of his cock through his jeans, his hand rubbing against it.

I watch as he undoes his fly and pulls it out. His hand fists around it, and he pumps in time with Diego's fingers pushing in and out of me. Keeping my eyes on him, I lick my lips. I'm so very close. Diego's fangs brush against my neck, his tongue lapping across my skin.

With one final push on my clit, my pussy tightens around Diego's fingers as I come. Diego and Bane both groan. Cum splashes out of Bane, splattering onto the wooden floor in the hallway. Riding out the last of my orgasm, my breath is sawing in and out of my lungs.

Diego rests his head on my shoulder. I can feel his breath against my skin. Bane's still watching us, his deflating cock hanging out of the fly of his jeans. My legs are like jello as Diego lowers me to the ground. I can barely hold my own weight from the intensity of my orgasm.

"Fuck, you're amazing." Diego whispers in my ear. "I can't wait to sink my cock inside you." His words make me shudder.

"What about right now?" I rasp out.

"Would you want an audience for that too? Or would you prefer that Bane join in?" My pussy clenches at the thought. I look down the hallway, but Bane is already gone. In his place stands Jax, and he looks less than impressed, his arms folded across his chest as he stares at us.

"Demetria, I need to speak with you." There he goes, demanding again.

"Rain check?" I smile at Diego before following Jax.

Chapter 13

Jax

Demetria already has Bane, and Diego wrapped around her little finger. I can smell her release flooding the hallway and it's making me rock hard. I leave her there, hoping she will follow me back into the kitchen.

While Diego was entertaining our guest, I was preparing some food for her. Hopefully, as soon as she has some sustenance in her system, she will be up for talking. Or maybe the endorphins from her orgasm will make her more open. Either way, I need answers.

"You want to know what happened," her soft voice calls out, more statement than question.

She's so close to me, near enough to have me tensing up. I grab the plate of eggs and toast off the counter and turn, passing it to her. Her eyes widen as she looks from me and back to the plate again.

"Thanks..." she takes the plate from me and shifts toward the dining room table before she stops, quickly changing her direction to the breakfast bar instead. But that doesn't stop her gaze moving back to the blood soaked table. I make a mental note to order a new one.

"Coffee or tea?" I need to pull her attention away from it, I can see the slight tremble in her hands as she places the plate down.

"Coffee, two sugars, and a splash of milk, please." Demetria seems a little more confident now that I've drawn her attention to me instead.

At least she's polite.

I move to the coffee pot and set to making her order. I can hear a fork scraping against the plate, so at least she's eating. When I finish the cup, I place it down beside her. She gives me a small nod but carries on shoveling food in her mouth, gulping down coffee between bites.

The need to press her for more information is at the forefront of my mind, but I also don't want her to freak out again. I've shared a lot of revelations with her in a small amount of time and I'm not sure how much more she can take before she fully snaps. And that's not something I want for her.

I have a fierce need to protect her, just like the others do. I have an inkling of what it is, but it's not something I want to mention to Bane or Diego. Not yet anyway. I need to know what their feelings are towards her before I make my intentions known.

There is a deep need inside me to claim her as my own, but I have a feeling both Diego and Bane are feeling exactly the same way. It's not completely unheard of for vampires to share a human they care about, but it is uncommon given how territorial we can be. In exchange for blood and sex, they give the human doses of vampire blood to prolong their life. Even a meager amount is enough to replenish the aging cells. I've heard of all sorts of orgies happening between groups such as this, but I know what I'm feeling for Demetria is not just about blood and sex. There is more to it than that.

But the thought of getting too close to her leaves me anxious. After my sire killed the one human woman I cared about, I've pushed myself away from them, not wanting to get close to another in case they are snatched away from me again. Besides, they're fragile things.

I've slept with human women over the years, but one night flings and nothing more. However, I've had too many approach me wanting my blood. They don't care about me for anything other than wanting me to prolong their lives.

I'm not sure I'm ready to get close to her. What if we can't protect her from the wolves? What if they get their hands on her and then she's gone again? I don't think my heart could take it if I lost someone else I care about.

The sound of the plate pushing across the countertop pulls my attention back to Demetria. Her eyes are on me now and I can still smell the lingering scent of her orgasm. My need to be close to her crawls back to the front of my mind. Leaning on the breakfast bar opposite her, I look over at her.

"I'm sorry for everything you have been through, Demetria." Her eyes widen at my statement. "Something like this should never have happened in our territory."

"It's not your fault, Jax."

"It's our territory and I should have known there were wolves here. For that, I am sorry."

"I don't understand why they are here. The one I think is in charge made it sound like they'd been here a while." I quirk a brow at her, waiting for her to give me more information. "He said he'd been watching me. I think... I think he killed my parents."

Her admission hits me like a ton of bricks. What connection is there between what happened here and what exactly happened to her parents to make her think these wolves killed them?

"Could you tell me more?" I urge her on.

"Two years ago, my mom called me late one night. She was screaming down the phone that there was a monster in the house. I thought she meant vampires, but when I got there, there was blood everywhere." She sniffles. "Something had ripped apart my father. I found my mother naked and covered in blood. The cops said it was a home invasion."

"But you don't think it was?" She shakes her head at me. There are all sorts of monsters in this world. A half crazed wolf could easily be the culprit.

"Nope. The wounds looked exactly like the ones inflicted on Ginny." A stray tear runs down her cheek. I can't stop myself from leaning forward and wiping it away with my finger.

"I'm sorry, Demetria."

"The one in charge said he's been watching me for a while. What if he killed Ginny and my parents? Is it all my fault? Are they dead because of me?" I can see her hands shaking as she clenches her fists tightly.

"Sometimes wolves go crazy. We end up with a few strays passing into other sectors. If they don't find their mate there, then they go searching for them. There are two types of mates for wolves. A true mate, the other half of their soul, and a blood mate."

"So I'm not his true mate, then?"

"You most certainly are not," I growl out. Her entire body tenses at my tone of voice. "You have nothing to fear from me, Demetria. We will protect you."

"But what about when I go home? What then?"

"Stay here." A voice speaks from behind her, and Demetria spins her head around to look at Bane.

He comes closer to her, standing behind her. Her shoulders loosen as she relaxes from his close proximity. Bane passes her a packet of pain meds and she smiles up at him, nodding her thanks. Popping two into her hand, she swallows them with a gulp of coffee.

I eye them both. There is definitely a connection between Bane and Demetria. They calm each other, even though she should be terrified. Bane's presence is enough to ease her anxieties, and she seems to do the same for him. He's protective of her, and would easily rip someone apart for her, but he seems more talkative around her.

For now, I'll keep my distance. I don't want to get attached to her; I don't want to lose someone else. And if what I think is true, I could lose my closest friends because of her. I clear my throat.

"He's right, stay here. For as long as it takes for the threat to be exterminated."

"I can't just stay, I mean..." she stops to think. "Maybe for a little while, but I have a life. I have a job."

"Right now, Demetria, your safety is our priority."

"I guess..." She seems so unsure of herself right now.

It's no surprise. She's in an apartment with three vampires she's only just met. Two of which she has definitely grown intimately close to. I wait for a pang of jealousy, but it never comes.

"This is such a shit show. I just... I don't understand everything that is happening. If these wolves killed my parents, as well as Ginny…"

Bane steps up behind Demetria. He towers over her as she sits on the barstool, but he stoops slightly and wraps an arm around her chest. She shifts one of her hands, and it rests on his bare forearm.

"It's not your fault, Demi." He whispers close to her ear.

"But how isn't it? They're after me, and so far, three people I care about have been ripped apart." She looks exhausted and deflated by the situation.

"It really isn't. This is just some sick game to the wolves. Whether it was you or someone else, I believe they would have done whatever it took to isolate their prey. I think they want to push you to the breaking point."

She shakes her head, black hair falling across her face, hiding her facial expression from me. Reaching across the breakfast bar, I lay a hand over the one she has resting on the table. As my skin touches hers, she jumps slightly. Her crystal blue eyes flick up to mine. I can see she's scared, maybe even feels a little hopeless, but we won't let anything happen to her. She's ours to protect.

Chapter 14

Diego

Demi walks past me as I enter the kitchen, saying she needs rest and time to let the pain meds Bane found kick in. She's slept already, but I can't blame her. After I made her come in the hallway, I headed to Bane's room to let him know about the pain med situation. He said he'd sort it and I went straight to my bedroom.

When Demi came, I found my own release in my pants and desperately needed to change. Even as I'd shook my wet jeans off, I found my cock hard again and jacked off with thoughts of her tight pussy squeezing my fingers whilst Bane watched us.

When I get back into the kitchen, I notice Jax is clearing away the dishes. His shoulders are hunched as he works. Bane lingers by the breakfast bar. It's as good a time as any to work out exactly what we are going to do.

"So, what's the deal, boss?" I say as I drop down into a chair at the dining table. Laying my hands on the stained wood, my nails scratch into the surface as I think of the wolves and what they did to Demi and her friend again.

"We know they want Demetria. From what she's said, the leader of this nomad pack wants her as his mate. And it sounds like he's going to stop at nothing to get her."

"We keep her here, we protect her." Bane shifts on his feet. I wonder if a part of him wants to go to Demi.

"We can't keep her here forever though, Bane. She's already made that clear." Jax finishes drying his hands on the dishcloth and leans back against the counter.

"We could always fuck her till all she can think about is our cocks. I mean, mine alone should be enough for her to never want to leave." I grin and Bane snarls at me. "What?" I shrug.

"Enough, Diego. We don't need your stupid jokes."

"Who said it was a joke?" I mutter. Another snarl rumbles from Bane. I don't know what his deal is. He wants to fuck her as much as I do, he came just watching me finger fuck her.

"For now, she stays here. We make her as comfortable as we can, and we make sure one of us is with her at all times. Bane, I want you to call more guys in to work the doors, and make sure we station someone at the stairs to the apartment." Jax is always the one to give the orders.

"When she's done resting, I'll find out where she lives. The least we can do is get some of her clothes. What about her job, though? Doesn't sound like she will be up for missing work." I really don't want her to go, but we need a backup plan in case she refuses to take some time off.

"Good thinking. We'll deal with the work situation later. For now, I'm going to head down to the club and check everything is okay. We've already had Harley covering for Diego since we've all done a disappearing act since Thursday night."

"She deserves a pay rise. Though not having to see your ugly face at the beginning of her shift might be all the compensation she needs, Jax." I smirk as he whips his head around to pin me with a glare.

Bane sulks as he makes his way to the door. He was probably hoping Jax would get him to stay upstairs with Demi, but I pulled the short straw on that one. I snigger and Bane glares at me over his shoulder. He exits the apartment and heads back down to the club to call in a few more guys.

Jax walks past me but stops to rest a hand on my shoulder. I look up at him, an eyebrow raised in silent question.

"Try to keep your hands to yourself, Diego. Jack off all you like, but no more repeats of the hallway." I give him a curt nod and he pulls his hand away, leaving in the same direction as Bane.

He's delirious if he thinks I'm not going to touch Demi. She calls to me and it's a song I can't resist. Jumping up, I make my way to her bedroom. It feels like I'm being a creeper just lurking outside, but it feels wrong to be away from her.

Reaching for the door handle, I let out a soft laugh as I remember that Bane broke it off last night when Demi was having a nightmare. I wonder if Jax has mentioned anything to him about it.

Cracking the door, I look in through the gap. The lamp on the side table is still lit, giving the room a soft glow. She's laying on her side, the comforter wrapped around her. One of her long, pale legs is on top, the bottom of the pair of boxers Jax loaned her peeking out. Her black hair is fanned out across the pillow and the sweatpants she was wearing have been dropped haphazardly on the floor beside the bed.

She looks so peaceful in sleep. A part of me wants to enter the room and lie beside her, to feel her body close to mine. Shaking my head, I try to push those thoughts away. I stalk away from the bedroom and head back to the living area.

Looking out of the window, I can see the street where the front entrance of the club sits. Dusk is falling fast. The barriers for the line thread around the side of the building. Humans and vampires alike come in their hundreds, wanting to enjoy the mischief they can get up to behind its doors.

We're one of the few clubs in the area that allow the consumption of human blood directly from the vein on site. So far, everything has run smoothly. We have security inside the building who watch for any patrons that are trying to push the rules. We've only had a couple of instances where we have had to eject a vampire and send the human to the hospital for fluids. Our safety record is something we pride ourselves on.

A figure on the other side of the street draws my attention. He's slouching under one of the main street lights, shaggy brown hair brushing his shoulders. At first, I think he's watching the club, maybe a customer who is considering entering. But then I notice his eyes are looking at the window I'm standing behind.

He shouldn't be able to see me. Jax had one-way glass fitted in all the windows. I can look out, but no one can see in - the window shows a reflection of the outside world. His eyes are definitely looking this way though, like he can see me watching him through the glass.

My cell phone beeps, and I pull it from my pocket, looking down at the screen.

How's Demi?

It's a text from Bane. He's not even been gone for thirty minutes and he's already checking up on her. Dude's got it bad.

Sleeping. Chill dude, I got this.

I fire back the text, wondering if I should let him know about the figure I saw. My eyes flicker back up to the window, but the man is gone. I tilt my head to the side, scouting the surrounding area to see if he's lurking anywhere nearby, but he's gone.

I'm about to text Bane to tell him to keep an eye out when a whimper catches my attention. With my vampire speed, I'm outside Demi's door instantly. She's writhing around the bed, her limbs flailing and tangling in the sheets as she moves. In seconds, I'm crouching beside the bed. My hands grasp Demi's shoulders. She shrieks, but her eyes are still closed.

"Demi, shh. It's okay, you're safe." Her body thrashes even as I attempt to stop her movements. "It's just a bad dream. Wake up." I shake her slightly.

Her eyes fly open. I can see the faint evidence of tears in the corners and her breath is coming out in pants again as she takes me in.

"Diego...?" She whispers.

"It's me, Demi, you're okay." Moving my hand to her face, I push her hair out of the way.

"He was here. He wanted to take me." Her voice trembles. "He got me, took me somewhere. I tried not to cry out." A single tear rolls down her cheek. "He likes my fear. But... he... he stripped me. I tried to fight back."

"I promise you're okay, he's not here. I won't let him take you. None of us will." My hand drifts to her cheek, and she places her shaking hand over mine.

She seems calmer, and now would be the perfect time to leave. I move my hand away from her face and place a gentle kiss on her knuckles, leaving my hand around hers as I stand. Her crystal blue eyes track my movements, her gaze never leaving me.

"I should go, let you rest." I go to release her hand, but her fingers wrap around mine.

"Please... don't go." She says. I hear her heart rate spike, her vulnerability laid bare by her body's responses.

"Jax would prefer it if I left you be."

"I don't care what he wants, *I* need you here." Her grip on my hand tightens, and I look down at our connected hands.

"Okay..." I let go of her hand and slip around to the other side of the bed.

Kicking off my boots, I sit on top of the covers and lay back against the pillows. Demi snuggles down next to me, pulling the sheet back over her shoulder.

"You can get more comfortable if you want. I don't bite..." she pauses for a split second. "That's your job, considering you're the one with the fangs." My eyes shift to her face, and I can see the smile on her lips. I let out a soft chuckle.

"I'm not sure you'd want me getting too comfortable, Demi. To do that, I'd need to take off my shirt and jeans, and well… I'm going commando."

Her eyes widen, and I can see the spark of lust within them. She hums slightly, considering what I've said. Moving her hands on top of the covers, she reaches for my shirt. Pulling it up, I lift my back off the bed and drag the fabric over my head, depositing it on the floor.

Her hand drops to my chest, fingers tracing the tattoos on my skin. She brushes them across the swirling black pattern, down my pecs, and further down over my abdominal muscles. I shiver at her touch, my cock twitching inside my jeans. The head pushes against the rough fabric and I groan from the sensation.

Her fingers don't stop their movement, going all the way to the waistline where my tattoos are cut off by the fabric. Undoing the button, she grasps the zipper and lowers it slowly over my growing bulge. She reaches inside, but before she can connect with my throbbing flesh, I grab her wrist, halting her movement. I need to stop her, even if it pains me to do it.

She looks up at me, questions in her eyes, even as she licks her lips. "Why do I feel so drawn to you?" Her voice is unsure, but only for a fraction of a second.

I don't understand why either of us is drawn to the other. I've never felt this way about anyone before, but with her, my cock is perpetually hard. If I let her touch me right now, I can guarantee I will come straight away. I want so much to sink myself into that wicked mouth of hers. To feel her tongue as she laps at my pre-cum and I pump into her depths until I explode.

"Fine! I'll join you. But turn off the light, and no touching."

Demi nods, rolling quickly and dousing the light. As the room is plunged into darkness, I slip out of the bed. Pushing my jeans down my hips and letting them drop to the floor, I step out of them. I turn, lifting the covers, and slip beneath them, lying still on my back.

She shuffles closer to me. Just another inch and her glorious body will be flush with mine, but she keeps her distance.

Stupid Diego, you didn't want her to touch your cock. Not the rest of you.

Putting my arm under Demi's head, I pull her closer. She gasps as her soft body connects with mine. Resting a hand on my stomach and her head on my chest. I feel hair tickle the underside of my arm as she wriggles to get herself comfy. Gently, I kiss the top of her head once she stops moving.

The touch of her hand on my skin leaves a trail of fire. I only wanted her to turn the light off so she couldn't see just how hard I am for her; how much I want her. As her hand edges lower, I take it in my own and stop her from taking this any further.

"Sleep, Demi."

She lets out a long breath. One of her legs brushes against mine, but it doesn't take long before her breathing evens out and she slips into sleep. I lay there, holding her close and staring up at the ceiling in the darkness. I don't know how I got so lucky for her to let me into her bed, but I don't want to fuck this up.

Chapter 15

Demi

The cock in my pussy leaves me feeling full as I rock over its length. A gasp leaves my mouth as they fill me to the hilt. My hands run over the chest below me, feeling every part of the scarred skin. Opening my eyes, I look down at Bane. His eyes are fully red as he thrusts in and out of me.

I feel another cock rubbing against my ass, already slick with lube. Pushing up against my rosebud, I can't stop the gasp as they breach the ring of muscle. Turning my head, Diego is behind me. His eyes are closed and his hands resting on my ass as he slowly rocks inside me, pushing his hard cock in, inch by delicious inch.

When they're both fully seated within me, they stop moving, letting me get accustomed to the sensation. They're stretching me to the max, and it feels amazing. Once I've relaxed enough, I begin to move, their cocks dragging in and out of both my holes. Bane grips my hips and slams me down onto his cock each time Diego pulls himself back before rocking back inside me.

A noise to my left pulls my attention as they move in and out. Another figure steps out of the shadows. It's Jax and whilst he's fully naked, I can't quite make out his body in the low light. His eyes watch me as his friends fuck me. Stepping up to the side of the bed, his hand rests on my cheek. His fingers run over the seam of my lips, and I open them for *him, licking the end of his thumb and sucking it into my mouth.*

His eyes flare, the red taking over just like Bane's. With a hand in my hair, he guides my mouth to his waiting cock. I want to see all of him, but I want to taste him more. Wrapping my lips around him, I suck him down. My eyes connect with his as he thrusts into my open mouth, not caring when he hits the back of my throat repeatedly and I start to gag.

I should pull away, but fuck if this isn't hot. They fill every one of my holes and I can feel my orgasm rushing up on me as tears prickle at the corners of my eyes and saliva drips down my chin. I'm so fucking close...

My eyes spring open and a yawn passes my lips as I stretch my body out on the bed. That was one hell of a hot dream, I was so close to coming; I bet if I touched my pussy I'd be dripping wet. I roll over into a mass of warmth; Diego is still beside me. That explains the sex dream, I fell asleep with him in my bed, and he stayed.

His arm is slung over his eyes, and the cover is tantalizingly low on his hips. The tattoos I found yesterday reach down below where I can see. My eyes track down his delicious body all the way to the tented fabric at his crotch.

I want to see more, to touch all over, this pull I'm feeling towards him won't let me go. Grasping the cover in my hand, I drag it down slowly as it reveals more of his skin. When his cock is finally on show, I can't help the gasp that escapes from between my lips.

He really is gorgeous everywhere; his long, hard cock stands at attention, nestled between short hair at his groin. It's only then I notice the glint of metal at the end, and I rub my thighs together.

Pushing up onto my knees, I shift further down the bed to get a closer look. As well as the ring through the end of the darkened head, there are bars in a ladder formation up the length.

Jesus Christ, a Jacob's ladder.

Reaching out, I run the tip of my finger up his length, over every bar. His cock jerks at the touch and I lick my lips.

I wonder if he tastes as good as he looks?

Leaning down, I swipe my tongue over the head, licking up the faint trace of pre-cum leaking from him. My hair falls down, forming a curtain across the side of my face as I envelop his steely length. A soft moan has me raising my eyes to his face. His arm is still over his eyes, but his lips are now parted.

Sinking down over him, I flatten my tongue to take more of him in. The bars on the underside brush against my mouth and my pussy tightens, wanting to be filled by his hard flesh and the metal adorning it. Would the bars and the ring hit me in all the right places as he thrusts inside me? I'm dying to find out.

Bracing myself on the bed, I move up and down his length. My tongue swirls around his head, licking up every drop of pre-cum. Closing my eyes, I move quicker, taking his length deeper and deeper with every stroke. His moans are coming in earnest now, and it drives me on.

Fingers thread through my hair, and I lift my eyes back to his face. Those black orbs are searing into me, and his fangs are peeking out between his lips. Using his hands, he guides my movements, his cock pushing deep and that metal bar hitting the back of my throat. I let out my own moan at the sensation.

"Fuck, Demi!" Diego calls out, his hands tightening their grip on my hair.

I get a few more strokes before his hands slip out of my hair and grip my shoulders, dragging me up his body, until his lips connect with mine. My damp pussy pushes against his cock. There's only a small scrap of material between us both; one I wish more than anything wasn't there.

Rocking against his cock, we swallow each other's moans as our tongues dance together. This time though, I manage not to cut myself on his fangs. Pushing me away, his red-rimmed eyes look into mine, and the side of his mouth lifts.

"Turn around, I want your pussy on my face."

Letting go of me, I shift my position, my hands on either side of his thighs. His cock is right in front of my face, still glistening with my saliva. Diego grips my hips, pulling me back so my pussy is over his mouth. There's a ripping sound as he tears apart the boxers I'm wearing. The cool air hits my wet, overheated flesh and I shudder.

I suck his cock back into my mouth, the metal bars brush across my palette and it's an odd sensation. His hands move up and down the insides of my legs and over my ass, but he doesn't once touch where I need him most.

I can feel his hot breath tickling the inside of my thigh as he plants a kiss there. His tongue darts out and licks either side of my mound. A moan escapes my throat. He must like it because he thrusts his cock up into my mouth.

He finally gives me what I need. His tongue licks me from my clit to my dripping wet pussy, the metal bar through his tongue hitting me in all the right places. My thighs tighten around his head, and there's another moan from both of us as we move in sync. I suck down his cock as his tongue delves into my opening.

My hips make small thrusting motions, wanting him deeper inside me. I'm so close now, and from the movement of his lower half, I can only imagine he is too. He thrusts into my mouth as I lower myself down.

I take as much of him as I can, my tongue running along his burning flesh. Taking his balls in my hand, I knead them in my palm. I dart my tongue over the slit and metal at the end of his cock. It seems to be enough to give him the final push. His cum spurts inside my mouth, and the groan he emits makes his tongue vibrate inside me.

With his cum filling my mouth, I swallow every drop. My tongue sweeps over every inch of him to make sure I don't miss any. Pulling my mouth back from him, I lick up the sides and give his balls one last squeeze.

A finger pushes inside my tight opening, along with his tongue, as his thumb brushes over my clit. I'm finally pushed over the edge. My thighs clench and my body shudders as my orgasm hits me like a tidal wave.

Diego's finger and tongue still thrust inside me, prolonging my orgasm, but I can't stop myself from collapsing on top of him. Resting my head on his thigh, I struggle to catch my breath. Even as I lie there, his tongue runs up and down my folds, lapping up the juices from my release and sending small shivers through my body.

Rolling me onto my back, Diego shifts on the bed so he is poised above me, settled between my thighs. His lips glisten with my juices. Pushing them to mine, his tongue teases its way into my mouth, and I can taste myself on him. I feel my excitement build as his hand lifts my t-shirt and his fingers tweak my nipple. The metal at the end of his cock rubs against my clit and I gasp at the sensation on my already sensitive flesh.

How can he be hard again already? He's only just come.

But I'm wet and ready for him. His cock moves back and forth through my juices, and I just want to feel him inside me.

Wrapping my legs around his waist, I pull him closer. The head of his cock nudges at my opening; his piercing rests against my clit and sends small shock waves through my entire system. My fingers tangle in his hair as I hold his lips against mine. So damn close, I just need him inside me.

"DIEGO!" Jax's voice thunders through the apartment and I'm shocked the walls aren't shaking with the ferocity.

Before I can even blink, Diego is across the other side of the room in all his naked glory. His cock is still hard and covered in my juices. Pushing up on my elbows, my legs are still open, and my pussy is pulsing.

The door slams against the wall, and Jax is there. He looks almost feral as he glares at Diego, his fangs bared as he snarls at him. Striding across the room, he grabs Diego by the back of the neck and all but drags him from the room, throwing him through the door.

He turns back to me, his eyes stopping on mine before trailing down my body. My nipples are hard, with the t-shirt still bunched up around my breasts. His eyes go lower until he's focused entirely on what lies between my legs.

There is a look of lust in his eyes, and I wonder if I can tempt him to finish what he stopped Diego from completing. The continual need to be with them all makes me push my usual boundaries. Tweaking my nipple, I watch as his tongue darts out to wet his lips. Moving my hand down my stomach, I reach my pussy and run my fingers through the dampness before pushing two inside. Jax's nostrils flare as he takes me in.

If he won't let me fuck Diego, then maybe I can get him to finish me off. Thrusting my fingers in and out of myself, I moan, throwing my head back and closing my eyes. I continue masturbating, not stopping any of the noises I make as I bite my lip.

The door slamming startles me, and I open my eyes. The room is empty and I'm alone again. Letting out a huff, I flop back on the bed and look up at the ceiling, pulling my fingers from myself.

Just one more orgasm, that's all I wanted. Is that too much to ask for?

Chapter 16

Jax

Slamming the door behind me, I lean back on the wall beside it, my fists clenched at my sides. I wanted so much to rush across the room and taste her sweet nectar, which I could smell as soon as I entered the apartment. Walking in on her half-naked, and Diego, completely nude, had nearly done me in.

Her rosy pink nipples were hard, her lips bruised and the folds between her legs swollen and drenched. It would have been so easy to kneel on the floor, drag her to the edge of the bed, and sink my tongue inside her. I wanted nothing more than to sweep through her folds and dip inside her.

I can almost taste her on my lips already. My cock is throbbing in my slacks, making them uncomfortably tight. Since throwing Diego out of the room, he's already taken off. Probably to put on some clothes.

I hear the bathroom door in her room open and shut again, cutting off some of her scent, but it's still driving me crazy. When the shower turns on, I huff out a breath and push away from the wall, storming into the kitchen. Diego didn't make it as far as his room. In fact, it doesn't even look like he attempted to make it that far at all.

He's standing buck ass naked in front of the open fridge, a carton of orange juice pressed to his lips, gulping down the contents. Pulling the carton away, he wipes the back of his hand across his mouth and his eyes fall on me.

There's a smirk adorning his lips, one that I'm going to have to wipe off his face. I'm across the room in less than a second. I wrap my hand around his throat and shove him back against the counter. The granite has to be digging into his back from how hard I'm pushing him against it.

Diego drops the carton of juice, the sticky liquid splashing on my leather shoes. My hand flexes around his neck, but his smirk never falters. I let out a feral snarl and pull him towards me before slamming him back into the granite with enough force to crack it.

"What did I say, Diego? No repeats. You are supposed to be protecting her, not trying to fuck her!" My voice raises as I reach the end of my sentence. "And now I find you naked in her room, your cock as wet as her pussy."

Diego grunts, opening his mouth to talk, but my grip is too tight. I flex my fingers again, letting my hand loosen somewhat on his neck. Diego coughs and clears his throat.

"What's wrong with both, boss?"

Wrenching back my hand, I clench my fist and let it fly towards his mouth. It connects with his jaw, forcing his head back with the impact. Diego laughs as he brings his head upright, blood dripping from his split lip. He spits red on the floor, and I growl at him.

"Tell me, Jax, are you pissed because I almost fucked her? Or because you're so desperate to be the first to sink your cock into that tight pussy?" His eyebrow raises at me as the smirk reappears on his mouth, blood dripping down his chin.

I go to lunge for him again, but a hand on my shoulder stops me. I look to my right to find Bane glowering over my shoulder at Diego. He shakes his head at me and I shrug his hand off, stalking away from Diego before I do something more than punch him.

"Diego! Not helping." Bane keeps his gaze on Diego as he speaks. "Go put some clothes on." He jerks his head in the direction of the hallway.

My anger is still simmering just below the surface, but as Diego pushes away from the counter and leaves the kitchen, I feel it settling. Bane brushes past me and picks up the carton of juice that's spilled on the floor, throwing it in the trash. Grabbing a cloth, he wipes up the spilled liquid.

"I don't know why he can't just do as he's told." I huff out. "I told him not to touch Demetria, and then I come home and find him naked in her room."

I don't even mention the compromising position I found her in, or the fact she was trying to entice me by masturbating. The thought of what I saw is enough to make my cock twitch again. Bane stands up straight, dropping the soaking wet cloth in the sink, and looks over at me, his eyebrow raised.

"You know why, Jax."

The ever-stoic Bane has said more words to us since Demetria arrived than he has in the last few years. It's usually just grunts or looks that we have to interpret. I'm guessing he knows more about what's happening than he's letting on.

"Go sort yourself out." Bane looks from me to the bulge in my pants, and I clench my fists again.

I know exactly where I'd like to be right now, and how I'd like to be sorting out my issue, but I won't cross that line. Spinning on my heel, I walk away, heading for my office. Bane lets out a soft chuckle when he realizes I'm not heading to my bedroom.

Flicking on the light as I walk through the door of my home office, I shut it behind me. Heading straight to my liquor cabinet, I grasp the whiskey decanter and pour myself a healthy serving into one of the crystal glasses.

Taking a sip, I walk to my desk and drop down into the large leather seat behind it. There is so much to do. I still need to put an order in this month for the club, get someone out to fix the bedroom door that Bane broke, and kill some goddamn filthy mutts. All whilst trying not to kill Diego for laying his hands on Demetria and dealing with my constantly aroused state around the little human.

Pulling my phone out of my pocket, I hit one of the few names on my speed dial. It only rings three times before it's answered.

"Hello...?" I can hear grunts and moans through the line, and I roll my eyes.

"Achilles, it's Jax. We need to talk." There's a high-pitched giggle close to the mouthpiece. Wouldn't surprise me if he's balls deep in his flavor of the week.

"What can I do for you, mate?" The moans on the other end of the line get louder, and I hear flesh slapping together.

"I need you to come and retrieve a body from the club." It's business as usual. Achilles' antics are no issue of mine.

"What are we going with this time? Animal attack or heart attack? Do the bloodsuckers in your club not read the signs you put up?"

"It wasn't one of my kind this time. Some wolves are in my territory." There's a squeal and a thump over the phone and a few mumbled words I don't quite catch. "Achilles, you still there?"

"I'll be right over." He hangs up before I can get another word out.

I make my way to the large bookcase on the left wall. Pulling out the right book, the shelves begin to shift, revealing a coded door. Punching in the correct digits, the locks disengage and the door clicks open. I slip inside the opening and pull it closed behind me.

Making my way down the secret staircase, I bypass the door that leads to my office in the club and descend to the basement instead. When I get to the bottom, I punch in another code and exit into the darkened hallway. Taking the second door on the right, I enter the refrigerated room. Achilles is already inside.

He looks a little ruffled, his pure white hair not in its usually perfect style. There are red lipstick marks all over his neck and shirt collar, and I can't help but smile. At least someone is getting some.

You could be too if you just gave in to your desires. Even my inner monologue is an asshole.

"Sorry to pull you away from happy hour," I remark.

"It's nothing. Now tell me more, what do you mean wolves?"

I gesture towards the body of Demetria's friend laid out on the metal table in the center of the room. She's still covered in my suit jacket from the other night. Achilles steps closer to the table, inspecting the parts of her he can see without touching.

"A pack of wolves attacked her outside the club. I smell at least seven separate scents. They raped her, then ripped out her throat. I'm assuming she died instantly."

With a flick of his hands, black smoke floats from Achilles' fingers, making its way under the jacket. The fabric slowly lifts and edges to the bottom of the table, revealing her entire body. A gasp escapes him.

"Poor girl. Those savage, disgusting beasts!" He snaps. His hand reaches for Ginny's cheek but stops an inch away. "They are meant to cherish women, not rip them apart."

I look at her body, she's covered from head to toe in blood and bodily fluids. I can smell the lingering scent of the wolves even now, and it leaves my fangs throbbing and my fists clenching. The need to rip them apart rushes to the surface. I'm glad I decided not to let Demetria see her friend, it would have broken her heart all over again.

"Is there anything you can do about the semen? Even if you use your magic on the morgue attendants, someone is going to notice it."

"Of course." Drifting his hands over Ginny's body, the same black smoke that moved my jacket settles over her.

With a snap of his fingers, it's gone again and so are the other stains, leaving only the blood behind.

"Thank you." I reach my hand out and Achilles grasps it and gives it a firm shake. But he doesn't let go straight away.

"Is there more to this tale, friend?" He lifts a perfectly shaped, white eyebrow, his silvery eyes boring into mine.

"There is always more, Achilles. You should know that by now. But another time. I'll transfer payment shortly."

Achilles nods and lets go of my hand, moving closer to Ginny's body once more. With one hand just above her shoulder, but not quite touching her, they are both engulfed in purple and black smoke. Once it clears, they are both gone. The only trace that Ginny was ever here is the dried blood on the metal table, and my blood-soaked jacket.

Lifting my jacket from the table, I inspect the ruined fabric. I leave the refrigerated room and head to the end of the hallway towards the furnace, throwing the jacket inside. I don't want it anywhere near Demetria, especially when there is no way I'm going to be able to get rid of the blood that has seeped into the fibers.

I head out of the basement and up the stairs, pausing at the entrance that leads to the office in the club. Part of me wants to check on Demetria, but I deny myself as I step through the door. I sit down at my desk, gripping the hard wood as I try to push away the need to go to her. The desk strains under the pressure, and I can hear the wood starting to crack.

Slamming my hands on the surface, I lift the lid of my laptop and open the files Harley has filled in for ordering stock for the club. Settling into a familiar routine, it takes my mind off the woman upstairs in my apartment. Once I have all the orders complete, I rest back in my chair and pass a hand through my wavy hair.

My thoughts are straight back to her again, her long black hair that I want to run my fingers through and those enchanting eyes that watch our every movement. I can see the way she's pulled towards all of us. She can't even stop how her body is reacting to us. I understand her pull to me, and I can only assume the others' blood in her system is increasing her lust for them.

Settling my fingers on the keyboard once more, I make a few more orders. For one, I'm going to need a new dining table. I don't particularly care about the blood that stains it, but I don't want it to be a reminder for Demetria every time she sees it of what happened to her. I click on the six seater glass-top table and head for the checkout.

At least that's one less thing to worry about. Now all I have to think about is how to stop the others from getting too close to Demetria. We will protect her until the problem is gone, but after that, I need her to leave and be as far away from us as possible. We don't need her in our lives, we've done fine without her so far.

You only don't want her to break their hearts... your heart.

Chapter 17

Demi

Diego and Jax leave me feeling flustered. Fucking assholes, both of them. Pushing off the mattress, I glare at the door. I've been lying on the bed for at least ten minutes, staring at the ceiling and hoping that one of them might come back, but neither has.

Stomping into the bathroom, I look at myself in the mirror. I notice I have flushed cheeks, and my eyes look less sunken than they did. My skin is finally getting back to its usual complexion. Stripping off the t-shirt, I let it drop to the floor before stepping into the shower.

I turn on the jets of water and bask under the heat of them as it sinks into my tense muscles. After a quick shower, and washing my hair, I wrap myself in the towels I left on the rail and step back in front of the mirror. Opening the soft fabric from around my body, I check myself over.

The wounds from the wolves look much better. The skin is still pink and puckered, but they are nowhere near as red as they were when I first woke up a few days ago. Wait, was it a few days ago? I've lost track of time. The blinds in my room have been constantly shut and I've been sleeping on and off since I first woke up. I've no longer been paying attention to day and night.

Just how many days have I missed at work, and what the fuck is Michael going to be thinking? Rushing back into the bedroom with just a towel wrapped around me, I look around for my bag. It's sitting next to the side table beside the bed. Moving over to it, I snatch it up and dig around inside, looking for my cell phone.

When I pull it out, my shoulders drop. The screen is fractured, the glass barely staying in place under my screen protector.

"Fuck." I hit the power button, hoping that maybe even with the damaged screen it might still turn on.

I grasp onto a little hope as the screen lights up, but it soon disappears again. There are black spots all over it, and I can't see anything through the cracks. Deflated, I drop my bag and phone onto the floor.

I spot something dark on top of the light covers on the bed, another set of clothes. Looking over to the door, I remember the fact that there isn't a lock on it anymore. Anyone can just walk in.

Pulling the t-shirt over my body, I lift the neck to my nose. Though the smell isn't strong, I know they aren't Jax's. I've come to associate damp pine with him, but these have the subtle scent of licorice, rich and sweet. That's all Diego.

Forgoing the sweatpants, I pull the set of boxers up my legs. I eye the stake on the side table. I'm not sure at what point I stopped feeling the need to pick it up anymore, but I leave it behind and head out of the bedroom.

As I get closer to the open-plan kitchen and lounge, I can hear the television on low. Peeking out around the wall, I check to see who is in the room. Spotting the back of Bane's head over the top of the couch, I let out a sigh of relief. I'm not sure I want to deal with Diego or Jax right now.

Padding across the wooden floor, my feet hit the plush carpet around the lounge area. Bane's head tilts a little in my direction. I have no doubt he's known I've been here the whole time, but it's only now that he's acknowledging my presence. I appreciate his attempts to be more human.

Rounding the couch, I flop on the opposite end to where he's sitting. These men are dangerous. As much as I shouldn't feel comfortable around them, I do. And I keep getting closer and closer. There's something about all of them that draws me to them.

Pulling a pillow to my chest, I hug it against myself and lift my legs up, curling them underneath me. A hand and remote suddenly appear in front of me, and I look over to Bane. He's looking at me with those crystal blue eyes, giving me a slight nod. I take the remote from him and flick through a few of the channels.

It's mostly news and a few older movies, nothing I want to watch. Noticing the Netflix button on the remote, I press it and it takes me straight into the home page. There is a profile set up for each guy. I select Bane's and it gives me every possible option of movie and TV show.

Clicking through the list, I stop on an action movie and hit select. Placing the remote on the arm of the couch, I look over at Bane again. He's got his booted feet up on the coffee table, and his arms folded across his torso. His t-shirt is tight, and his jeans are molded to his huge body.

Leaning back on the couch, I still hold the pillow across my chest and I turn my attention to the screen, but I'm barely watching it. It seems so mundane that I'm sitting here watching a movie with a vampire who looks like he could kill me with just a look.

"Where's Diego and Jax?" I blurt out.

"Out," Bane grunts.

No shit.

"Doing what exactly?" I pick at the corner of the pillow.

"Jax has business to see to and Diego left."

He really isn't the talkative type. I've noticed that since being here. He seems to talk in short sentences, sometimes not even whole ones, just singular words.

"Not really the talkative type, are you, big guy?" I pick up on the rumble that emits from his chest. Does he like the fact

I've given him a nickname? "Any chance I can borrow your phone? I need to call work."

Another grunt, but no actual answer. Fine. I'll be a good girl and watch the movie. When Jax or Diego gets back, I need to see if one of them is a little more willing to lend me a phone. I love my job, and I don't want to lose it.

I don't remember what happened during the movie by the time the end credits roll. There were explosions, car chases, good guys killing bad guys, but I zoned out for most of it. Bane and I sit in silence. I'm not sure if he's watching it either. One movie leads to another and at one point, I get up to go to the kitchen.

Opening the fridge, it's full of all sorts of food and drink. I still don't understand why vampires need so much human sustenance, I thought they only needed to drink blood. Eyeing the opaque drawer at the bottom, I can't stop my curiosity. I slam it shut as quickly as I open it when I realize it's filled with bags of blood. *Bleugh, nope!* Grabbing a can of soda, I close the fridge, trying to pretend I haven't seen those clear bags.

Popping open the can, I take a healthy gulp and glance around the apartment. I still haven't had much time to look around, keeping mostly to the bedroom that Jax has given to me. It's safer there, away from the three men that seem to call to me. Even when we aren't in the same room together, it's almost like I can feel them. I wonder if it's an after-effect of the blood they gave me.

Bane is still sitting on the couch. I notice now that there are two hallways. One that leads to the bedroom I'm staying in and another on the other side of the kitchen. The hallway is dark, and I can't see what lies beyond the shadows.

What's down there?

I hear the lock on the main door clicking before it opens. The smell of food floods the apartment and my stomach rumbles. Diego pushes inside, his hands filled with bags. Taking my can, I place it on the coffee table and head over to offer him a hand. Diego kicks the door closed behind him. His eyes fall on me before cutting across to Bane.

"Hi." I squeak, and he throws me that killer smile of his. My insides melt.

Fucking hell, Demi. Get a hold of yourself.

Even fully clothed, he's sex on legs. His black shirt is open at the front again, showing off those gorgeous tattoos - the ones I got to trace only a few hours earlier. His black jeans hug him in all the right places, and I end up digging my teeth into my lower lip as I remember what lies beneath them.

"You can't do this to me, Demi. You need more clothes in the communal areas." Diego looks me up and down, his nostrils flaring.

I grab the edge of the t-shirt, trying to pull it lower down my thighs, but it won't budge. Diego is in front of me now, his body towering over me as he looks down, those black eyes drinking me in.

My body instinctively leans closer towards him. The smell that I noticed on the t-shirt envelopes me as I get closer. These are definitely Diego's clothes, which means the first set was Jax's. Before I can get any closer, Diego is gone, shifting past me to the breakfast bar. He puts the bags down on the countertop and turns to grab a few plates out of one of the many cupboards.

"I got Chinese. Didn't know what you liked, so I got a bit of everything. My favorite is the chicken chow mein." He pulls each dish out of the bags, laying them out like a feast.

"You guys actually eat? Other than blood, I mean." There is a double snort, one from Diego and the other from Bane. "What? I wondered why there was so much normal food and drink in your fridge."

"You really don't know much about vampires, do you, *tesoro*?"

"You guys drink blood, heal really quick and apparently have heartbeats and feel as warm as any human." I eye the food, choosing something that looks like beef. I spoon some of it onto my plate before grabbing a fork and taking a bite.

"Of course we eat, and not just pussy." My eyes widen at Diego's comment, and I almost choke on the salt and pepper-coated beef I'm chewing on. "We drink alcohol, fuck better than any human, and if you ask really nicely, I can bite you whilst we fuck. It'll be the hardest orgasm you've ever had."

"Diego." Bane grunts. He's beside me now, reaching for one of the dishes. He takes the whole thing and puts it on a plate, moving off to the dining table and sitting down.

"What? I'm just making sure she knows more about us. Well, me. Your limp dick couldn't satisfy anyone, not even me." Diego puffs out his chest as he talks, a cock-sure smile adorning his lips.

Jesus Christ, he really has got a mouth on him.

Wait, Bane can't even satisfy Diego… what am I missing?

He's totally wrong, I've seen and felt Bane's cock and I know for a fact that there is nothing limp about the beast between his strong thighs. I can feel my cheeks flushing as I think about Bane with his fist wrapped around his cock, jacking off as he watched me and Diego.

Shaking off those thoughts, I add some noodles to my plate along with the beef and move to sit next to Bane. My eyes fall onto the dining table. The blood is still there and I squeeze my eyes shut. There's no way I'm sitting here. I turn and head for the couch instead. Bane stops eating as he notices my change of direction. Without a comment, he stands and grabs his food. Making his way over to sit beside me, our thighs brush together as he takes a seat.

Diego follows and sits down on the floor on the other side of the coffee table. He's directly opposite me and places some prawn crackers down between the three of us. I grab a handful and smile as I drop them on my plate. Scooping a little of the beef and noodles onto the edge of the prawn cracker, I take a bite, chewing slowly before swallowing.

We eat in companionable silence, with just the sounds of us chewing and forks scraping across the plates. A door slams down the hallway I was curious about earlier, and Jax appears from the darkness.

He looks a little frazzled. His shirt is untucked, and half the buttons are undone. His golden blonde hair is tangled in places, the waves in disarray from what looks like him running his fingers through it repeatedly. His emerald eyes look around the room wildly until they settle on me. As they do, I see the tension release its hold on him, his entire posture relaxing.

I want to ask him if he's okay, but knowing Jax, he'll just be an asshole all over again, making me hate him even more than I already do. Diego stops with his fork close to his mouth and looks Jax's way.

"Everything okay, boss man?"

"Everything's fine, Diego." Jax sniffs the air. "I see you've been keeping your hands to yourself."

Jax looks over at me at the same time that Diego does, and I shrink back in my seat. A hand on my thigh is the only thing stopping me from bolting. I look over to Bane and he smiles at me. It's weirdly comforting. Balancing my plate on my lap, I reach my hand for his and lace our fingers together. He gives them a squeeze, calming my nerves.

"I did. I know how to follow rules… sometimes, anyway." Diego jokes.

"Good." Jax moves to the counter and dishes up some food for himself. He grabs one of the chairs from the dining table and brings it over to where the rest of us are gathered, placing it down on the other side of the coffee table next to Diego.

As if by some sort of unspoken cue, Jax starts eating, and everyone goes back to their own food. I pick a little at mine, the thought that the asshole clearly doesn't want Diego touching me really bothers me. What has it got to do with him, anyway? It's not like he's saving me for himself. I was there ready for him and instead he stormed out of the bedroom and left me wanting.

These three have a weird relationship. I don't know much about them other than that Jax owns Dark Desires, Bane works the doors, and Diego is the bartender, but they all seem comfortable around each other. Aside from Diego disappearing earlier, every single one of them has been in or around the building. I can only assume they each have a room in the apartment, as they've changed clothes more than once already.

I look between all three men; Jax is the prim and proper one, with a severe case of dickhead syndrome. The majority of his actions so far have led me to believe he's still a douchebag. A very good-looking one, but a douchebag, no matter what. I think he's more pissed by the fact I brought wolves to his front door and now he has some helpless little human crowding his space. As much as I know things are tense between the two of us, it doesn't stop me wanting to feel his lips on my skin and have him thrusting his cock into all my holes.

Diego is hotness personified. He oozes sex. Everything about him makes me want me to strip him naked, sink down on his metal-adorned cock, and ride him till I collapse. Then let him fuck me some more till I fall into oblivion. Just having his eyes on me makes me hot and flustered. I was so close to having his cock inside me; I need him to fill me and finish what he started.

Bane is, well, Bane. He's huge and should terrify me, but he doesn't scare me one bit, not anymore. The first time I saw him on the door, and he flashed his fangs, I nearly bolted. But he's really not all that bad, at least to me anyway. Bane's more like an enormous teddy bear. He's gentle with me, like he's worried I might break, but he still makes me horny as hell. His kisses scorch me from the inside out, and I bet his cock would do the same. I want him to pin me below his huge body as he quenches my lust.

As much as I want each one of them to fuck me. Most of all, I want them to fuck me together, just like in my dream. I've never had a threesome, never mind an orgy. I once asked an ex if he'd be up for a threesome with another guy after we watched a steamy porno where the girl was fucked by multiple men at the same time. I wanted to experience it just the once, but he was so straight-laced, he shut me down straight away and told me he didn't want to share.

I'm like a wolf in heat; wanting, no, *needing* sex to satisfy the desires taking over my body. As soon as I think of wolves, those glowing amber eyes appear in my mind. Claws and fangs dripping with blood, and muffled whimpers. It's enough to push any thoughts of sex with the three hot vampires straight out of my head.

"Demi." A soft voice pulls me from my thoughts. Fingers flicking in front of my eyes to get my attention. I blink rapidly, trying to pull myself back to the present and to Diego.

"Huh? Sorry. What did you say?"

"I asked if you're finished. You've been playing with your food for the last five minutes."

"Oh shit, I was a million miles away. Yeah, I'm done." I put my fork back on the plate and hand it to Diego.

At some point, Bane and Jax must have left, their spaces now empty. I was so inside my own mind; I didn't even notice Bane letting go of my hand and leaving.

Way to keep alert, Demi.

Diego gathers up the rest of the dishes and takes them over to the sink, dropping them down into the soapy water. Jax and Bane both reappear at the end of the other hallway.

"I have informed Achilles of what happened, and we've dealt with the situation in the basement." Bane gives Jax a curt nod before looking my way, a goofy smile adorning his lips.

Bane walks behind where I'm sitting on the couch, his hand trailing across the skin on the back of my neck as he does. He heads for the door and turns, giving me a small wave, which I return before he walks out of the apartment door.

"Demetria. Bane mentioned you needed a phone." My ears perk up and I nod enthusiastically. "Here, use mine." He passes me a sleek-looking iPhone. It looks like one of the newer models.

"I need to call work. I don't even know what day it is at this point, but I've got to have missed at least one shift." He nods as I begin to dial the number.

"Understandable, and it's Sunday, if you'd like to know." My fingers pause on the screen as Jax says the day and I glance up at him. Shit so much time has passed already.

"Fuck, Michael is going to be so pissed with me. Someone will have already told him I missed my shift yesterday."

"Please inform this Michael that you have a virus and don't want to risk patients." I hate the fact he wants me to lie, but it's for the best. I can't exactly tell the truth.

"Okay." I hit the call button. It's only a few rings before Michael answers. "Hi, Michael, it's me."

"Demi, where have you been? Why aren't you answering your phone? Whose number is this?" Michael rapid fires the questions at me. I open my mouth, but he doesn't give me a chance to respond. "You missed two shifts. Angela rang me in a panic when you didn't turn up yesterday morning, and now I'm at the hospital trying to find someone to cover for you. I was about to send a search party."

"I am so sorry. I got hit by a virus or something. I've spent the last two days throwing up." I look at Jax, hoping my answer is adequate for him. "And would you believe I broke my phone on Thursday night when I went out? I've been waiting for a new one to arrive in the mail."

"Wow, be careful Demi. You know what they say. Bad luck comes in threes." He chuckles down the phone.

"I will. Thanks, Michael. I'm expecting I'll be out for maybe a week." I don't want to push it too much.

"Sure thing, Demi. Take care of yourself. And don't forget..."

I cut him off. "Fluids and rest, I know." I let out a soft laugh. "Bye, Michael."

"That's my girl." I hang up and hand the phone back to Jax, who's looking at me with a peculiar look on his face.

When his hands curl around the phone, his fingers brush against mine and I feel a jolt, like an electric shock, through my fingers. He flinches. Barely, but I notice it, he must have felt it too. He snatches his hand away and pushes his phone back into the front pocket of his slacks.

"Seems as if you will be here for a while." A look of what I assume is disgust flickers over Jax's features. "Bane is taking you back to your apartment in the morning. Grab clothing and anything else you'll need for a prolonged stay."

With that, he spins on his heel and stomps back down the hallway to whatever the hell lies down there. I look over at Diego, who is washing the dishes we used at the sink. He looks over at me and shrugs.

"Captain Asshole is back in the building then." My words cause Diego to snort, laughter shaking his shoulders as he works.

Tiredness sweeps through my body. I've done nothing all day but watch movies with Bane, yet somehow I'm still exhausted and a yawn creeps through my lips.

"Get some sleep, Demi. I'll be working at the club tonight, but Jax will be in his office down the hall." He points in the direction that Jax went, water and soap suds dripping from his hand.

Standing, I grab my half finished soda and head back to the room that is currently mine. The door handle is still broken, so I just push it to. Scrambling under the covers, I pull them up to my chin but leave the light on. I close my eyes and let sleep take me.

Chapter 18

Demi

I manage the entire night without a single nightmare. Rolling over in bed, I smack straight into something hard. Opening my eyes, I follow the body up from the chest to their face. It's Bane. No wonder I slept so peacefully. He's laid back on top of the covers, his legs crossed at the ankles and his head resting on one arm.

He's fully dressed and the only thing he isn't wearing is his boots. It's like the first time I woke up in bed with him all over again. Only this time I don't plan on climbing on top of him. Not saying the temptation isn't there, but I have bigger plans for today. And one of those is to finally get my hands on some of my own clothes.

Shuffling away from Bane, his arm moves out. Touching the bed where I just moved from, his hand grazes across mine. He wraps his fingers around them, one of his eyes popping open, his eyebrow raising.

"Where you going?" His voice is sleep-addled and rough.

"Well, big guy, I'm going for a shower, and then you're taking me to my apartment." A grin cracks across my lips at the prospect of being able to wear my own clothes.

"Okay." Bane lets go of my hand and in seconds he's stood at my side of the bed. Reaching under my arms, he lifts me and lets my feet drop to the ground.

Leaning down so his head is beside mine, he runs his nose up the side of my neck, inhaling deeply. His hands cup my ass and pull me closer to him. I'm practically molded to his body, his thigh shifting between my legs. The movement pushes the fabric of the boxers I'm wearing against my clit, and I let out a soft moan.

Bane lets out a rumbling sound right next to my ear, and I melt against him. Planting soft pecks against the skin on my neck, he moves to my mouth. His lips brush against mine before he pulls away. Placing another kiss on my forehead, he moves away from me, leaving me bereft.

"Breakfast?"

What the hell?

Glaring at him, I turn and storm towards the bathroom.

"Stupid fucking vampires not finishing what they start." Slamming the bathroom door behind me, I can hear him chuckling on the other side and it makes me even angrier.

I swear to God if one more of these assholes leaves me feeling sexually frustrated, I'm out of here. Fuck them, and fuck the wolves. I'm sick of having a constant lady boner. Stripping off the clothes I'm in, I jump in the shower and quickly wash my body and hair. I need my own clothes and toiletries, stat.

When I'm done, I wrap a fresh towel around my body and dry my hair the best I can with another. A hair elastic would be perfect right now, but unless I have one in my purse, I can't imagine the guys having one lying around ready for me to use.

Walking back into the bedroom, the door is closed and there's another set of fresh clothing on the bed. A smile crosses my lips. Grabbing the boxers, I pull them up my legs, followed by the t-shirt and sweatpants. I'm not sure what exactly I'm going to wear on my feet. I don't even know where my heels are anymore, not that I'd want to wear them, anyway.

Pulling my purse over my shoulder, I head out to the hallway. I can smell freshly brewed coffee and bacon. As I reach the kitchen, Bane is standing behind the stove, his back to me. There is already a cup of freshly brewed coffee on the breakfast bar.

Adding two sugars, I give it a quick stir before taking a taste. A sigh escapes my lips as I inhale the rich aroma. Sipping on my drink, I admire Bane's physique as he works. He's a giant, that's for sure, and the muscles in his arms flex as he stirs the pan in front of him.

The toaster pops, making me jump, but I quickly put down my cup and head over to it. Pulling out the toast, I put it on the breadboard and slather each piece with a generous amount of butter. I pile them onto the plate that's set beside it before moving it over to the breakfast bar.

I catch something different across the room and I give it my full attention. The once blood soaked table is gone and in its place is a beautifully designed metal and glass one. I roll my eyes and chuckle to myself.

When I turn back around to see what else Bane needs me to do, the answer is nothing. He's already plated up the food and is heading my way. Placing both dishes down, he takes my hand and guides me to the seat.

Once I'm comfortably sitting down, he sits beside me and starts digging into the heaping pile of bacon and scrambled eggs. I pick at the food at first, before finally digging in, letting out small, appreciative noises as I eat. The eggs and bacon are both cooked to perfection.

Taking a sip of my coffee, I look over to Bane and find he's already finished.

Where the hell does he put it all?

He uses a slice of toast to wipe up the crumbs of egg and bacon fat from the plate before shoving it into his mouth. He rubs his belly and grins over at me. There really is a teddy bear under all that muscle.

My belly is full, and I can't finish the large meal Bane put in front of me. Grabbing both plates before Bane has a chance to, I empty the leftover food into the trash and take them to the sink. Turning on the faucet, I wash them and leave them in the drainer.

Drinking the last dregs of my coffee, I ponder another cup, but honestly, all I want to do is go to my apartment and slip on some of my own clothes. I appreciate the fact the guys have been lending me theirs, but it's about time I have something that actually fits. Glancing down at my feet, I look back up to Bane, but he's busy typing away on his phone.

"Big guy," his fingers stop moving and he looks up. "I'm gonna need some shoes, maybe a jacket if we plan on going outside." He gives me a nod and disappears in the blink of an eye.

When he returns, he's holding a hoodie and a pair of flip-flops. Taking the shoes first, I drop them on the floor and push my feet into them. They're only a size or two bigger than my own feet, so definitely not one of the guys'. I wonder who they belong to.

"Harley's," Bane answers the question without me even having to voice it. I have no idea who Harley is, but a pang of jealousy races through me and I can't stop the frown that mars my face.

Bane steps in front of me, the hoodie still in his grasp. He cups my face with one of his large hands and tilts my head up to look at him. Leaning down, his lips whisper across mine and I rise up on my tip-toes so he doesn't have to lean down so much. Even that brief touch is enough to wipe any jealousy away.

He rests the hoodie around my shoulders, and I push my arms into it before zipping the front. Like most of the clothes they have given me so far, it absolutely drowns me, but it's comfy and smells faintly of Diego.

"Come," Bane grunts out, turning on his heel and grabbing a set of keys off the counter.

He holds the apartment door open for me. I'm almost there, but I pause. It's been a few days since I woke up in the apartment, and now I'm about to go outside for the first time since the attack. I'm suddenly nervous. Bane takes my hand and raises it to his lips, brushing a soft kiss across my knuckles.

"No one will hurt you. Promise." I look up into his blue eyes. I can see the truth there. He won't let anyone hurt me.

Come on, Demi. Pull up your big girl panties. Or boxers, seems as what I'm wearing aren't even mine.

Rolling my shoulders and taking a deep breath, I lift my head and take a step outside the apartment. Bane follows behind me, still holding my hand, and pulls the door closed behind him.

We're in a small hallway with another door to the left, but absolutely no windows. I spot a keypad on the outside of the door. He leads me towards another at the end and when we get there, he enters a code into another keypad beside it. I hear the locks disengage.

Overkill much.

Leading me through the opening, we're finally outside on what resembles a fire escape. I'm guessing from the fact it's entirely enclosed with a metal fence that it isn't, though. I haven't seen any other doors in the apartment that could lead outside, so it's probably just how it was built. I take my time walking down the steps. Bane doesn't try to rush me, letting me set my own pace.

Once we reach the bottom, he enters another code, and pushes open the heavy-looking steel. He makes sure it shuts behind him before walking me over to a black BMW. Opening the door, he waits for me to climb in before shutting it after me and heading to the driver's side.

With a few grumbles when he gets in, he pushes the seat back to give himself enough room for his long legs. I'm guessing this isn't his car. A small laugh escapes me. He whips his head around to glare at me before a smile cracks across his own face.

Bane starts the engine. I give him the address for my apartment and we take off. He doesn't say a word. Not that I was expecting much enlightening conversation from him; he's definitely the silent brooding type.

We pull out of the alley next to the club; it looks so different in the daylight. There's no line outside and the huge sign above the door isn't lit. In fact, the entire area looks like any other, but I know what lurks behind the building. An alley where two of us went in, but only one came out alive.

Quickly brushing the tears from under my eyes before they can fully form and stare out of the window as we drive down the street. I'm not really looking at anything in particular, just watching the trees and people as we pass by. Fiddling with the cuff of my sleeve as Bane drives. It's odd being outside after I've been cooped up inside their apartment for a few days.

My nerves push to the forefront of my mind; I'm not really sure what I expected. I went to hell and back and I'm still standing - I plan to keep it that way for a while yet. I look over to Bane, but his eyes are set on the road. Reaching for the radio, I turn it on, not really caring what we listen to. I need something to fill the silence.

Getting myself comfortable, I lie my head back on the headrest. I close my eyes, letting out a sigh before humming along to the music.

Chapter 19

Bane

Being this close to Demi in the car is driving me absolutely insane. All I can smell is her. I flex my hands on the steering wheel as I drive. Jax said it was best to take his car so we could load it up with whatever she needs from her apartment, but part of me wishes we'd taken my bike instead. The thrill of the ride would have been a distraction.

The thought of her thighs wrapped around me makes my cock twitch. Her arms would have been tightly around me, and her breasts pushed into my back as she held on.

Yeah, the car was definitely the best plan.

I'm not sure I could have stopped myself from pulling over on my bike and fucking her over the bike.

The kiss we shared was enough to set my whole body on fire, and I can only imagine what it will be like when I sink into her tight heat. I *will* do that at some point, and nothing Jax says will stop me. Diego has already gotten to see what she feels like, something he's had fun tormenting me with. He's gotten to taste her and feel her clenching around his fingers.

Absent-mindedly, I tap my fingers on the wheel. I need to stop thinking about having her body wrapped around me, 'cause, hell... if I don't, I'll be pulling the car over and leaving cum stains all over the back seat. Then Jax will really have something to complain about.

I watch her out of the corner of my eye as she turns on the radio. It's some boring classical music station, the usual listening for Jax. He might look like he's only in his early to mid-thirties, but he's got a few hundred years on me and Diego. I much prefer rock or metal - definitely more my jam.

When Demi starts humming, it's like music to my ears. Maybe classical music isn't so bad after all. The sound of it soothes my nerves, and any hard-on I was getting disappears. We finally turn onto her street, and I count down the numbers until we reach her apartment. I pull into a space a few buildings down.

Getting out of the car, I speed around to her door and open it. Demi's turquoise eyes drift open and look up at me and my offered hand. I pull her up and out of the seat. She goes to pull her hand away, but I keep it firmly in mine, lacing our fingers together as I let her lead the way.

Demi only lets go of my hand as we reach the front door. Rooting in her purse, she pulls out her key and slips it into the lock. A sigh of relief escapes her as we enter the building, and she takes in a huge lungful of air. As she leads me down the hall towards the door at the end, my hackles begin to rise.

I drag in a deep breath. Wet dog scent is everywhere. It's the same smell from the alley. Grabbing her hand, I stop her in her tracks. A gasp escapes her as I let out a feral growl. Pulling Demi back, I place myself between her and the door at the end. My fangs itch, wanting violence, but I know I need to protect her too.

"Stay here!" I bark the order, and she takes a step back from me. Demi gives me a small nod, her narrowed eyes lead me to assume she sees my red eyes and descended fangs.

Taking another step towards her door, the smell of the wolves gets even stronger. It's not only the scents I found on her and her friend's body, but it's at least a few of them. My muscles tense and my fists clench. I'll rip them apart for what they did to her.

Glancing at the entryway, it's open a crack. The wolves have clearly busted the handle to gain entry to her property. Edging closer, I move on silent feet. If they're still inside, they've probably already heard us, but I don't want them to know the exact moment I'm going to bust through the door.

Another door opens closer to the main entrance and I whip around, snarling. Demi turns as well, taking in the small, older lady with gray hair in the open doorway.

"Agnes."

"Oh my, Demi. You're okay." Agnes rushes towards Demi, or at least, she goes as quickly as she can. She wraps her arms around her. "I went to the store this morning, and when I came back, I saw your apartment door was open." Letting go of Demi, she fusses over her like she's one of the family. "I went to check on you, but you weren't there and the place was a mess. I was so worried about you. I've rung the police, useless bastards that they are. They still haven't gotten here."

"I am so sorry, Agnes. I've been staying with friends for a few days. It was on a bit of a whim, hence my attire." She motions to the oversized clothing she's wearing and Agnes nods.

As the two of them talk, I look back over my shoulder at Demi's open apartment door. Agnes doesn't seem like the kind of person who could hurt a fly, so I leave the two of them to their conversation and approach the apartment.

Stepping through the door, the wolves' scent is stronger now, I scrunch up my nose in disgust. What did they do, rub their mangy hides all over the place or something? When I get inside, Agnes is right. They trashed the place. There are all sorts of things scattered on the floor, the couch cushions have been ripped apart and the TV has been smashed to pieces.

A gasp behind me has me spinning. Demi is standing at the door, a hand covering her mouth as she takes in the devastation. I don't even think as I step closer and wrap my arms around her, making soothing noises as I hold her close.

"I'm sorry," I whisper against her ear.

A sob escapes as she lays her head on my chest, her small arms encircling my waist.

"I can't believe someone would do this." She hiccups. "I have nothing of value."

"It was the wolves," I growl, anger rising at their audacity. "Their scent is all over your place."

A shudder runs through Demi's body, and I tangle my fingers in her hair, stroking it as I hold her tightly. My eyes move around her apartment again, taking in the devastation. I'm not sure if she's going to be able to salvage anything. I need to send Jax an update on what we have found.

"Go pack what you can. I'll stand guard." With a kiss on top of her hair, I let her go. She moves back, nodding as she disappears into another room. Pulling out my phone, I send Jax a text.

The wolves have been to her apartment. They trashed the place.

Get her things and get back here ASAP.

Not sure what the hell he thinks I'm doing, so I don't bother to reply as I shove my phone back in my jeans pocket. Tilting my head towards the door, I hear two sets of footsteps approaching. I ready myself. They smell human, but you can never be too cautious.

"Portland PD, if there is anyone in there, put your hands in the air."

Two humans burst through the slightly open door, both with their guns drawn. As soon as they see me, they swivel in my direction.

"Get on the ground!" One of them barks the order, but I just stand my ground, lips lifted in a sneer.

"Bane, I... oh fuck." Slipping my eyes to her, I see Demi standing in the doorway with a duffle bag over each shoulder and a backpack in her hand. They slip down, thudding against the wooden floor.

The officers' guns turn on her, and she automatically lifts her hands. I'm in front of her in a flash, and one officer gasps as it dawns on him what I am. His gun lowers slightly, but his friend keeps his aimed at my chest.

"I said down on the ground." The other officer snarls. "Both of you. Don't make me shoot you."

"My name's Demetria Arnold. This is my apartment. I came home and found it broken into. I'm just getting some things to take to where I'm staying with a friend."

My fangs flash at the cop who still has his gun on me. He flinches before straightening himself back out and keeping his hand raised.

"Miss, if you could please step towards me slowly with your hands still raised. I need you to show me some identification." The officer who has already lowered his gun beckons her towards him. He keeps his voice calm, which is more than what his friend is doing.

I'm not sure I trust the other guy. His heart is racing and his finger is resting over the trigger, ready to squeeze off a shot. Demi goes to move from behind me, but I stop her before she can shift from behind the cover of my body.

"No!" I glare at the officer with the gun. "Not whilst he has a gun aimed at her."

The calmer officer takes a step forward, and I can't stop the growl that escapes from between my lips. His next step falters as his eyes cut from me to Demi, who is peering around my arm. He places himself in front of the gun-crazy officer and holsters his weapon, showing his own hands.

Clever man. He's realized that aiming a gun at a vampire isn't the best idea. Showing his empty hands, he beckons Demi forward again. She looks up at me and I give her a nod. Hands still in the air, she shuffles around me.

I watch her every move as she gets closer to the officer. The other one has finally lowered his gun, but he's still holding it in his hand like a lifeline. Not that it will save him if he dares to harm Demi. I will end him whether he has a gun or not. A bullet will hurt like hell, but it'll heal once I've consumed blood.

"I need to go in my purse for my wallet." Demi's voice sounds tense. I'm not surprised. Only a few minutes ago she had a gun pointed at her.

"Of course, Miss Arnold. Just nice and slow."

Following his instructions, Demi reaches into her purse and pulls out her wallet, and hands the officer her driver's license. He checks over the flimsy bit of plastic, looking from the photo to Demi. With a nod, he hands it back to her and turns to the twitchy officer.

"It's all good, Mack. This is Miss Arnold, and this is her apartment." The one named Mack still doesn't look convinced as he holsters his weapon. He keeps his hand over the grip, ready to pull it out again.

"You sure, Jimmy?" Officer Jimmy nods and turns back to Demi.

"Is everything okay here, Miss?" He looks between the two of us. I fold my arms across my chest, a growl rumbling through it. Officer Jimmy takes a small step back. "We got a call from a neighbor. A Miss Agnes MacKay."

"As fine as it can be, Officer. And yeah, I saw Agnes when I came in."

"Do you know who could be behind this?" Demi goes to open her mouth but I rest a hand on her shoulder.

"Not a clue. As far as I can tell, only a few things were taken. Mostly clothing." I'm not surprised. It's the one thing in Demi's apartment that will smell like her the most, the best way to track her.

"And you're sure everything is okay?" He eyes me cautiously. "You wouldn't prefer to go down to the station?"

Demi shakes her head and looks back at me. There's a look of confusion which mars her usually sweet features.

"Everything is fine, Officer. This is my friend, Bane." She gestures towards me with one hand. "I'm staying with him for a little while. Probably a good thing, cause at least it means I wasn't home when the wol... intruders got in."

Officer Mack raises an eyebrow. With Demi almost messing up, they don't look convinced about the whole situation and his hand still rests on his gun. I'm pretty sure he just wants to shoot me. But fuck him, I'll shove that gun where the sun doesn't shine if he isn't careful.

"You're going to want a locksmith to come out and make sure the apartment is secure. And if Mr. Bane would be so kind as to give Officer Mack the address of where you are staying, we can get out of your hair. A word in private first please, Miss Arnold."

Officer Jimmy motions towards the open door, and Demi follows him. Officer Mack pulls out a notepad and pen, stepping in front of me as I attempt to follow her out of the door.

"Your address?" He taps the pen against the paper and I start to reel off the address for the club while listening in on Demi's conversation with the other officer.

"Look, Miss Arnold, if you find yourself in any trouble at all, call me - anytime, day or night."

"Honestly, officer. I'm absolutely fine. My friends will take care of me." The conviction in her voice warms me.

"Of course, Miss. I just want to let you know that you have options if you decide you don't want to stay with them."

God damn humans getting into our business. He's probably worried I'm going to hurt her, drink her blood, and leave her corpse out in the cold. The human officers of the city have seen what vampires suffering from bloodlust can do. Not that they are allowed to say a word of it to anyone. If they did, the Council would make sure they met their demise.

"I promise, officer. If I run into any trouble, you'll be the first to know. But you must believe me when I say I'll be fine. Is that all?"

"Yes, ma'am." Demi moves back into the apartment. Officer Jimmy watches her from the door. His eyes flick to me one last time.

Officer Mack meets him at the door and they both leave. Demi surveys the mess the wolves have caused to her apartment again, her shoulders slumping down. This is her home, and they came in here and destroyed it. One more reason I can't wait to get my hands on them.

I shoulder her bags, grabbing them from where she dropped them in the bedroom doorway. Taking Demi's hand in mine, I pull her apartment door to. As we walk outside, I send another text to Jax letting him know someone needs to come secure it for her. I'll tell him about the clothes they have taken when I see him in person.

Chapter 20

Jax

An hour, that's how long Demi and Bane have been gone, and that's almost how long I've been pacing back and forth across the office in the apartment. My only distraction was the delivery of the new dining table. With the last text from Bane about her apartment needing securing, I act fast. Phoning around a few places, I end up paying more than double the normal amount because I want them out there to fix it on the double.

Those asshole wolves have broken into Demetria's apartment and wrecked it. Why? I don't know. They must have known she wouldn't be back there yet after the state they left her in. If it were up to me, I would keep her here for the rest of time, if only to make sure no one can ever harm her again.

Wait, no. I want her to leave as soon as the wolves are dealt with.

Grabbing the bottle of whiskey, I drink it straight from the decanter before dropping it back down. My fists clench and relax repeatedly as I resume my pacing. Laughter sounds from my doorway, and I turn to glare at Diego. He's standing in the door, leaning against the frame.

"She's gotten to you as well."

"No, she hasn't." I bark. "I'm sick of these wolves. They've attacked on our territory and broken into a human's apartment."

"Sure, keep telling yourself that, Jax. She's got you wound so tight." He laughs. "How blue are your balls right now?"

I growl at him, lifting the bottle of whiskey back to my lips, and take another gulp. The liquid burns down my throat and I welcome the fire. Two hands rest on my shoulders, massaging my tense muscles. I let them droop as Diego pushes his fingers into all the right places.

A groan escapes me as he hits just the right spot. I put the bottle back on the table with a thud and Diego crowds behind me. The full length of him presses against me, and I can feel his cock twitch against my ass cheeks.

"Man, you feel tense." He whispers in my ear. "I can always give you a hand." He licks the shell of my ear and a shudder races through my spine.

We've been close before, but over the last few years, I've pulled away from humanity more than the other two. They seek pleasure wherever they can find it, but I don't trust myself to get close to anyone but them.

His hands skate between my shoulder blades and down my spine. When he reaches my backside, one hand clutches my ass, and the other reaches round to my cock. Brushing the back against my erection, I can't stop it from twitching.

Diego rubs up and down my clothed length, and I jerk back into him. I need this. Demetria is well and truly under my skin. All I can think about is pounding into her before I sink my teeth into her neck.

No, Jax. That's not what you want.

Unzipping my pants, Diego reaches his hand inside my boxers and grasps my steely cock in his fist. The sensitive end brushes against the material and I let out a groan. His blunt teeth nip against the skin of my neck just above my shirt collar and already I know I'm close.

"Just let go, Jax." He whispers against my neck.

I've been so on edge since Demetria got here and I've given myself no release. My balls tighten and my spine locks up as I ejaculate. My cum soaks the inside of my boxers, seeping through to the fabric of my slacks. Diego spins me around and shoves me up against the table, the bottles rattling. His fist is still gripping my cock as he pumps up and down me at a leisurely pace.

"Fuck, Jax. It's been a while since I've felt your cum on me." Pulling his hand from my cock, he lifts it to his mouth and licks up the fluid.

My hand grips the back of Diego's neck and pulls his mouth towards mine. As soon as they connect, I thrust my tongue inside and I can taste myself on him. We both groan as our tongues battle together.

The apartment door opening has us both freezing, our lips still so close to each other, our breath coming out in pants. I hear Demetria giggling in the kitchen and push Diego away from me. Quickly doing up the zipper on my slacks, I stare at the stain on the front.

I'll have to change before I let either Demetria or Bane see me. But first I'll have to get back to my room, and that means passing them both. My gaze lifts to Diego; there's a twinkle in his eyes. He knows exactly what I'm thinking. With a laugh, he turns on his heel and walks out of my office.

Pulling my jacket from the back of my chair, I drape it across my crotch to hide the stain and follow Diego out into the kitchen. The smell of baked goods permeates the air and I find Demetria sitting at the breakfast bar eating donuts.

Diego attempts to grab one out of the box as he passes. She slaps his hand, but she's not quick enough to stop him and he shoves half the donut into his mouth. Her laughter rings out, filling the apartment. Bane is watching the two of them, a goofy smile on his face.

They're both so different around her. Bane usually keeps to himself when he stays here, not really spending much time outside the room he's claimed as his own. And Diego, well, he's just Diego, but he seems happier, more outgoing, and full of life.

"I'm glad to see you back safely, Demetria." Her laughter stops, and I want to hear it again. She turns to face me, swiveling around on the barstool. "I have sent someone to secure your apartment."

A smile cuts across her sugar covered lips. I think it's the first time she's really smiled at me. The others have been graced with her smile more times than I can count over the last few days, but when she looks at me, it's usually with a scowl.

"Thank you, Jax." I want her to say my name again. In fact, I want her to scream it out as I make her come.

The damp patch on my slacks is getting more uncomfortable the longer I stand here. With a shake of my head, I head for my room. I need to get out of these pants quickly. Slamming the door behind me, I slip out of them and throw them in the laundry pile, along with my boxers.

My shirt is next and I head into the bathroom, turning on the shower before jumping inside. Scrubbing my skin, I can hear Demetria laughing and giggling with Bane and Diego in the kitchen, and it's driving me crazy.

We're all drawn to her for some bizarre reason. There's a chance she's my true mate. It's something rare among vampires, but there's no way she can be that for all three of us. I can't let the others blood bond with her until I've claimed her first.

I have no issues sharing her with Diego and Bane, but as her true mate, I have to settle my bond with her first. But do I really want that? Every part of me should say yes, but I've already had my heart broken and I don't want that again. When my sire killed my human companion, I all but went on a rampage. I can't lose control like that again.

Just listening to her laughter as it drifts down the hall has my cock hardening all over again. Grasping my length in my fist, I pump it up and down. Closing my eyes, all I can see is her half naked on her bed after I found her with Diego. Her pussy dripping and her nipples hard enough to cut glass.

Pumping my cock in my fist, I imagine it's her tight hole gripping me. It doesn't take long before my balls tingle and tighten, spending myself against the shower wall.

Now I'm back under control, I clean myself and step out of the shower. Slinging a towel low around my hips, I move back into the bedroom. What I don't expect is to find Demetria sitting on my bed. I inhale deeply as her scent hits me with its full force. Her eyes are on my body, looking me up and down. They stop on my crotch and her tongue darts out to wet her lips.

"Shit, sorry. I should have waited outside." She quickly stands and heads for the door.

"What is it, Demetria?" Looking back over her shoulder, she slowly turns to face me again.

"Diego, he... well, he was just joking, but he mentioned earning my keep." Her hands are clasped in front of her. "He said maybe I could work in the bar. I just need something to do, I'm going stir crazy."

"Okay."

"I knew you wouldn't... wait, what?" Her eyes are wide. "Did you just agree?"

"Yes, Demetria. I can be agreeable sometimes." Running my hand through my wet hair, I nod. "Plus, it means we'll actually be able to work and not keep having to watch you."

"Oh... Captain Asshole is back again. But good, good. If it gives me something to do, then whatever."

With a last look over my body, she turns on her heel and stomps out of my bedroom into her own. I've lied to her again. None of us mind watching her, but our work *has* been suffering a little since she turned up. There is always at least one person in the apartment with her, but she's done nothing but watch movies and even I'd be bored out of my mind by now. This way Demetria will have something to do, and we can keep on top of the club and still watch her, but with the extra help of the staff.

Chapter 21

Demi

Things have finally settled down in the apartment. I've all but moved into the room Jax gave to me, bringing a handful of my possessions from my place, as well as what's left of my clothing. Bane told the others about the fact that some of my clothes were missing. They think it's so the wolves can make sure everyone in their pack knows my scent, meaning there's more than just the ones I met.

Security at the club has tripled after Diego joked that I should earn my keep by working the bar with him. Shockingly, Jax actually agreed. At least that way they could keep working and not have to worry about someone being in the apartment with me at all times.

Brushing out my hair, I plait it over my shoulder and pull on a tight black t-shirt. I check my appearance in the mirror. I've gone a little heavier than I normally do on my make-up, with black eye shadow on my upper lid and lower lash line. The red eye shadow covers my crease, brow bone, and just under the black of my lower lashes. With a heavy helping of mascara, I finish the look off with winged eyeliner and dab on a little lip balm, but otherwise leave my lips au naturale.

I'm not sure whose idea it was that I should be wearing such a short skirt, but I'm guessing it was probably Diego. Even with his comment about more clothing in communal areas, I know for a fact he's going to appreciate the sheer lack of material covering my legs. Moving back into the bedroom, I slip my sneakers on and head for the kitchen. Bane is sitting at the breakfast bar, waiting for me.

As soon as he sees me, his eyes light up. He quickly stands and moves towards me.

"Beautiful." I feel anything but. I do appreciate the compliment though.

"Thanks." I smile at him as he wraps an arm around my waist and hefts me against him.

His lips connect with mine, and it's like fireworks all over again. Every time he kisses me, something lights up inside me, begging me to strip him down and let him have his wicked way with me. Our tongues dance together, and one of his hands grips my ass, pulling a gasp from me.

I can feel the outline of his cock rubbing against my stomach and I push against him. Too soon, he breaks the kiss and licks his lips.

"Come on." He grabs my hand and drags me from the apartment and around to the front of the club.

The music is just like that night. It pulses through the floor as we get closer. I try to ignore what happened the last time I went through these doors. Squeezing my hand, Bane pulls me through the main entrance and straight into the club. This time the lights don't blind me, I'm expecting them. We push through the crowds and head straight for the bar where Diego is already serving drinks to customers.

When Diego sees me, a grin cracks across his face and he throws me a wink as he continues making the beverages. Bane drags me around the bar and through a small opening in the side. His lips brush across my temple before he's gone again, leaving me behind the bar as he disappears into the crowd once more.

"Hi," a cheery voice sounds beside me. It's the woman who served me drinks a few nights ago. "I'm Harley." She thrusts her hand toward me, and I take it in mine, shaking it firmly.

"Demi."

"Oh, I know." She grins. "You're all the staff have been talking about. The pretty, dark-haired girl who the bosses are head over heels for."

What the hell?

"They are definitely not head over heels for me." I wince slightly.

Are they?

"Deny it all you want, sweetie." Harley brushes her long blonde hair over her bare shoulder. "Ever tended a bar before?"

"For a few months in college." Harley claps her hands together.

"Fantastic. Hopefully, I won't have to spend my whole night teaching you what to do then." She grabs a glass from behind the bar and starts filling it from one of the pumps.

I watch as she pours the perfect glass of beer and places it on the bar, taking the bill the customer hands over before turning back to the register and retrieving his change. When she hands it back to him, she shoots him a killer smile before turning her attention back to me.

"We get a mixture of customers in here, as you've already seen for yourself. Pretty much everyone orders human drinks, but we get the odd customer who may ask for bottled blood."

Grabbing my hand, she pulls me past Diego and down to the other side of the bar. She opens the only fridge with frosted glass. Inside it are small bottles filled with red liquid. They look a little like the Starbucks frappuccino bottles you can get from the store, only it is definitely not coffee in them. Each bottle is labeled with a blood type. A small shudder runs through me, remembering the sachets of blood I saw in the bottom drawer of the fridge in the guys' apartment.

"Most vamps prefer to drink from the source whilst they are here. It's one of the few places you can get away with, as long as they don't drain the donor, that is." She gives a small shrug. "Just make sure you get the right bottle. We don't want anyone pissed off you gave them AB instead of A positive." The way she says it is so nonchalant. Like I'm just handing over a beer and not someone else's blood.

After a quick rundown of how the bar and register works, Harley grabs me by the shoulders. She spins me around and pushes me towards the bar, where there's already a crowd of customers waiting. It takes me a while to get back into the swing of things, but once I do, I'm serving drinks like a pro. Harley wasn't wrong when she said most people order normal drinks, I've only had one so far who has asked for a bottle of blood. I can't quite stop the grimace that flashes across my face as I push the bottle over the bar.

Sweet Child O' Mine blasts through the speakers and I sway my hips to the music as I continue serving drinks. As I'm finishing garnishing a few cocktails for a bachelorette party down the other end of the bar, I feel a hard body pressing against my back. I know instantly it's Diego, his licorice scent flooding my nostrils. His fingers grasp my thighs, pulling me flush with him as my hips move to the music. His arousal brushes against my ass as I move.

"The things I want to do to you, Demi." His voice whispers against my ear, and I drag in a deep breath.

I wonder if his list is anything like the things I want to do to him. He's been the most forward out of the guys. He constantly touches me when we're together and whispers dirty things in my ears, even though I can see the disapproving looks Jax throws our way. Bane has been sweeter, kissing my hair and holding my hand as we watch movies together. But Jax… I can see an intensity burning in his eyes as he looks at me when he thinks no one else is watching. I still haven't figured out if it's hatred or lust.

As I grind against Diego, I catch another set of eyes watching me on the other side of the bar. It's the guy who bought the bottle of blood earlier. We didn't exchange many words apart from his order, but he gave me a huge tip before he disappeared back into the crowd. He's watching me now though, and my body freezes up. Pulling away from Diego, I rush to gather up the cocktails.

"Everything okay, Demi?" Diego's eyes burn into me as I shoot him a smile.

"All good, just don't want to piss off anyone off by letting their drinks get warm." I throw him a wink before heading down to the bachelorette party. As I pass the bottled blood guy, he smiles at me, his fangs glinting in the light.

"Here you go, ladies." I place the drinks down on the bar; one woman thrusts a fifty into my hand and I quickly grab her change.

Glancing around the bar, I look for someone else to serve, but the only person I see is the bottled blood guy. Looking down at the other end of the bar, I notice Diego and Harley are both busy with their own customers. Huffing out a breath, I approach him slowly.

"What can I get you?" I have to lean over the bar. No supernatural hearing for me makes it hard to hear people over the music.

"I'll have the same again, please, sugar." His words whisper across my ear, I don't realize how close he has gotten until now. "Unless you're offering something warmer?"

His hand touches my forearm as his fingers wrap around my wrist. The claws on the tips of them press into my skin. Unlike when Diego and Bane touch me, this guy sets my nerves on edge.

"Not offering anything extra here, buddy. My blood is all mine, thanks." I try to tug my arm away, but his grip is relentless.

"Shame, you smell like such a tasty treat. Your arousal is making me so hard." His thumb rubs small circles on my wrist as he holds me tight. "Are you sure I can't interest you?"

"She said no!" That deep voice has my eyes darting past the guy in front of me.

Bane towers over the man. His hand grips the guy's shoulder as he yanks him away from me. The sharp claws on the man's fingertips rip into my skin as he's pulled away, opening five gashes down my wrist. I gasp in shock as pain rips up my arm. A towel is thrown over my wrist as my eyes rise to meet Diego's. The red rim around his eyes is back, and I can see his fangs pressing into his lower lip.

"Come on, we need to get you out of the main room." With an arm around my shoulder, Diego drags me straight to the opening at the end of the bar.

Turning my head, I see Bane holding bottled blood guy by the throat. The guy's legs are dangling at least two feet from the floor. But his eyes are on me, just like every other vampire in the bar. As soon as we hit the opening, Diego lifts me from the ground and speeds me away.

Everything's a blur, and I squeeze my eyes shut to block it out. We suddenly stop moving, and a door slams closed. When Diego puts me down, my head is spinning. I've seen them move at their vampire speed before, but actually doing it is a whole other ball game. I try to look around the room he's brought me to, but the way everything seems to move just makes me want to barf. The pain in my wrist hits me, and I place my hand over the towel.

My blood is already soaking through it. *My blood... shit.* My eyes cut to Diego's, he's taken several steps back from me already. His breathing is heavy as his chest rises and falls with his fangs on full display. I see his internal struggle, like he's trying to hold himself back from me.

"Leave if you need to, Diego. I've got this. I'm a nurse, after all. I just need a first-aid kit."

Those black and red eyes watch me as I hold the towel against my arm to staunch the flow of blood. Diego's nostrils flare with each inhale, but he still doesn't move. Maybe I can just find the kit on my own. Stepping closer to the door, I don't even see him move. The next second, my back is pressed against the solid wood.

Diego leans toward me, his lips ghosting up my neck, sending shivers down my spine. His body is close, and I can feel his erection pushing against my belly. What is it with these guys? They make me a horny, wet mess with barely a touch. Pressing my thighs together, I can't stop myself.

"Drink from me, Demi." His words are barely a whisper against my ear. "My blood will heal you."

The thought should revolt me, but instead, I find myself giving Diego a small nod. He leans back, the lower half of his body still holding me against the door. His lips crease up into a wicked smile. Lifting his wrist to his mouth, he bites down into it with his fangs. When he pulls it away, his lips are tinged with his own blood.

Blood beads at the two puncture holes in his wrist, and I'm fascinated by it as they start to run down his skin. Without a second thought, I grab his arm and bring it to my mouth. Locking my lips over the holes, I drink from him. He tastes like heaven. The sweet honey undertones hit my tongue and I moan. When I first woke up after the attack, this is what I tasted. The lingering remnants of Diego's blood. When I found out what it was originally, I wanted to be sick. But now as I swallow each mouthful, I don't want to stop.

I can feel heat pooling in my belly, my body moving of its own accord as I writhe against Diego's hard body. I need more; I need him inside me, fucking me into oblivion. Wrenching his wrist from my mouth, I feel his blood coating my lips. His eyes focus on me before he slams his mouth over mine, his tongue thrusting inside, and his erection rubbing against me.

Lifting me by my ass, I wrap my legs around him. My hands thread through his hair as I hold him close. Carrying me across the room, Diego drops me down on top of a crate against the wall. He pulls his lips from mine, and staring down at me, he grabs my skirt, pushing it up over my thighs.

His hand cups me over my panties, and I rub against him, needing friction.

"Fuck, Demi!" Diego growls out. "You're so wet for me."

Slipping his fingers inside my panties, he thrusts two of them inside me. My back arches up at the sudden invasion as I moan. His cock is straining against the denim covering his legs and I want him inside me. Diego's free hand moves to his belt, pulling it open before popping the button on his jeans and lowering the zipper.

As his fingers continue to thrust into me, he pushes his jeans down his legs. His cock stands proud, nestled in the thatch of short hair and his piercings glitter in the light. The head of his cock is swollen and red, pre-cum beading at the tip. I lick my lips at the thought of how he tasted before.

Pulling his fingers from me, I moan at the loss. I'm so close to coming, I need him to end this exquisite torture. Fabric tears as he rips my panties from me, stuffing them in his back pocket. A wicked grin adorns his lips as he looks down at me whilst he fists his cock.

Leaning over me, he rubs his length through my juices. His piercing catches my swollen clit, causing my whole body to shudder. Bringing his lips to mine, we crash together. Our tongues fight as we taste each other. Rocking his hips against mine, he rubs his length through my slick folds, but he doesn't enter me.

"Fuck Jax and his stupid fucking rules. You're mine, Demi."

Positioning the head of his cock at my entrance, I wrap my legs around his waist. All I need is for him to move, to thrust inside and fill me up.

Chapter 22

Jax

Working through the paperwork on my desk, I glance at my phone again. I've been waiting to hear from Achilles, but so far there has been nothing from him. He's been trying to uncover information about the wolves in our territory. All I want to do is find them and end them before they can hurt anyone else. Or worse, come back for Demetria.

The soft vibration from my cell phone gets my full attention. It's a news bulletin about a missing woman. Swiping across the notification, I wait for the page to load. Lila Moore has been missing for over two weeks without a single lead as to what happened to her. Glancing at the image of the young woman, she's all blonde hair and blue eyes.

Scrolling down to the bottom of the article, there are links to more missing women cases. At least eighteen women have gone missing in the last five years, and none were eventually found alive. The police have identified at least nine of the bodies they have found on the list of missing. Hikers found some of the corpses in the woods, others on the side of the road. Each one ripped apart; their throats torn out. The official cause of death, animal attack.

Even with all the similarities in the deaths, the police haven't pursued the cases any further, stating that while tragic; they were all accidents. Women partying hard during camping trips, runaways…they all get lost in the woods, only to be attacked by animals, which there are plenty of in the Portland area.

To me, 'animal attack' is a story that the Council uses to cover up deaths caused by a supernatural creature. An easy way out of having to explain that whilst some of us are good, there are bad supernaturals in every species. Just like humans, there are those who want to cause havoc and not follow the rules. Those that think they are above everyone else.

Human deaths haven't bothered me in many years. All humans die in the end, it's the one inevitable event in their lives. But with this many missing and murdered women - at least some of whom I now notice resemble Demetria - I'm wondering if it's all linked. By the looks of the articles, the wolves have been in our territory for at least the last five years, kidnapping and killing with no one to stop them.

I'm so lost in my own thoughts that I barely hear the soft knock on my door.

What would Harley be doing here?

"Come in." Dropping my phone on the desk, I wait for Harley to enter. The leather of my chair creaks as I lean back on it.

"Sorry, boss. Bane said I should come get you." She twists her hands in front of her. "It's Demi." As soon as her name escapes Harley's lips, I'm on my feet.

"What happened?" My voice booms louder than I intended, making Harley flinch.

"One of our patrons got a little handsy. When Bane came to remove him, the guy's claws caught Demi's wrist. Diego rushed her to the backroom before it set anyone's bloodlust off."

I'm out of my office in a flash, leaving a bewildered Harley behind. As I move through the bar, I spot Bane by the door. He gives me a small nod; I take it to mean the trash that touched Demetria has been taken care of. I can still smell the faint trace of her blood in the air, and I follow it down the hallway to the backroom.

But what greets me when I enter isn't what I was expecting. Diego has my woman across a crate; her lips are tinged with his blood. The lower half of her body is naked, legs wrapped around Diego's bare ass. He's poised, ready to thrust inside her. Both of their arousal as well as their blood taints the air and the beast inside me roars.

They're both so lost in their lust they haven't even realized I've entered the room. Shifting across the space, I grab Diego by his shoulder and throw him clear across it. He smashes into the shelves, sending boxes crashing to the ground. Diego is on his feet in seconds, tugging up his jeans as he goes.

A feral snarl bursts from his chest as my claws extend, and my fangs lengthen. We crash together and fists fly as we both fight for the upper hand. With a strike of Diego's claws, he leaves his side wide open and I ram my knee into it with enough force to send him to the ground.

As Diego lands on his stomach, I pounce. Shoving his face into the ground, I straddle his back, my knees pushing into his rib cage. My claws dig into the back of his neck, holding him down as he struggles to get out of my grasp. But I'm older and far stronger than him and this is the first time I've really shown him the extent of my power.

"She's mine, Diego!" I roar, spittle flying from my mouth. "If you touch what is mine one more time, I'll put you six feet under."

"Fuck you, Jax." Diego continues to wriggle under me.

I'm so focused on keeping him down, I don't see the booted foot that smashes into the side of my face. It's enough to knock me off balance. Diego makes his move, rearing his body up and pushing me off him. Our positions are reversed, only with me on my back, his fists pummeling my face.

"Stop, just fucking stop!" Demetria's voice cuts through the air, but Diego doesn't listen. Neither of us do.

"She isn't just yours, Jackson! She's mine too." Another punch from the left. "Get that into your thick skull." My face cracks back to the right.

Then his weight is gone. Bane holds Diego tightly across his chest, crushing him against his own body. I push up into a sitting position. My face aches all over and I feel blood dripping down from a cut above my eye.

"Get him the fuck out of here before I rip out his goddamn throat!"

Bane drags a kicking and snarling Diego out of the backroom. As I shove myself up off the floor, my eyes cut to Demetria. She's dressed again, her skirt back in place, but it isn't enough to hide the scent of her arousal from flooding the room. Brushing off my suit, I straighten my shirt and turn towards her.

"What the hell did you think you were doing, Demetria?" I stalk towards her. Her lips are still strained red and the sight of it sends blood rushing to my cock.

"What do you mean?" She snarls. "The fact that I was about to fuck Diego? Or the fact I kicked you in the face?" My cheek throbs at the mere mention of her boot connecting with it.

"Everything! All you do is tempt them both, but they can't have you, Demetria." I'm in front of her now, having backed her against the wall.

"And why's that Captain Asshole? Cause you think you own me?" Her eyes are full of fury. "I am no one's. Not yours," she jabs her finger into my torso, "not Diego's," she jabs me again, "and not those fucking wolves." She smacks her tiny fist against me.

With my nostrils flaring as her scent surrounds me, I grab her wrist and pull it away from my chest. Demetria goes to raise her other hand, but I snatch that wrist too, slamming them against the wall above her head.

"You are mine, sweet Demetria. Diego has no right to touch what is mine."

"You don't even like me, so why do you even give a damn who I fuck?"

Demetria thinks I hate her, and that sends a jolt to my heart. I've been pushing her away from me with such ferocity, what else did I expect her to think? I feel the slight movement through her arms, her knees rising to hit me in the groin, but I deflect her with my thigh.

"I don't hate you, Demetria."

"Well, I fucking hate you!" She spits in my face and snaps the hold I have on myself.

Slamming my lips down on her, a small squeak causes them to open, and I thrust my tongue inside. Dominating the kiss, I push her back into the wall, my hardened cock pushing against her as I hold her in place. Her teeth slam down on my tongue and blood fills her mouth, but all it does is make me groan as I plunder her mouth further.

When she kisses me back, I release her hands and lift her from the ground. Demetria's long legs wrap around my waist as I push her back into the wall again. Her lips wrap around my cut tongue as she swallows my blood. A moan leaks from her and I shove my erection into her crotch. At this angle, my swollen flesh rubs against her clit through my pants.

Demetria rests her head back against the wall as I thrust against her, my lips tracing down the side of her neck until I reach the juncture of her shoulder. Licking and nipping at her flesh, she rolls her hips against me. My fangs scrape across her skin, leaving tiny cuts which I lavish with my tongue as she tries to ride me.

I want to rip the clothing from our bodies and bend her over. To sink my length between her folds as I tangle my fingers in her hair, pulling her back until she screams my name and can no longer stand. Then, when she thinks she can't take anymore, I'll flip her over and sink back inside her as she cums all over my cock and I fill her to the brim. I'll cut across my neck and let her drink my lifeblood, sinking my own teeth into her neck until we seal the true mate bond.

Sealing the bond... it's like a bucket of cold water being dropped over my head. Releasing my mouth from her neck, I all but drop her on the floor. Demetria stumbles to keep herself upright, glaring at me. Her lips are swollen and bruised from our kiss, and now both mine and Diego's blood mark them.

I stare at her. My cock is pulsing, begging to be sheathed inside her. Everything in me is telling me to claim what is mine, but I can't. I can't bind myself to her. Until the wolves are gone, I refuse to make her mine. If we can't stop them - if she dies - I won't be able to live without her. I'll rip my broken but still beating heart from my own chest and end it all, letting oblivion take me.

Storming past her and out of the room, I don't give her a single glance as I pass.

"I fucking hate you, Jackson." She screams after me.

Bane steps in front of me, stopping my progress, his hand on my chest as his stormy blue eyes stare down at me.

"Stop being such an asshole, Jax. You know she's ours. Just claim her already. Let *us* claim her." So many words from the usually quiet giant.

"I can't..." I shrug his hand off me and carry on down the hall.

"Check the basement." His words follow me as he heads for the backroom to comfort Demetria, or whatever the hell it is he plans to do.

Slamming open the emergency exit, I inhale the night air, clearing Demetria's scent from my lungs. I head out into the alley behind the club and make my way to the stairs that lead to the apartment and the ones beside that.

Taking the stairs two at a time until I reach the bottom, I unlock the door and step inside. I already know where to go, even if I couldn't hear the muffled voice drifting from the end of the hall. Opening the door, I step inside and leave it to close behind me.

A vampire who looks to be in his late thirties is strapped to the wall by thick manacles. His face is mottled with bruises, which I'm sure are courtesy of Bane. Shrugging off my suit jacket, I hang it on a hook by the door.

"Let me the fuck go!" He growls, blood splattering from his mouth. "You can't fucking keep me here."

"This is where you're wrong. This is my territory and my club. I can do whatever the hell I want." I step closer to him, and he shrinks back as best as he can. "You touched what's mine, and I can't let you get away with that."

My arm lashes out, my fist connecting with his mouth. He spits blood on the floor. A few drops land on my shoes and I snarl. His eyes are blood red now, his fangs on display. Just how I wanted him. Walking to the desk, I pick up a set of pliers and make my way back over to him.

"Do you know what happens to vampires who touch my things?" A shake of his head is all I get as he stares at the tool in my grasp.

Grabbing him by the throat, I force his head back against the wall and pull his jaws open. I close the pliers on one of his fangs and yank down hard. The sharpened tooth rips from his gum and he bellows as blood flows from the wound. Letting the lengthened incisor fall to the floor, I force his mouth open again and close the pliers on his other fang. Another yank and I detach the last fang from his mouth. A scream rips out of him and he chokes on his own blood as it flows down his throat.

"I rip out their fangs and add them to a jar in my office," I whisper into his ear. "But you… I think you need more than just a warning."

Letting the pliers fall to the floor, my claws latch onto his crotch. They slice through the material into the flesh beneath it. He continues to scream as I rip through the skin until there isn't much left of his pathetic cock. He's sobbing now, whispering pleas for mercy, but he won't get any of that from me.

"Wait, there's more." I grin.

Trailing my sharpened nails up from his waistband to the neck of his shirt, I cut open the material, baring his chest to me. My claws glance across his skin as I make my way back down to where his heart lies. Pulling back, I look him over; his mouth is bloody, and tears pour from his eyes. There's a hint of urine in the air, a look at his crotch confirms he's emptied his bladder.

"Please... I'm sorry... I didn't know she was yours." He sobs, but it falls on deaf ears. "Just let me go... you'll never see me again."

"Oh, I know I won't. But I can't let you go."

Drawing back my hand, I punch it through his ribs, my claws puncturing through skin, muscle, and bone. Curling my fist around his still-beating heart, I let my sharpened nails dig into it before I rip it from his chest. There's a look of shock on his face as he sees the thumping organ within my grasp. Then the light fades from his eyes and his body slumps, his head falling down to his chest.

Dropping the heart on the floor, I stomp down on it for good measure. My anger over the wolves, Diego, and Demetria has gotten the best of me, and I took it out on him. Not that he didn't deserve it, he shouldn't have touched my mate.

Cleaning myself up at the sink in the corner of the room, the dead man's blood swirls down the drain. I still haven't heard from Achilles, but if I let him know I have a body to dispose of and cash to line his pockets, I'm positive he will get back to me. Then I can ask if he's heard anything about the wolves.

Wiping my hands on the towel, I notice the flecks of blood staining the edges of my cuffs. Another shirt ruined and heading for the furnace. Grabbing my jacket on the way out, I pull out my phone and text Achilles about my little situation. With that done, I pocket it again and take the stairs back up to the apartment.

Chapter 23

Demi

That absolute asshole.
Cock blocked again from finally getting what I want with Diego by Captain Asshole himself. Not just that but then he had the audacity to kiss me. And what a kiss it was. Dominating and intoxicating all rolled into one.

"I fucking hate you, Jackson." Those are the words that left my mouth as he stormed away, leaving me horny and unfulfilled.

Bane walks into the back room and looks me over, taking in the blood still smeared on my lips. Pulling me into his arms, he holds me close. My anger settles back to a simmer as he runs his fingers through my hair.

"Thanks, big guy." Shifting my head, I tug him down and lay a soft kiss on his lips before pulling away.

Bane smiles at me and takes hold of my hand. Lifting my arm up, he inspects my wrist. Apart from the dry, flakey blood, I wouldn't have even known what had happened. After drinking from Diego, I all but forgot why I was doing it in the first place. Bane running his fingers over my wrist sends shivers through me.

"Come." One day I'm going to get more than a few words out of Bane, but I'm guessing it's not going to be today.

Turning on his heel, he walks out of the back room and down the hall towards the restrooms with me close behind him. Instead of heading there, he pulls me to the other side of the corridor. We head through a black door marked 'Employees Only' revealing a small single bathroom with only a toilet and sink.

Grabbing a few paper towels from the dispenser, Bane runs them under the tap before taking my arm and rubbing the wet towel against my flesh. Once all the blood is gone, he runs it over my lips, gently dabbing the mixture of blood from them. Snatching a few more towels, he dries my arm before throwing them in the trash.

"So, does this mean I can go back to work?" I'm not hopeful after what happened, but I really don't want to go back to the apartment just yet.

"Okay."

Yes, score another point for Demi.

I look down at my skirt. There's no way I can go back to the bar wearing just this, especially since Diego destroyed my panties. Dick. I remember him pocketing them after he ripped them from my body.

"Eh, big guy. I'm gonna need something to change into. Diego kinda destroyed my panties." I gesture at my lower half, and he nods.

Bane is out of the door and back again before I can even comprehend where he went. He thrusts out a folded piece of black material and I take it. Opening it out, I see it's a pair of shorts with the 'Dark Desires' logo on one side. *Good enough.* Slipping them up my legs, I pull them on. I hoped I would be able to wear them as panties, but my skirt is too tight to wear the extra fabric underneath. I shimmy out of my original outfit and Bane takes it from me.

Bane holds the door open for me, and we head back down towards the main bar. Harley is serving a couple of customers down the other end, and Diego is standing just inside, a bottle of blood in his grasp as he chugs it down. Even in the low light, I can see some of the cuts on his face slowly knitting themselves back together. It's amazing to watch what blood can do for a vampire.

I wonder how many people know that drinking a vampire's blood can heal their wounds as well. It's not exactly something the Council advertises. Can you imagine what would happen if people knew that small tidbit of information? Some asshole would probably think it's a good idea to capture and drain a vampire to sell their blood on the black market.

As I get closer to the bar, Diego turns his attention to me, dropping the empty bottle of blood in the trash.

"I'm sorry." I blurt out.

"It's not on you, Demi. It's Jax. He's got a goddamn stick rammed so far up his ass."

Cradling my cheek in his hand, he runs his fingers over it. A smile adorns his lips as he leans down and kisses my other cheek. His lips are only there for the briefest of moments before he pulls away from me again.

"Now, get your ass back to work. We got customers to serve." Dragging me the last few feet behind the bar, he pulls me past him and smacks my ass.

I'm still horny, and also panty-less, but it's better than being locked up in the apartment again, pulling the guys away from their real jobs. I get straight to work, busying myself with putting some of the clean glasses back on the shelves. After the incident with blood bottle guy, I'm getting a few looks from the patrons, but I ignore them and get on with my task.

Pouring a few glasses of beer, I stack the glasses on a tray and hand them over to the waiting customer. Once he's paid and gotten his change, he's replaced by someone else. The night seems to rush by, making and serving drinks, cleaning and restocking glasses, wiping down the bar top. It's not long before the club finally closes and Bane and the other bouncers usher the last few stragglers out.

"Do I expect to see you again, Demi?" Harley's voice rings out behind me as I put the last few glasses away.

"As long as Captain Asshole doesn't decide to keep me locked in his tower again." I laugh at the thought. Fine, he's protecting me from the wolves, but Harley doesn't know that.

"I'm sure if you show him a good time, he'll let you do anything you want." She runs her tongue over her ruby red lips and flutters her eyelashes.

I can't stop the laughter that bubbles through my lips. Even after that kiss, I'm pretty sure there is no way Jax is ever going to want me to cross that boundary. He says he doesn't hate me, but he certainly doesn't like me either.

"Ready to go, *preciosa*." Diego's arms wrap around my waist as he kisses the top of my head. "Harley, we can walk you out."

"That'd be great. Thanks, boss. Let me just get my things." Harley throws a wink my way as she drops the towel and rushes through a door I hadn't even noticed between the counters of the bar.

Diego turns me in his arms and smiles down at me. At some point, he cleaned up his face so there's no blood on it anymore and nearly all of his wounds are completely gone. Only the deepest wounds are still healing. There's not a single trace of the bruises that covered one side of his face either.

Leaning down, he kisses me full on the lips. It's not like our other kisses - it's soft and sweet. His tongue brushes across the seam of my mouth and I open them for him. A clearing throat has us both pulling away. Harley is standing there staring at us, a huge smirk on her face.

"Can't leave you two alone for a minute, can I?" Harley shakes her head and moves off towards the front of the club.

"Guess that's our cue to leave as well." Diego grabs my hand and tugs me along.

It's cold when we get outside and a shiver runs through me. I can see my own breath each time I exhale. I didn't even think of bringing a jacket when I left the apartment. It was so much warmer earlier, but now, even without a single cloud in the sky, the air is chilled. Diego wraps his arm around my shoulder and pulls me close as we follow Harley to her car.

She stops in front of a silver Civic and clicks the locks. Turning back to me and Diego, she gives me a one-armed hug.

"Told ya, Demi. Head over heels." She whispers next to my ear. When she moves back, she's grinning like the Cheshire Cat. "Treat her right, boss man. She's a keeper." She winks at Diego before spinning around and getting into her car.

Once she's inside, she starts the engine and gives us a little wave before pulling away from the curb. Diego leads me down the side of the club to the steps I know lead to the apartment. He's quiet for once, which is very unlike him. He clearly isn't going to listen to Jax, but I think their fight earlier has made him take a small step back.

I swear Captain fucking Asshole needs to stop impeding my orgasms.

There's only so much more I can take. He's declared me as his, even though he doesn't seem to want me himself. Maybe it's time we had a proper talk and I find out what the hell is going on.

When we reach the bottom of the steps, Bane steps out of the shadows, making me jump back.

"Jeez, big guy. Are you trying to give me a heart attack? Gonna have to fit you with a bell or something." Diego snickers at my comment and I glare up at him. "Don't start. I'm thinking I'm going to need to get myself a chastity belt. At least that way you can't start anything that Jax is going to interrupt, again." I huff, folding my arms across my chest.

Brushing past them both, I stomp up the stairs, my two shadows following closely behind me. When we reach the top, Bane leans over my shoulder to input the code. I really should ask the guys what the code is in case I ever end up in a situation where they aren't here and I need to get in.

Entering the apartment after the second security door, I let out a breath. It's late already, but I know after the night I've had, I won't be able to settle. It's not like the hospital when I come home from a shift and collapse in bed. I'm still wired and need something to help relax me.

Leaving the two guys at the door, I head to my room to change into my PJs and preferably put some underwear on. Rifling through the drawers, I can't find a single pair that isn't something my grandma would wear. I barely had any as it was when I got my things from my apartment. Most of them were ripped to shreds by the wolves, and those I did salvage weren't the nicest pairs - probably why they were still there.

Pulling on some plain, black cotton panties, I slip into some sleep shorts and a tank top, throwing my hoodie over the top. I head back into the living room: Diego is already gone, but Bane is sitting on the couch with the TV on. Grabbing a drink from the fridge, I make my way over and lower myself down beside him.

Bane's arm loops around my shoulder, pulling me close. I rest my head on his chest, feeling the heat of him through his thin shirt. I welcome the warmth. His fingers run through my hair, soothing me.

"I need to go shopping tomorrow, if I'm expected to work in the bar tomorrow night. Between Diego and those damn wolves, I'm lacking in the panties department." I think about the panties Diego ripped off me earlier, and the fact he pocketed them. *Dick.*

"I'll take you."

"Thanks." I've seen the way Bane has protected me, so he's probably the best to go with.

Curling up against Bane's side, I let my hand rest on his chest. The feel of his heart rhythmically beating under my fingers soon has my eyes closing as I drift off to sleep.

When my eyes open again, I'm in my bed. It's already well into the morning, and the sun is peeking through the curtains. Warmth at my back tells me one of the guys slept in here with me last night. I don't think I had any nightmares, their presence always seems to keep me calm in my sleep. Letting out a yawn, I stretch my arms above my head.

The temptation to snuggle deep into the blankets and close my eyes again is real, but raised voices coming from down the hall have me climbing out of bed. Bane is laying on his side, his hand reaching out to the empty space I just made. When he doesn't find me, he grabs onto my pillow, pulling it back into his chest.

How much would he hate me if I took a picture of him while he sleeps? He might look big and scary, but really, he's the sweetest guy I've ever met. He's always jumping in to protect me, even from the other guys. I still don't get why Jax has so much of an issue with Bane and Diego showing me attention when he doesn't give me any. But that's his problem, I guess.

As I move out into the hall, the voices die down. Jax and Diego are in the kitchen looking equally pissed off at each other. I shoot Jax a glare as his eyes lock with mine. I'm done with his bullshit.

"Good morning, Demetria." His voice is rougher than usual, but man if I can't help but want to shudder when he says my name. He's the only one who calls me by my full name. Even my parents used to call me Demi.

"Captain Asshole." I mock salute him as I walk over to the coffee machine and make myself a cup. Diego smirks, and I roll my eyes at him.

"May I ask about your plans for the day? I have some things I need to take care of." Jax doesn't even comment on the fact I saluted him.

"You may not." Turning my full attention to Diego, I sip my coffee. "So Bane's taking me shopping later. After the incident last night with my panties, I'm gonna need some more."

"I'd love to go with you, beautiful, but some asshole," Diego glances in Jax's direction, "has given me orders to clean up the backroom. I think it's so he can keep me away from you." A snarl has my eyes moving to Jax. I stick my tongue out at him.

"Guess it's just me and the big guy, then. I suppose I'll have to ask Bane what color panties he'd like to see me in." I pop a few slices of bread into the toaster and lean back against the countertop. "Want me to see if I can find you something to get that stick out of your ass, Jackson?" Cue another smirk from Diego. After what happened last night, I'm going to call him Jackson from now until the end of time.

"Just be careful." Guess that's the only response I'm going to get from Jax considering he's already taken off down the hallway toward his office. Shrugging, I push off the counter and grab the butter and some strawberry jelly out of the fridge.

"Fucking asshole," I murmur as my toast pops up.

Grabbing it from the toaster, I take it over to the breadboard and slather it in butter and juicy strawberry goodness. Taking a bite, I moan as the sweetness of the jelly hits my tongue. I can feel Diego behind me, his arms loop around my waist as he pulls me to him.

"He can't help how he is sometimes. Jax went through a lot with his sire before he met me and Bane." His lips press against the side of my head, and I lean back into his warmth as I take another bite of my toast.

"Doesn't mean he should be telling me who I can and can't sleep with, then claim I'm his. I'm my own person, Diego. And once this shit is over with the wolves, I'll be going back to my life, and you'll be going back to yours." Diego turns me suddenly, his hands on my shoulders.

"Do you really think I'd let you go now I've had a taste of you?" Diego lets out a laugh. "You couldn't get rid of me even if you tried."

I'm at a loss for words. Even though I feel a weird connection to them, even Jax, I figured once all is said and done everything would go back to how it was. But maybe not. A throat clears across the room and I find my giant standing at the end of the hall, leaning up against the wall.

Bane has changed his clothing. He's wearing a navy blue shirt that stretches deliciously across his wide chest. If he flexes, I'm sure he'll burst out of the damn thing. His charcoal gray jeans hug his legs and his blond hair is brushed to one side, flopping down slightly over his forehead.

"Ready?" Bane angles his head toward the door.

"Guess so." Rising on my tiptoes, I give Diego a small kiss on the cheek. "Enjoy your punishment." I'm out of his reach before he can move, grabbing the rest of my toast and joining Bane.

"Totally worth it," Diego shouts out at our retreating forms.

Chapter 24

Bane

The drive to the mall doesn't take us long, thanks to Jax lending us his car again. I assume he's worried I'll get too distracted with Demi on the back of my motorcycle and end up having an accident. Once I get us parked, I'm out of the door and on her side of the vehicle before she even gets her seatbelt off.

Taking her hand, I help her out of the car. Demi looks absolutely stunning today, just like every day I've seen her so far. Her long, black hair is braided down her back, and her soft make-up and eyeliner make her turquoise eyes stand out. She's wearing tight black leggings that hug her ass, a fitted band t-shirt, and one of Diego's hoodies she seems to have stolen over the top.

Lacing my fingers through hers, she happily accepts them, her own curling around mine. Walking the short distance from the car to the entrance, I hold open the door, letting her inside ahead of me. The security at the entrance looks me over and I give them a curt nod as I follow Demi inside.

The mall is huge, and as soon as we step inside the air-conditioned building, my senses are on high alert. With my head on a swivel, I take in everything around me as Demi walks around like she isn't being hunted by wolves. Even with everything going on, including the death of her friend, she hasn't broken. Either that or she is really good at hiding it.

Stopping in front of the mall map, she scans the list of stores, her finger running over it to find the one she wants. Once she does, she pulls on my hand and I let her lead the way. We walk past several stores crowded with small groups of people and I check every single one of them for danger. So far, I'm picking up only humans and a few vampires. No wolves, which is a good sign.

Pulling me into a store, I catch the name *Victoria's Secret* as we cross the threshold. Once inside, I'm surrounded by lingerie and all manner of swim, sports, and sleepwear. If Demi wanted panties, then I'm pretty sure this is the place to be. There is every style and color you could think of.

Demi lets go of my hand as she heads straight toward a few rows of underwear, leaving me trailing behind her. The store is perfumed; the scent makes me want to sneeze. As I shuffle through the racks, I notice they are definitely not made for someone my size. I brush up against most of the items hanging from them. Demi is lost in thought, rifling through the lingerie. As I get closer to her, I spot her pulling things down and adding them to a pile on her arm.

"Lilac or blue?" Demi spins on the spot, holding up two almost sheer lace pairs, thrusting them in my direction.

My eyes widen as I look at both, imagining her body wrapped in them before I pull them down her long legs. I let out a grunt as I look between the two and Demi's hopeful face. I've never had to go shopping with a woman before, and it's not the most comfortable position I've ever been in. Give me feral vampires any day of the week, those I know how to handle.

"Both?" There's a question in my voice.

"Good thinking, big guy." Demi beams at me as she adds them to her growing pile.

When I think she's done, she heads to another collection, adding even more lacy lingerie to her pile. Her hands are full, but she turns to me and holds them out expectantly. Without a second thought, I reach out and take them from her. Another smile cracks her lips, and she looks at me, grabbing the new phone Jax gave her from her back pocket. She turns it to face me, and I hear the click of the camera.

"I can't wait to show this to Diego." Demi giggles as she pockets the phone again. I'm going to need to delete that photo before we get back. There is no way Diego will let me live it down if he sees a photo of me drowning in this much lace.

Before I can respond, she's off again, leaving me standing there completely dumbstruck at how I even ended up in this situation. I sense someone approaching behind me and turn so quickly I almost drop everything. There's a small human woman staring at me. Her name tag announces she's called Frankie.

"Would you like a basket, sir?" I nod my head, and she lifts the plastic up toward me.

I drop the pile inside and she smiles up at me coyly. Her hand brushes against mine as she passes me the handles. She leaves one of her hands on top of mine and I just stare at the offending limb.

"Let me know if there is anything at all I can do for you. Maybe a demonstration of our latest range?" Her eyes rove over me like I'm the prey, and she's the predator. Clearly, she doesn't know who or what she's dealing with.

"Baby, I need you to come help me pick something for after our date this weekend? Something you can rip from me." Demi's voice washes over me as she shifts around my side, one hand skirts round my back and the other lays over my heart.

My eyes drop down to her, and she looks up at me, her lips curving up into a wicked smile. Demi's hand moves up my chest and slips around the back of my neck as she pulls me down so our lips connect. My lips part with a sigh, and she thrusts her tongue inside. Holding the basket in one hand, I use the other to pull her against me, molding her body to mine as our kiss goes from playful to demanding.

When we part, Demi gasps for breath and she gives me a wink as she sinks back down onto her feet. Turning her body, she keeps one hand on my arm as she looks at Frankie. The poor assistant is standing there with her mouth wide open as she looks between the two of us.

"Thanks for helping my big guy, Frankie." Demi's fingers trace down my wrist till her fingers lace with mine. "He decided we needed to come to the store for new lingerie, especially considering he keeps ripping mine."

Frankie's expression now resembles a fish gasping for air, like she can't quite grasp the words to respond to Demi's forwardness.

"I don't suppose you have a dressing room? I'd really like to try some pieces before I buy them."

"Yes... of course." Frankie stutters and I can't stop myself from grinning. Demi really has left her flustered.

Turning on her heel, Frankie heads toward the back of the store and, hand in hand, we follow her. She gestures for us to enter the dressing rooms ahead of her. They are simple in design, with each cubicle behind a dusky pink curtain. Inside is a small bench, a full-length mirror and hooks to hang items of clothing.

Demi drags me inside and stares at a perplexed Frankie before she closes the curtain in her face. As soon as she does, she's bent at the waist laughing, her breath heaving in and out as she rests her hands on her knees. She makes no attempt to control her laughter.

"Oh God, did you see her face?" Demi rushes out between bouts of laughter. "I don't think she knew what to say."

Dropping the basket on the bench, I silently move in front of Demi. When my boots are in her field of vision, she lifts her head slowly. Her eyes are watering from her laughter and her cheeks are glowing a rosy red. Cupping her cheek in my hand, I raise her head and sweep down to kiss her again.

Demi's arms wrap around my neck and I lift her from the ground. My hands cup her ass as her long legs wrap around my waist. Pressing her against the wall, I dominate her mouth, exploring the depths with my tongue. I've been trying my best to follow Jax's rules about not getting too close to Demi, keeping my kisses brief, but her possessiveness over me with Frankie has snapped something inside me.

I'm not like Diego; I haven't been pushing the boundaries, but I can't take it anymore. I watch Demi every time she enters a room and capture each smile she gives me. The scent of her has been driving me insane, and I've spent far longer than I care to count locked up in my room, jacking off to thoughts of her.

I swallow each moan as we kiss, letting her body rub against mine. My cock is rock hard and pushing against the seam of my jeans. It's pleasure and pain combined, driving me to devour her. When I break the kiss, her chest rises and falls rapidly. Her lips are bruised, and her fingers are still tangled in my hair.

Sliding ever so slowly down the full length of my body, Demi drops to her knees before me and it's a sight to behold. Her turquoise eyes watch me as her fingers move to the buttons of my jeans. She's asking for permission, and all I can do is nod.

With deft fingers, she undoes my jeans and lets my cock spring free. The head is angry and red, and the veins are prominent down my length. Demi's eyes widen and she licks her lips as she stares at me. A drop of pre-cum wets the end.

Demi's small hand grasps the base of my cock, her fingers nowhere near touching. The warmth of her touch seeps through my skin and my length twitches at the feel of her on me. Drawing in a deep breath, I try to calm myself. I've wanted her to touch my cock since I saw her and Diego in the hallway in the apartment.

Swirling her tongue around the head is almost enough to bring me to my knees and I slam a hand onto the wall next to the mirror to steady myself. I don't let my eyes leave Demi as her tongue licks up and down my length, her hand moving in jerking movements at my base. It's taking everything in me not to thrust my length further into the warm cavern of her mouth.

"Demi..." my voice is low, and her eyes lift to me and she smiles.

Her lips wrap around my weeping head as she takes me as far as she can go, even then they barely touch the circle of her hand. The sight of my cock disappearing between her lips as her tongue flattens against my length has my hips jerking and she moans around me, the vibration doing crazy things to me.

Demi glides over my length, sucking and licking, I can't stop my hips from moving in short, shallow thrusts. Her other hand shifts to massage my balls and it's game over. With a groan and one last thrust, I come in her mouth and she swallows every single drop, her tongue cleaning my length.

Pulling her from her knees and back up my body, I kiss her again. It's only brief, ending before it can even start. Tucking my softening length back in my jeans, I re-button them.

"My turn..." My hands reach for her, but she holds her hand in front of me. Stilling my movement.

"I think we've done enough to make Frankie back off." Then it hits me.

"Jealous?"

"Of what, exactly? This is just a temporary thing, right?" If Demi thinks this is just a brief fling, she really doesn't understand what she means to us. Even when the wolves are dealt with, I don't plan on letting her go.

Straightening her clothes and grabbing the basket, she whips open the curtain and leaves me standing there. She passes Frankie as she heads for the checkout and throws her a smile. The woman's cheeks glow red, leaving another sales assistant to ring through Demi's purchases. I'm there to hand over my credit card before she can even fumble for her purse.

"You didn't have to."

"I know."

Grabbing the bags, I make my way to the exit. Demi loops her hand through the crook of my arm, oblivious to the thoughts running through my head.

After another hour of shopping, Demi is done, grabbing a few more items from various stores. Each time I pay for her purchases, and after a while she stops trying to reach for her purse. With the bags loaded in the trunk, I drive us back to the club. It's quiet outside, too early for any of the workers to be milling around.

With the bar being closed and me being with Demi, we don't even have any of the other security around the building yet. It'll be a few hours before they get here and cover the doors whilst Demi works the bar. Pulling the car around the corner from the side alley for the club, I get out and head straight to Demi's door, opening it for her.

Stepping out of the car, she smiles up at me.

"My knight in shining armor."

Both of us move to the trunk to grab her things, loading up with her bags, I don't even hear the approaching feet. It's only when Demi gives a muffled yelp that I realize something is wrong. Spinning around, I smell them. The scent of wet dog. Scents I'm now familiar with as the wolves who attacked her.

My hackles rise, my fangs and claws lengthening as I drop the bags. One of the filthy mutts has his hands all over Demi.

He has one arm holding her close to his body as she flails to get free, the other over her mouth. He's flanked by three mutts in human form and another three in their shifted forms.

Letting out a snarl, I leap forward and crash straight into one of the shifted wolves. His teeth sink into my shoulder as I rip my claws into its side. Blood spills over my fingers as I dig them through skin and muscle and a whimper escapes through his closed jaw. More fangs sink into my left calf as the other wolf tears into my leg. I can smell the mixture of our blood in the air.

Kicking out my other foot, I hit the wolf attached to my leg in the head. He lets go for a moment, shaking his head, and spraying my blood from his teeth all over. My calf is throbbing, but I know I need to get to Demi. Tearing my claws from the other wolf's side, I slam my fist into the side of his head.

His body drops to the floor, unconscious. But there's no reprieve as his companions jump on me, keeping me on the ground. I thrash like a feral animal, but it's no use. They don't let up. Something sharp scratches my neck and a burning pain radiates from the area. The wolves on top of me back away, giving me the room I need to rise.

I stumble to my feet, but my limbs feel heavy, and my vision is unfocused. The wolves have both shifted and are back in human form, keeping a steady distance from me. I lash out, but miss them completely, teetering on my feet. My eyes focus for a brief second and I see the terror on Demi's face as the wolf holding her smirks.

"Don't worry, bloodsucker, we'll take good care of her. My Alpha has so many plans for this one. And when he's finished with her, the rest of us will make sure that pussy is never empty." He cackles, and his words hardly register as I fall to my knees.

Trying to stand again, I get my foot under me but fall straight back to the ground, face planting the tarmac.

Darkness consumes me as whatever they drugged me with takes hold.

Chapter 25

Demi

Consciousness creeps back to me and I blink my eyes open slowly. My head is throbbing, and my arms feel like they are being ripped out of the sockets. I seem to be upright, but my feet can barely touch the floor. My entire weight bears down on my arms, which are pulled high above my head. Something is tight around my wrists, chafing at my skin.

Lifting my gaze, I take in the rope that is bound around my wrists holding me from the ceiling. I drop my eyes again. I'm still clothed, minus my hoodie which is a small relief - the only thing missing is my shoes and socks. Even though I'm still dressed, the parts of my skin that are bare are covered in goosebumps. It's cold in here, wherever *here* is.

Where the fuck am I?

I glance around the room if you can even call it that. The walls are concrete, but the ground is rough and rocky, covered in dips and rises. There's a steel door opposite to where I'm hanging, with a small opening at eye level.

Where's Bane?

The memories are fuzzy, but I start to piece them together. We went to the mall and then arrived back at the apartment where the wolves attacked us. They took him down, I didn't think it was possible. I tried to scream, but with a hand over my mouth, no one heard me. One wolf jammed a needle into

Bane's neck. He fought some more, but whatever was in the needle took effect and he collapsed on the ground. Then something struck the back of my head, and everything went dark.

"You're awake. Good." That voice, it's the leader of the wolves. The one who killed Ginny. He sounds like he's somewhere off to the side, but I didn't spot him when I looked around.

"Just let me the fuck go. I'm not your mate." I snap. "And even if you think I am, I'd rather be dead."

He steps out of the shadows to my right as I tilt my head to look at him. I can see him better than I could that night. There is nothing special about him. His clothes are torn, his hair is filled with as much grease as I remember, and he's covered in dirt. As he gets closer to me, a shudder passes through my body. I can't help it.

"Told you I'd find you, little one, and it looks like the bloodsuckers have taken good care of you." He stops in front of me, his hand grasping my jaw, holding my head up to look at him. He inhales deeply. "Maybe they took care of you a little too well. Their stench covers you, but don't worry, I can remedy that. You'll carry only my scent, inside and out. Everyone will know you're mine."

"I'll never be yours." I spit in his face. The saliva hits his cheek, and he wipes it away, smirking up at me.

I wrench my face away from him and look away, focusing on the floor and his boot-clad feet. Drawing his face closer to mine, his nose trails up the side of my neck. Unlike when Bane does it, I feel disgusted. His every touch makes me want to puke. Darting out his tongue, he runs it up the side of my neck. I pull on my bonds, hoping they will loosen, but all they do is cut into my wrists, making the skin burn.

The door to the room opens, and two more men walk in. I recognize one of them as Alaric; he was in the alley that night. The other is a man I haven't seen before, but he's as dirty looking as the other two.

"Alaric, Hank, take my mate to the showers. Make sure she's clean. I don't want to smell bloodsuckers on her anymore. Burn her clothes, I have others for her."

The rope around my wrists loosens, and I fall to the floor in a heap. Rough hands grab me, pulling me to my feet. They wrap around my arms and half drag me out of the room. I try to fight, but I'm exhausted and my head is still throbbing.

The two men continue to drag me down a darkened hallway, and the rough ground bites at my feet. I lift my head to try and work out where we're going. The walls on either side of me are carved from rock, and there are lanterns strung in lines, barely lighting the way.

"Glad to see you're back with us. I told Rufus it wouldn't take long." Alaric speaks to my left. *Rufus? Is that the name of the leader?* "We were taking bets on how much time it would take for the fangs to fuck up."

Hank lets out a rough laugh like it's some sort of inside joke. I drop my head back down and let them pull me along. I don't have the energy to fight them right now, especially not two wolves - they'll take me down before I even get a few steps.

We stop in front of another steel door, and Alaric shoves it open. I lift my head slightly as we enter. Unlike the other room I was in, the walls and floor here are covered in grimy, gray tiles and there are a few showerheads attached to one wall.

Alaric keeps hold of me as Hank steps to the closest tap and turns it on. The spray starts off brown and dirty before finally becoming clearer, but even then it doesn't look like the cleanest water.

"No wonder you guys smell so bad. I'm betting you never shower." I snark.

Thrusting me forward, Alaric shoves me under the water, fully dressed. It's ice-cold and feels like thousands of tiny needles piercing the bare skin of my arms. I shriek and try to get away from it, my feet scrambling against the wet tiles. A growl sounds behind me and Alaric crowds against me, one arm slung under my breasts, holding me under the water.

"Rufus said to get you clean. We wouldn't want to disappoint him now, would we, little bitch?" I cough and splutter as the water crashes over my mouth and nose.

"Shame!" Hank says from behind where Alaric and I stand. "I'd love to watch him punish her. Maybe he'd even let us fuck her mouth."

Alaric barks out a laugh next to my ear and I startle. I'm shivering all over, the cold water freezing me to the bone. Rufus, the leader, wants me clean and I want out from under this water.

"Soap?" My voice trembles because of the cold.

"Hank, grab me some soap. Then we can get her clean." Alaric hefts me a little higher. My feet are now flat on the tiled ground, and he's letting me stand unaided. "Strip." His voice rasps against my ear.

"No!"

Alaric's grip on me loosens a touch and I slam my head back into his face, making him grunt. Snatching my arms in his, he spins me so I'm facing him and slams me back into the tiled wall, knocking the air from my lungs. His clawed fingers rake down the front of my clothes, ripping through my t-shirt and bra like they're butter.

His hands reach for my leggings and I try to bat them away, but his claws make quick work of the fabric, leaving me in just my panties.

I hear Hank shuffling back over to us, holding the soap out. Alaric snatches it from Hank's open hand and turns his full attention back to me. I put my arms over my chest, trying to hide myself as best as I can.

"No need to hide, little bitch. We'll be seeing everything soon enough."

My eyes dart up and I see the leering smirk on Hank's face over Alaric's shoulder. I take in a shuddering breath and hold out my hand for the soap, but Alaric tuts and shakes his head at me.

"Oh no, that's not how this works." He steps closer to me again and my back connects with the tile behind me. "Rufus said to make sure you're clean. The only way to do that is if I do it for you."

Alaric's hand reaches for me. I try to duck away from his touch but fail miserably. He pushes my back against the tiles again with one hand, as his other skirts across my breasts. Soap still in his hand, he roughly massages it against my skin. As soon as his finger glances across my nipple, I react.

My knee drives straight up into his crotch, ripping a gasp from him. Staggering a little, he drops the soap and grabs his family jewels with his hands, his breath coming out in pants.

"You fucking bitch." He grunts through clenched teeth, amber eyes glaring at me. "Hank, hold her."

Hank lunges forward and grabs me, spinning me in his arms and pulling me back against his chest as he tugs my arms behind me. Alaric slowly bends, picking up the soap he dropped.

"I'm going to fucking enjoy this, little bitch." Alaric stalks closer, malice shining in his eyes. "Rufus said we couldn't fuck you, but that leaves so much we can still do."

Then his rough hands are on me, soaping up my skin. He runs the soap over my breasts. My nipples are rock hard, not from pleasure but from the cold. He doesn't seem to care as he tweaks one nipple between his fingers, hard. A yelp of pain escapes me.

I squirm in Hank's arms, fighting with what little strength I have to get away. Alaric's hands move from my chest as he rubs the soap down my stomach and sides. He drops to his knees before me, lathering up both my legs, his hands moving roughly against my skin. When he reaches the apex of my thighs, he pushes them open.

I try to close them, but he holds them wide. Skirting his hand up the inside of my thigh, I jerk against Hank's hold.

"Please... I can wash myself."

"And where would the fun be in that, little bitch?" Alaric laughs again. "I'm going to make sure you are squeaky clean for your mate, inside and out." My eyes widen.

With no warning, he pushes past the fabric of my panties and forces two fingers inside me. A scream erupts from my lips at the invasion, but Hank covers my mouth with his free hand. Alaric continues to thrust his fingers in and out of me, aided by the soap covering them. His rough nails scratch at my insides and the soap makes it sting.

"That's it, little bitch. Squeal for me." Alaric says as he laughs. I can feel Hank's arousal now, pushing at my behind and all I can think is how thankful I am for the fabric between us both. My mind and my body are going numb. I see black spots behind my eyes as I struggle to take in a breath.

Ripping his fingers from me, Alaric stands suddenly. He lifts his hand to his mouth, licking his fingers. I can see slight tinges of blood on his digits as he does it. *Disgusting piece of shit.*

"God, you taste sweet. Like the finest wine." He sucks his fingers into his mouth before pulling them out with a pop. "Turn her!" He snaps at Hank.

Hank does as instructed, letting go of my arms. He spins my body and grabs me again, yanking me so my chest is against his. Alaric's hands are on me again as he washes my back and sides, grazing his nails against my ass as he moves lower and lower.

I feel his breath on my backside. The stubble on his face brushes against the globes of my ass. Grabbing onto each cheek with a hand, he grips me hard, his nails biting into the skin, making me wince.

"Maybe I should wash you here too?" Alaric prods a finger at my anus as I whimper behind Hank's hand.

Shaking my head violently, I twist and turn my body, pulling my legs back together and clenching. The fabric over my ass is pulled down and Alaric's finger circles my back passage, rubbing soap around my entrance.

"ALARIC!" Rufus' voice booms and the finger probing at me pulls away. I sign, my body relaxing just a little.

"Yes, sir." Alaric jumps to his feet, turning his back on me. Hank's grip across my mouth loosens.

"Get her dressed and take her to the others. I want her to get accustomed to her new accommodations." I have no idea who the others are, but I'm not sure I want to find out.

"Next time, little bitch." Alaric keeps his voice low as he chuckles.

The water turns off and I almost crumple, the cold water has left my entire body shaking. Hank shoves me away from the shower and I trip, falling into Alaric's open arms. They're both soaking wet, but they don't seem as affected by the cold as I am.

Must be a wolf thing.

Hank lifts what looks like an old scrap of satin fabric and holds it in front of me. He shoves it over my head, and wrenches my arms through the holes. My eyes drop to the fabric. What I thought was a scrap of material is a dirty, torn babydoll that barely covers my breasts and ass. It clings uncomfortably to my still wet skin.

Alaric grabs me and drags me out of the showers, back into the darkened tunnel. We turn in the opposite direction to where we came from. The dirt on the floor clings to my feet and lower legs, and before long, it's like I've not even had a shower at all.

I can hear another voice getting closer as we move through the tunnels. We stop in front of two other wolves I've never seen before. One unlocks the door they are guarding and pushes it open. Alaric drags me inside. There isn't much light in here but what I can see horrifies me.

Scattered around the cave-like room are multiple cages, most of them filled with half-naked women all clad in attire similar to my own. I count only two cages that are empty, and one of them has the door wide open. As Alaric pulls me closer, I start to fight again, but he doesn't let go. His grip on my arms only gets tighter, claws digging into my skin and slicing into it. It burns like paper cuts.

My eyes dart around. There are chains hanging from the ceiling and manacles attached to the walls. A red-haired woman is laying across a wooden table, her arms are restrained above her head at one end of the table and her legs are spread wide. My breathing hitches as a man steps up to the table and leans over her. His hips start thrusting as she sobs. My swallow is audible as I tear my eyes away from the scene.

"Please... just let me go." I plead.

"Can't do that, little bitch." Alaric whispers against my ear, licking my ear lobe and making me shudder.

No matter how much I struggle, I can't get free. As we move further into the room, all I can hear are the moans and pleas of the other women, and my panic escalates. Alaric shoves me down towards the ground and pushes me into the cage. The metal bites into my knees as I scramble to get my balance, and the dirt on the floor smears across my hands and knees.

The sound of the cage door shutting echoes around the cave, and a few sobs sound around me. There is hardly any room to move, and even though I can see out of the cage, I feel like the world is closing in around me. I've finally snapped; sobs wrack through me and tears flow down my cheeks. I thrash about, kicking at the metal surrounding me.

The cage jolts as Alaric slams his boot into the side of it. A few whimpers come from the other cages around me.

"You fucking bitches need to quieten down!" Alaric hollers. "If you don't, the boys will find much better uses for your mouths."

All at once, there is complete silence, apart from the noises coming from me. Even the woman being raped has gone quiet. Something tugs on my hair, yanking my head back to the side of the cage. My cheek connects with the metal and it digs into my skin. Wetness drips down the side of my face as a sharp edge digs into my cheekbone, cutting it.

"That includes you, little bitch." He gives my hair another yank. "If you don't stop, I'll shove my cock so far down your throat, the only sounds coming out of your mouth will be you choking on my dick." With that, he lets go of my hair and stomps away.

The clang of the metal door shutting makes me jump and I curl into a tight ball. I dig my teeth into my lip to silence my cries.

They'll come for me, they have to come for me. Please don't leave me here.

I rock back and forth, my breathing rasping in and out. The only other sound in the cave is flesh slapping together. I close my eyes and shove my hands over my ears. I'm stuck here, and all because I couldn't make do with granny panties.

Chapter 26

Diego

I'm pacing the kitchen like a wild animal. Demi's gone, ripped away from us, and I have no idea where she is. I'll tear the world apart if that's what it takes to find her. I shouldn't have listened to Jax, I should have blood bonded with her when I had the chance. But instead, I let him stop me before things went too far, even though my instincts told me to claim her.

Every time I'm close to her, something deep within me pushes me to feed her my blood, to let her drink from me as I sink into her tight heat. There's a chance that if we'd bonded, maybe it would be enough to find her. The blood bond would have made a thread between us. I could have followed it until I found her and then tear those sniveling wolves to shreds.

A snarl rips through my lips, and I slam my fist into the wall. The plaster gives way under the force of my punch, dropping to the wooden floor by my feet. A sharp pain slashes through my knuckles and I know when I pull back my hand, the skin will be torn and bloody.

"Diego." Jax barks out from behind me.

I don't even think as I spin around and launch myself at him, slamming him back with enough force to shake the wall behind him. My bloody hand wraps around his throat, squeezing him tight, but he doesn't fight back.

"This is all your fault!" My voice is harsh as my fangs split the skin of my lower lip with the speed they erupt from my gums.

Smashing my fist into his side, I hear the bone crack as it connects with his ribs, but I don't stop. Jax's breath rushes out of him with every hit. He just stands there, not even trying to defend himself as his head hangs down against the hand curled around his throat.

"I know." He croaks. "We'll find her. We have to."

"And how are we meant to find her, Jax?" I snarl. "You wouldn't let Bane or me form a blood bond with her. You know how hard we've fought every day she's been here not to give in to our instincts. Now she's gone, we've lost her." The emotions hit me like a ton of bricks. The wolves will be long gone; we'll never find her.

Dropping my hand from around his neck, I watch as Jax slumps down. He looks as lost as I feel. The sound of movement from Bane's room catches my attention, and I'm there in the blink of an eye. He's been unconscious since we found him in the alley by the car, a nasty chemical smell running through his veins, but it has gone now.

Looking him over, I watch as he tries to open his eyes but one of them is sealed shut with blood. Bane's face is mottled with bruises, and I can see the half closed wounds through the tears in his clothing. Once we can get him out of bed, we'll have to give him a few pints of blood to replenish what he lost to help speed along his healing.

Bane runs a hand across his face, wincing as he catches his swollen eye. The other opens and looks straight at me.

"Demi?" My head drops and he pushes himself up on the bed. He fights to stand but I stop him with a hand on his shoulder. Even now, in his weakened state, I'm struggling to hold him down.

"She's gone, Bane." My voice is barely a whisper. "The wolves took her."

The roar that he releases rips through me; it's full of so much sorrow and pain. Bane can feel her loss as much as I can. His fingers claw at my arms as he tries to push me away and get out of bed again.

"No, no, no." His grip on my forearm tightens. If he squeezes any harder he's sure to snap the bones. "We have to save her."

"We don't know where she is. Her scent disappeared a block from where we found you." I can feel my heart fracturing as I speak. I need her as much as I need human blood to keep me alive.

Bane's shoulders droop, the fight draining from him as he slumps back onto the pillows. As he drops, he releases my arms, but not without leaving small cuts in the skin where his claws pressed in.

"I know how to find her." A voice behind me has me spinning and I glare at Jax at his declaration. He's leaning up against the door frame. I really did a number on him, and he can only just hold his own weight.

"How?" Bane perks up slightly. He swings his massive legs over the side of the bed and pushes himself up beside me.

"Achilles... he can do a locator spell. He's already on his way over, but it's going to take a few days to prepare it." Bane lets out a weakened snarl, like the thought of leaving Demi with the wolves is too much.

"Do it, Jax. And he better find her, or so help me God, I'll fucking end you." My lips pull back and I bare my teeth at him, my hands clenching at my sides.

"I'll do everything in my power to bring her back." A pained look splinters across Jax's face as he scrubs a hand across it.

Jax may have denied his feelings for her, but I can see how much the loss of Demi is affecting him. He knows I was right when I blamed him in the kitchen. He knows it's his fault, but he deserves my words. I understand why he didn't want to get close to Demi given his past, but he shouldn't have stepped in our way.

Shoving past him, I head straight for the kitchen. First things first, I need to get Bane some blood so he can finish healing. Then Achilles better hurry the fuck up and get here because we need a plan and preferably one that ends up with us finding Demi and bringing her home.

Opening the fridge, I grab a handful of blood bags from the bottom drawer and slam it closed. As I turn, Bane is already behind me and I push them in his direction. Taking one of the bags, he pierces the top with his teeth and drinks the entire thing before grabbing another.

Jax lingers by the wall. He looks utterly defeated, not his usual Captain Asshole self as Demi has been calling him. The wound in my heart cracks open a little further as I think of her laughter, and her annoyance at Jax, pretty much all the time. She's right though, he is Captain Asshole.

The smell of magic fills the air in the kitchen, but the scent is a familiar one. *Achilles*. A portal opens next to the dining room table and he strides through. His white hair is half pulled up into a ponytail, keeping the strands out of his face, and his amethyst eyes are glowing with the use of his magic.

As soon as he's through, the portal snaps closed behind him and he surveys the room, nodding at me and Bane before he turns his attention to Jax.

"Jackson." He greets my solemn nestmate. "You said you have a human to find. Am I presuming it's the friend of the girl you had me deal with?" Jax gives him a nod. "Show me to her room, please."

Jax signals for Achilles to follow him, and they head for Demi's room. Bane and I follow behind them. When we get into her room, Achilles is rifling through her things. I want to snap at him, but I stop myself - he's only trying to help us find her.

Picking up the t-shirt she wore to bed last night, his magic engulfs it, smoke swirling around the fabric. It's like a miniature storm is happening within the cloud as it flashes purple, green, and a whole rainbow of other colors. When the smoke dissipates, Achilles turns to Jax, then me, and Bane.

"This could work, but I think there's something stronger I could use." The t-shirt is one of the most recent things worn by Demi and Achilles' magic should be able to track her with that. What the hell does he mean there is something stronger?

"Explain." Bane barks. He looks ready to punch Achilles, but I place a hand across his chest.

The warlock in question smirks. "You all took part in healing her, correct?"

"Yeah, but what does that have to do with finding her?"

"It's simple, really. You gave her your blood and seeing as she is your true mate, the traces of your blood still linger." His comment is blasé, there is absolutely no hesitation in his words.

"She's our what?" The words spill from my mouth. It's rare for vampires to find their true mate. Most bonds between a vampire and another are the blood bond. It's the same across a lot of supernatural species.

"Demetria is our true mate..." My eyes snap to Jax.

"How long?" Bane's entire body shudders under my hand and I can sense his anger growing.

"I've known for a while." Jax lets out a sigh. "Since I danced with her in the club. It's why we've all been so drawn to her, why her blood calls to us so strongly. Our very nature wants us to complete the bond."

"And you didn't think to tell us?!" I move across the room till I'm standing toe to toe with Jax. "You didn't think this was information we should have known?" I practically spit the words in his face.

Bane is by my side in a split second. His large hand wraps around Jax's neck. Those wicked fangs of Bane's gleam in his open mouth, as a growl builds in his chest rumbling dangerously from him. His red eyes glare up at Jax as he squeezes his fist tighter.

"If the big guy can refrain from murder, I need all three of you to help find your mate." I forgot for a second the warlock is still here. Jax's revelation made everything else in the room disappear.

With a snarl, Bane drops Jax to the floor and he lands in a crouch. Jax isn't the type to let anyone give him a beating, but he knows he is in the wrong for so many things. Maybe he's accepting what we dole out as punishment.

"Fine. What do you need?" I give my attention back to Achilles.

"I need blood from each of you and three days." That's too much time for Demi to be gone. We have no idea what sorts of things they could do to her in that amount of time. Would they kill her? "Calm yourself, Diego. They obviously want her for a reason. They won't kill her."

I don't know if I can believe him, but there has to be some hope in this situation. Demi is my true mate. Without her, I don't see the point in life anymore. Moving over to Achilles, I watch as he whips out a wicked-looking knife; the metal is curved, and the handle glistens with different colored jewels.

Slashing the blade across my open palm, the blood wells up from the wound and a wooden bowl materializes in Achilles' other hand. He positions it below the cut and I squeeze my fist tight as he holds it below to catch the blood.

"That's enough." Moving, I let Bane take my place, and Achilles repeats the process before moving on to Jax. I look at my hand as the wound seals itself like it never happened. "Three days, and I'll be back with a location."

Achilles runs his hand over the bowl and it disappears into a puff of smoke along with the knife. A portal opens behind him and he steps backwards through it. He lifts his hand in a small wave before it snaps shut again, leaving all three of us in Demi's empty room.

"Now what?" Bane looks to me for an answer, not Jax.

"Now we prepare because when I get my hands on those wolves, they will wish they were never born."

Storming out of the room, I leave Jax and Bane behind, heading straight for the room we use as a gym. I'm angry with myself for not listening to my instincts, and I'm angry at Jax for lying to us. I need to get some of my frustration out of my system and if beating the shit out of a punching bag helps, then so be it.

Chapter 27

Demi

I slept fitfully through the night with the cage digging into my skin where I lay. A few of the wolves came in, approaching different cages and dragging women out of them one at a time. Their screams dragged me from what little broken sleep I managed.

Refusing to move, I lay there, opening my eyes just enough to be able to see through my lashes. Some of the women try to fight as they are dragged out of the cave, their screams echoing off the walls. Others curl in on themselves as the wolves carry them away.

When the first woman returns, a petite blonde from the cage next to me, her left eye is swollen shut and she hangs from Alaric's arms. Her open eye is unblinking as she stares into nothing. I can just about make out the wetness on her face from her tears. Blood drips from her lips and there are white stains marring her skin.

That's the moment the trembles in my body start. The wolves are doing what they want to the women and then caging them like animals. I watch each woman they take during the night, and my shaking gets worse till the cage I'm in is rattling around me.

Rolling over, I rub my eyes but all I do is get the dirt caking my hands in them. I keep blinking, my eyes watering. When my vision finally clears, the woman in the cage opposite me with the swollen eye is staring straight at me. I go to open my mouth, but she presses her finger to her lips, so I slam it shut again.

The door rattles behind me, and her eyes widen like saucers. I can see the look of terror on her face. A small whimper escapes through her lips. The metal crashes against the rock wall and several of the women jump in their cages.

"Grubs up, bitches." Alaric's voice echoes through the cave.

He approaches each one, throwing something inside. When he gets to mine, he sneers at me before tossing a piece of stale bread onto the floor. My stomach rumbles. It's been forever since I last ate and I'm starving. Launching for the bread, I grasp it in my hands, not even caring about the dirt covering it.

I take a bite; it tastes horrible, but it's something to fill the empty space in my stomach. I watch Alaric as he moves to the next cage. Instead of throwing the bread in, he just stops and stares down at her. She curls up on herself and whimpers again.

"Awww, my favorite bitch." He crouches down at the end of the cage, a huge grin cracking his lips. "I'll come for you again tonight." He reaches his hand inside the cage and strokes her leg, but she pulls it away from him.

Alaric lets out a snarl. Pulling his hand back, he slams his fist into the cage, and she yelps. The look of anger on his face disappears and he reaches back inside the cage and places the piece of bread down by her feet.

"It's okay, my sweet little mate. We'll take care of each other's needs later." It sounds more like a threat than anything, but his use of the word mate perks my ears.

Is she like me? Is Alaric wanting to claim her, like Rufus wants to claim me? What is with these wolves, wanting to take what isn't theirs? There is a deep-seated anger building inside me. I hate these wolves and when I get out of here, I'll kill them all.

Alaric moves along the rest of the cages, throwing the stale bread at the last of the women. When he's done, he kicks a few of them on the way out before slamming the metal door behind him. I look back over at the woman next to me.

"How long have you been here?" I whisper. Her head lifts and her eyes cut to mine.

"Too long... a few months maybe." She stutters. Her voice is barely a whisper. "Sasha and a few others were here before me, but Thea came after." She points to a few of the other cages as she speaks.

I look around, taking in the state of the women locked up around the cave. There's hardly any fight left in them as they curl up in their prisons as far away from the doors as possible.

I wonder when the last time anyone was allowed to clean themselves. The woman across from me has blonde hair that is matted and greasy, her pale eyes dull and hopeless. I don't even want to think about what she has been through for the last few months whilst they have held her captive. I saw what they did to Ginny in just one night.

What have all these women endured? When I get out of here, when Jax, Bane, and Diego come for me, I'll free them, too. There are a few whispers around the cave, other women talking to each other.

"Demi." I blurt out. "Me, I mean, I'm Demi." I need to fill the almost silence, even with the whispers it's still too quiet.

The woman watches me, taking in the information. It takes a few minutes, but she finally opens her mouth to speak.

"Lila..." Her voice is still a whisper.

"What do they want from us, Lila?"

"The one who called me mate keeps saying something about a blood moon and a blood bond." She brushes a matted strand of hair away from her face.

"That's Alaric. Or at least, that's what the others keep calling him."

"He's an asshole." I can hear the anger in her voice. "He won't let the others touch me apart from to bring me back here once he's done with me. He says I'm his, and as soon as the blood moon comes, we'll be joined forever." A shudder runs through her body, but I don't think it's from the cold. "I just want to go home."

Pulling her knees up to her chest, sobs wrack through her slight frame. I want to hold her and tell her everything will be alright, but I'm not sure if I even believe that myself. I'm just dozing off again when the metal door slams against the wall. My eyes snap open and I look around the cave. Most of the women are curled up in balls, shuffling as far away from their cage doors as possible.

Hank stops at the door of my cage. Squatting down on his haunches, he inserts the key into the lock and opens it.

"Come on, Rufus wants to see you." I glare at him as he leans on the door.

Without another word, he reaches in and grabs my ankle. I kick out at him with my other foot, but it's like hitting a brick wall. With his hand around my ankle, he drags me out of the cage, not caring about the fact the metal is scraping my back and cutting my skin through the thin fabric.

Once he has me fully out of the cage, he grabs my upper arm and drags me to my feet. Everything aches from being in such a confined space. I swipe out with my hand, my nails claw across his face, and draw blood. A growl rumbles through his chest, and when he looks at me, his eyes are glowing, and I can see fangs jutting out of his mouth.

"Stupid bitch!" His fist connects with my face, knocking my head to the side. *Fuck!* My jaw aches and I taste blood in my mouth. Spitting it in his face, I bare my own very human teeth at him.

With both my hands now in his, he drags me out of the room and a guard closes the door behind us. He's taking me down the darkened tunnel again, past the showers. I start to squirm; I don't want to end up back in the other place hanging from the ceiling again.

"Why can't you bitches just stop fighting?" He growls at me as he pulls me along. "It'd be so much easier if you just accepted your fate."

"A fate of what, exactly? Being raped and murdered by monsters?" His eyes cut to me with a glare.

Another growl comes in my direction... guess he doesn't have an answer for that one. We pass the room I first woke up in and I let out a small sigh. Taking a right, we head down another tunnel. This one is a little brighter, with more lights hanging along the walls and someone has put thick rubber mats on the floor. We stop outside another metal door and he knocks on it.

"Enter." With a shove, the door opens, my eyes widen at what I see.

This room looks almost normal. The same rubber flooring from the tunnel covers the entire space. There's a basic kitchen set up on the left, okay, so it's a camping stove on top of a unit and a small fridge under it. A rickety table is in front of it, with four mismatched chairs around it. In the middle of the room is a dirty-looking couch and a coffee table in front of it with a few books on the top.

Following the room round, I spot another opening, with a curtain half closed over it. Beyond it is a bed with rumpled sheets. There's another curtain to the right of that one, which is currently pulled closed. It's kind of homey, well, if it wasn't for the fact there was a bloodthirsty, murderous wolf living in it.

"Ah, my precious mate." The closed curtain draws back, and Rufus makes his way out from behind it, buttoning his pants as he walks. A huge grin is plastered across his face. "How do you like your accommodations?"

"They'd be great if I was a dog like yourself. But as a human, I find them kinda lacking." Rufus' eyebrow raises at me as he ponders my comment.

Way to go, Demi. Why not just piss off the crazy murderer?

"It's not for long, my sweet. Once we're mated, you'll move into this room with me." He moves closer and stops just in front of me, looking down at my face with those creepy eyes. "Come, I'll give you a tour."

"I'd rather..." Pulling me away from Hank, Rufus yanks me forward and I almost fall. His fingers lace through mine and he holds them so tight I swear he's going to break them. Rufus brushes my hair from my face, his eyes glancing at my cheek.

"What happened here?" He turns his head to glare at Hank.

"She attacked me, so I stopped her." I roll my eyes.

Like I would have actually been able to do him any serious damage.

"And you couldn't do that without marking her skin?" Hank goes to open his mouth, but he's cut off. "Get out!" Rufus commands.

Hank lowers his head in submission and backs out of the room, shutting the door behind him. Rufus runs his fingers over my cheek. I wince as they brush against where Hank hit me.

"Don't worry, little one. I'll make sure they don't hurt you again. You're mine, your punishments will be dealt with by only me." I have no idea if he thinks that's any better, he's fucking crazy. "Now, on with the tour."

Moving to the 'kitchen' area, Rufus points at the meager items there, telling me what each item is like I'm an idiot. When he moves to the couch, he presses up behind me and I can feel his erection pushing at my ass.

"I can't wait to bend you over this, and maybe when you're good, I'll even let you ride my cock," his words whisper in my ear. He must think they sound sexy, but all I want to do is kick him in the balls and run.

As if to show what he means, Rufus pushes me over the back of the couch. His clothed cock rubs up and down between my ass cheeks. My nails dig into the material on the back of the couch, and I bite my lip.

Must not throw up.

Rufus holds me by my wrists and keeps thrusting against me, small moans escape from his lips. I let out a grunt as the material of his pants chafes against my naked skin, and he takes it as encouragement as he thrusts harder.

Leaning over my back, his lips brush across the nape of my neck and he bites into my skin, his blunt teeth dig into my flesh.

"Fuck! I'm not sure I can wait a few more days till the blood moon." His tongue darts out and licks across my ear lobe. "My wolf wants to fuck you into submission."

Rufus' body against mine disappears and I collapse against the couch. My head leaning on the musty-smelling cushions, I risk a glance over my shoulder. Rufus is palming his erect cock through his pants, his eyes almost entirely black with lust, with the glow of amber seeping through.

"Come, I want to show you the best bit." He grabs my hand and tugs me back up, dragging me across the room and through the curtain.

It's a bedroom, but there are yet more chains. Some hang from the ceiling, some are attached to the walls and there's a closed chest at the end of the bed. As we get closer to the bed, he throws me down on the mattress, and I bounce slightly against it.

Then Rufus is on me, his legs straddling my thighs. I start to kick out my legs trying to get him off me, but he digs his fingers into my hips. His claws dig into my skin, splitting it and tears roll down my cheeks at the sudden pain.

"I've had these added just for you." His claws trace up my sides and over my breasts before moving up both my arms. Slamming my eyes shut, I keep wriggling. "It's for when you've been a naughty girl. Like right now. I'm going to have to punish you for attacking Hank."

There's a clicking noise as something wraps around my wrists. I tug at them, but I can't move. Rufus moves back down my body, ripping my legs apart. I try to pull them away, but something wraps around my ankle and there's another click. Then another.

My eyes open and I lift my head up a little. I'm spread-eagled across the bed, each limb wrapped in a manacle. I pull with all my might, but it just makes the metal bite into my skin. I scream, and pull, then scream a little more.

Rufus stands at the end of the bed, looking proud of himself. Opening his jeans, he pulls out his cock and fists it. I scream and cry as he jacks himself off, pumping up and down his length. His eyes close, and just when I think he might come, he stops. Kneeling on the bed, he crawls up between my legs. He lifts the grimy babydoll up so the material is scrunched above my breasts.

"Your fear smells so delicious. Can you see how hard it makes me?" His hand is back on his cock. He's so close to me now and I can't do anything to stop him.

Rufus goes back to his cock, leaning over me as he does. His mouth moves all over my body, teeth biting down on my nipples, and I scream. Covering my lips with his, he forces his tongue into my mouth.

With his hips thrusting, his teeth sink into my lower lip. If he bites any harder, he'll go right through it. He groans, and then I feel it; wetness all over my torso. Letting go of my lip, he sits back, his eyes running over my stomach. Removing his hand from his cock, he rubs his cum into my skin, leaving a sticky mess.

Blood drips from my lip and I can't stop panting. It feels like I'm suffocating. As Rufus smiles down at me with blood running down his chin, I close my eyes and lose my grip on consciousness.

Chapter 28

Jax

Rage courses through my veins, that, and despair. Those wretched wolves stole Demetria and it's all my fault. It's barely even twenty-four hours since she went missing and I'm already wearing a hole in the floor of my office. Diego and Bane refuse to talk to me, and I deserve it.

I kept the fact that Demetria is their true mate from them. I denied them and myself from fulfilling the true bond with her, and all for my own selfish reasons. A bond that would have made finding her so much easier. Now we are left having to rely on Achilles and hope he can track her with his magic.

She's gone, and I don't want to think about what they are doing to her. The leader intends to forge a blood bond with her, a bond that requires a blood moon. The next one is in three days, the same amount of time Achilles said he needed for his tracking spell.

Fight them, Demetria. Fight until we can find you. We will find you.

We closed the club as soon as Diego and I found Bane in the alley. I've told the staff to take a few days off, using the excuse of a ruptured waste pipe in the men's restroom. A few of them queried pay, but I've assured them they will get what's due even with the closure.

Harley rang my personal line a few hours ago to ask if Demetria wanted to join her for dinner, seeing as she wouldn't be working behind the bar. I didn't have the heart to tell Harley that Demetria is missing. I just made up an excuse about her being sick, the same one I asked Demetria to tell the hospital.

My grip on the whiskey glass in my hand tightens and the glass strains under the force. With a roar, I launch it across the room. It shatters as it hits the wall next to the open door, where a hulking Bane is leaning up against the frame. He looks from me to the shattered glass, and then back to me while shaking his head. With a sigh, he turns and walks away.

Running my fingers through my hair, I fist it within my hands. I'm so angry at myself. If I had let my true feelings for Demetria out and let the bond happen, I would have been able to find her already. The connection would have solidified, and I would have known exactly where she was. Instead, I denied us all.

Stupid, stupid, stupid. I scold myself for the millionth time, not that it will do any good.

Muttering as I pace the floor, I think of all the ways I'm going to destroy the wolves who are trying to claim *my* mate as their own. I will make them pay for crossing onto my territory, for killing Demetria's friend and others. But most of all, I want to watch the light fade from their eyes as I kill them for taking what is mine.

I have two days to prepare for what is coming, to steel myself to the fact that I might be too late. To accept that I might find nothing left of the woman I'm in love with. Leaving my office, I head to my room and change out of my suit into sweats and a t-shirt. I'll head to the gym; I need a distraction.

Walking through the door into the gym, I find it completely empty. I have no idea where Bane and Diego are, but that's probably for the best. I flip on the music system in the corner, and *AC/DC's Highway to Hell* blasts through the speakers scattered around the room. Stepping up onto the running machine, I set it for twenty miles. I start at a walk, but it soon becomes a run, and my feet pound against the platform. My pace is rhythmic as I focus on my reflection in the mirror, watching my arms pump up and down at my sides.

The door opens behind me and I watch as Bane and Diego enter the gym, heading for the sparring mats in the center. Diego catches my eye and scowls in my direction, flipping me the bird. Bane doesn't even look my way as he wraps his knuckles. A broken bone isn't much of an issue as it'll heal with blood, but it sure as hell still hurts. Diego follows suit, binding his own hands.

When they are both finished, they enter the ring, tapping knuckles together and getting into position. Bane is all coiled muscles, ready to pounce and claim the win. But Diego, smaller in build than Bane, is wily and fast. And not opposed to taking cheap shots to take down his opponent.

The motion of the machine beneath my feet slows to a stop, pulling my attention from the two men. I step down and make my way to the mini-fridge in the corner and pull out a bottle of water. Vampire or not, we still eat and drink, and definitely still sweat, though considerably less than humans.

I take a swig and turn my focus back to Diego and Bane, watching as the two men clash together. Neither lets the other get the upper hand. When Diego lays a kick on Bane, the giant is quick to retaliate with a hit of his own. I can't help but study them dance around each other, like a well-choreographed routine. Diego and I come together perfectly beneath the sheets, but these two fighting together is a sight to behold. The mutts won't know what hit them.

Moving over to the punching bag, I set down the bottle. I don't even bother to wrap my hands; I want to feel the pain, I deserve it. I strike a few combinations of hits against the leather, not caring when the skin on my knuckles eventually splits. I leave my blood all over the fabric as I circle around the bag. My anger seeps from me as I take it out on my inanimate opponent.

I keep it up for what feels like hours. It leaves my body exhausted and every muscle hurts. My knuckles are a mess as the skin has tried to heal, only to be split open again. With one last kick, the punching bag can't take anymore and the heavy metal chain that attaches it to the ceiling snaps, sending the bag across the room until it crashes into the weight machine. The rest of the room is empty, I'm not even sure when Diego and Bane left.

Wiping the back of my hand across my forehead, I clear the sweat away, no doubt replacing it with blood. I'm done and need sleep. I shouldn't have gone so hard on the punching bag, but the pain felt good. Tomorrow I must get the two men who have been my constant companions for the last few decades to talk to me. We need a plan; we need to be ready for when Achilles comes.

Stalking out of the gym, I leave the bag where it rests and head for my room. Once the door is closed, I strip off my clothes and aim straight for the shower. The water is ice cold when I start it, but it soon heats. I let the water run over my hands, cleaning the still open wounds. The blood swirls down the drain until eventually, it runs clear.

When my body is clean, I stumble out of the shower and wrap a towel low on my hips. My body wants blood, but it's hers I'm craving, Demetria's. If... *when* we find her I'm going to tell her everything. If she'll let us, we'll complete the bond and then I'll never let her go again. I'll show her how to defend herself and protect her from now until the end of time.

I collapse on my bed and let exhaustion drag me under.
We're coming, Demetria.

Chapter 29

Demi

When I wake up, I'm back in my cage, the door shut once more. I look for Lila, but she's gone. I push up too quickly, hitting my head on the top of the cage as I frantically search for her.

"Lila?" I call out, hoping they have moved her to another cage, but there's no response. "Lila!" I'm louder this time.

"Quiet down, they'll hear you." Another voice a few cages over hisses at me.

"Where's Lila?" I need to know where she is.

"They took her, now will you please quiet down." The voice calls back to me. This time, I shut my mouth.

I don't want the wolves to come, but at the same time, I need to know what happened to Lila. Did Alaric take her? She mentioned the blood moon, and him wanting to mate with her, the same as Rufus wants to do with me, but that can't be happening yet, can it? He said it was a few days before that happened.

There's more to each faction than I ever knew. When Jax told me about it, he said in the wolf sector they held balls each year so they could find their true mate, the other half of their souls. But not all wolves can find their true mates. Instead, some form blood bonds with their partners, the supernatural version of getting married.

But what Rufus and his men are doing is wrong. They're in the vampire sector, kidnapping women, and forcing them into the bond against their will. These wolves are crazy, and it's about time someone informed the Council about them. Unless they already know and are turning a blind eye.

I don't know what to believe anymore. I always thought vampires were merely blood-thirsty monsters, but I've seen a side to them I'd never imagined possible. Even from Jax. They've cared for me, looked after me, and protected me.

The door swings open and Hank strides inside. He's carrying someone bridal style, and I realize soon enough it's Lila. She's limp in his arms and her eyes are closed.

Kicking the cage door fully open with his foot, Hank kneels and throws her in. Lila lands with a thump, but doesn't open her eyes. There's blood and God only knows what other fluids between her thighs. The door clangs as it closes, locking her back in and Hank leaves the room once more.

I shuffle to the edge of the metal box and watch as Lila's chest rises and falls. I let out a small sigh. She's alive. We need to get out of here, all of us. No one deserves the torment these women are going through.

Please find us.

I send an unspoken prayer to anyone who is listening that the guys will find us. And that it is soon.

I spend what feels like forever watching women being removed from their cages by various men. The flimsy negligee they have been given barely covers their bodies. They lead most from the cave-like room, but some of the men seem to find it fun to chain the women from the manacles I saw when I first arrived. They do what they want with the women no matter how much they scream and cry, laughing at the pain they cause. These aren't men, they're savages.

A few of the women strike up whispered conversations when we're alone, but we keep our conversations brief. My focus remains on the door, scared of who will be taken when it opens again.

Alaric and Hank enter the cave carrying trays of something I don't recognize. I'm hoping it's food as my stomach is rumbling again. They systematically work their way through the cages, throwing the women scraps of the leftovers on the trays. When Hank reaches my cage, he doesn't have anything left.

"Rufus has requested your presence." He unlocks the cage and lets the door swing open, standing there expectantly.

I scramble out of the cage and stumble to my feet. His huge, meaty hand wraps around my upper arm, tightening his hold to the point of pain.

"I can walk, you know!" Hank's head whips in my direction. A low growl escapes through his lips as he glowers at me.

"Move!" He bellows in my face, spittle flying from his mouth. Using the back of my hand, I wipe away the droplets that land on my face.

"Say it, don't spray it, buddy." He gives me a firm shove and my feet start moving.

Hank takes me down the same corridor I've already been along to Rufus' room. With another shove, he pushes me through the open door and slams it behind me. Rufus sprawls on the couch, his arms hanging over the back.

"Come here, little one."

I shuffle across the rubber flooring until I'm standing at the side of the seat. His head turns slowly until his eyes settle on me. They rove across my body and I can't stop the involuntary shiver.

"You won't be in a cage for much longer. Soon I'll have you here with me, where you belong."

Standing from the couch, he makes his way over to me. He takes my hand in his, lifting it to his mouth and kissing the back of my knuckles. I snatch my hand back and there's a flicker of anger across his face.

"Soon you will follow my every order. You will want to please me in every way, like the good little bitch you are." He moves his hand along my bare arm, across my shoulder, and up to my cheek. I bite the inside of my mouth to stop myself from pulling away again.

"And what of the other women?" My voice trembles as his fingers caress my cheek.

"Alaric has his eyes on one of them already. Like you, she will be bonded." He smiles at me, but it may as well be a grimace. "I like to take care of my men, but our current stock is almost damaged beyond what is acceptable and we will have to replenish it."

That's his plan then; he'll bond with me and bond Lila to Alaric. The other women he will dispose of like they are rotten meat. Him and his wolves will murder them, and do whatever he does with them after that. I can't let him. We need to get out of here.

My eyes flicker to something shiny on the coffee table - a set of keys. I have no idea what they are for, but maybe they unlock the cages. If I can free the other woman, we can try to fight our way out. The idea is laughable, but dying on our own terms seems better than what's currently planned.

I take a step closer to Rufus, and force my hands to drift up his sides.

Don't puke, don't puke. I repeat the mantra in my head.

Leaning up on my tiptoes, I brush my lips against his and he takes it as an invitation. His fingers tangle in my hair, and pain flashes through my scalp as he rips my head to the side to deepen the kiss.

As soon as his tongue enters my mouth, I clamp my teeth down on it. I may only have human teeth, but with enough force I make them pierce through it. His hands tighten on my sides, and I can feel his claws digging into my skin. With a pained yelp, I let go of his tongue and spit the blood that is gathering in my mouth in his face.

Rufus shoves me toward the ground and I position myself so I fall straight into the coffee table, knocking the keys to the floor. I make sure to roll my body over them and grasp them in my palm. Now I just need to get them out of the room. A hand in my hair drags me back to my feet and I cry out at the burning pain in my scalp as Rufus spins me to face him.

"If you wanted to taste me so much, why didn't you just say so." Rufus' hand cracks across my face and splits my lip, the blow sending me to the floor again.

This time I'm not prepared and I instinctively hold my hands out in front to stop my fall. The keys fall to the ground as I land in a heap. I reach out slowly to grab them, trying not to draw attention to them, but a foot slams down on my fingers and I scream out.

"What do we have here?" Rufus reaches down and lifts the keys up. My eyes follow them up as he stands straight and pockets them. "I can't have this sort of disobedience."

His hand wraps around the back of my neck, and I scream again as he drags me to my feet. Moving out of the room, he pulls me along the hall, my feet barely finding purchase on the floor as he does. He barges through the door back into the room with the cages, and my eyes dart around the room.

One of the women is sprawled across the top of an empty cage. The man snaps his hips as he thrusts into her from behind. Her screams echo around the cave, bouncing off the walls. The other women hide behind their hands, curled up in the corners of their own cages.

"Enough, Derek!" Rufus bellows and Derek's hips falter to a stop as he looks up at us before stepping back from the woman. "I need to show my mate what happens to those who disobey me."

With his hand still latched around my hair, Rufus pulls me across the room to the table. He pushes me onto it so I'm face down, my hips catching on the edge. Letting go of my hair, he straps both my wrists to the sides of the table before walking away.

I hear his booted feet stop and a whimper sounds. I lift my head a few inches off the table but it's not enough to see where he went. I can only see the other end of the table in front of me and a little to either side. Rufus soon reappears with the woman I saw when we first came in. He pushes her against the other side of the table.

As Rufus traps her hands with the manacles on either side, her eyes lock with mine. Our faces are almost touching. Tears stream down her face as Rufus steps up behind her. There's a ripping sound as he uses his claws to rip open the little shred of clothing she is wearing.

"Now, mate, make sure you watch. And remember, this is *your* fault." The grin on Rufus' face is terrifying, promising nothing but pain.

"Please... don't." The woman begs.

Rufus raises his hand in the air, his long black claws glisten in the light before he brings it down. As he connects with her back, the woman's scream pierces the air. But he doesn't stop. Instead, he raises his hand and aims at her back again.

Rufus keeps going for more slashes than I can count. The woman screams through all of it and I keep apologizing to her, telling her how sorry I am. He's right, this is my fault. I shouldn't have tried anything with him. I'm not sure what I was thinking. I saw the keys and took a chance, but I failed and now she's suffering. All because of me.

"I'm sorry... I'm so sorry." I hiccup at the now unconscious woman. Tears fall down my cheeks onto the table below, and even though my eyes are now blurry, I can't take them off her.

"Now, mate. No more being a naughty girl." Rufus steps away from the woman. His claws are dripping with her blood, and he raises his hand to his mouth, licking up every drop.

Rufus makes his way round to where I lay, trailing his fingers over my back and down each arm before he undoes my bindings. My legs are like jello and I slump toward the floor, but he doesn't let me fully fall. His arms wrap around my chest and catch me. He lifts me and takes me back to my cage, lowering me down into it.

I crawl inside without him even needing to ask and flinch when the door slams shut again. I roll onto my back and look at the woman still strapped to the table. Derek approaches and undoes her bindings, scooping her up. I can't tell if she's alive or dead, but blood drips steadily down Derek's arms as he heads for the door.

As he goes to leave the room, Rufus stops him and whispers something in his ear. Derek nods and makes his way over to where my cage sits. He shifts the woman's body in his arms and lays her over the top of my cage. She whimpers at the movement, her eyes barely opening and looking down at me.

Derek steps up behind her and shoves himself back inside her semi-conscious form. Her fingers wrap around the bars on the top of my cage as he jostles her body. He goes at her until he's done, pulling out and stepping away.

Another man steps into Derek's vacated position, his cock already on display. He doesn't even wait, he just thrusts straight into her. A scream pushes through her lips and I grab onto her hands, lacing our fingers together. There are more men in the room now, waiting their turn with the broken woman lying over me.

Each one of them takes their turn with her. Her blood drips down her sides and onto me, soaking through the fabric and staining it red but I never take my eyes from hers. Even when one wolf slices his claws across her neck and life leaves her, I don't avert my eyes. They still continue to defile her long after she's dead.

Rufus is the last to take her, he comes with a howl, and the other men in the room join in chorus with him. He grabs her lifeless form and throws her broken body across the room before turning his attention back to me.

"No more defying me, mate, or every woman in this room will endure what she did." He gestures to the other cages. "Their deaths will be on your hands, just like your friend in the alley, your parents."

His words hit hard, and I whimper. Rufus killed them all, and he won't stop. Blackness takes over me and nightmares of my parents, Ginny, and monsters plague my brain.

Chapter 30

Diego

Achilles told us to be ready, so we are. He rang Jax an hour ago to tell him the preparations were complete and he was starting the spell to locate Demi. Bane and I left the room, heading for the basement and our weapons store before the call even ended. I finish strapping silver daggers across my body. I may have claws, but you can never have too many weapons, plus silver burns hurt like a bitch to wolves. I look over to Bane. He's dressed all in black, the same as me. A thick silver chain wraps around his chest and he secures it to a loop on his belt. When he spots me looking, he grins. He's ready to kill.

The door opens and Jax walks in. He's not in his usual suited attire; jeans cover his legs, and a t-shirt stretches across his chest. He has a sword strapped to his side, and when his eyes catch mine he gives me a nod.

"We'll get her back," Jax announces, "or we die trying." Bane grunts as he straps a gun to a holster on his leg. Magic permeates the air, and a portal opens behind me.

Achilles.

"I found her. She's not far." He humphs. "Stupid wolves should have run, not that it would have stopped me." His purple eyes glitter with mischief.

Before the portal can close, Achilles rubs his hands together, and the magic within the portal shifts. Beyond the portal is now a forest instead of Achilles' home.

"Ready?" Jax steps closer to the portal and I give him a nod.

"We must hurry. Tonight is the blood moon, and the next one isn't for a few months. It's the only time a wolf can make a blood bond." Achilles says, and I can't stop a snarl from escaping my lips. That piece of trash is going to force the bond on Demi. We *have* to stop them. "When the moon is fully bathed in red, that is when the bonding begins."

Without another word, Achilles steps through to the other side with Bane hot on his heels. I follow behind and Jax steps through after me.

I step out into a vast expanse of a forest. The sun has long since set, and the glow of the moon is hindered by the trees, foliage preventing the light from fully penetrating to the floor below. There's not a single sound, animals not daring come near this place. It's like they know what lurks within the depths of the forest: hunters that will end their lives if they are discovered.

The portal snaps closed behind us with a pop. Hopefully, it's not loud enough to draw the attention of any wolves who may be lurking. I grab two of the silver daggers from their sheaths and hold the hilts tight within my fists. Jax has his sword unsheathed, and Bane has his claws out at the ready. Black and purple smoke swirls around Achilles' hands as he starts walking.

I look up through the small gaps in the branches of the trees and I can just about make out the moon high in the sky. There are tinges of red at the bottom of it - the blood moon is coming. At least now I know for sure Demi isn't dead. The wolf always wanted her for this purpose, and I can only hope we make it in time.

We move on silent feet through the forest, stepping over fallen branches and roots. As we journey further in, the scent of the wolves I know we're looking for gets stronger. My fangs ache to rip through my gums, but I hold them at bay for now.

As Achilles steps out into a small clearing, I spot an opening in the wall of sheer rock. My nose is leading me in that direction. We edge closer, keeping our focus on any movement or sounds that we might come across. As we get closer the sound of music fills my ears; it's coming from beyond the entrance. I turn and catch one last glimpse of the moon before I step over the threshold into a cave, encapsulated within its darkness.

If it wasn't for the smell of wet dog, excrement, and human blood, I would have thought this was just a simple cave, but looks can be deceiving. We venture further in, and with my enhanced vision, I can see every tiny crack and rock that makes up the walls. Jax takes the lead, with Bane a few strides behind him. I take the rear, with Achilles just in front of me.

The subtle scent of my mate hits my nostrils and I growl. The closer we get, the stronger it becomes. I'm itching for a fight, and my hands flex over the hilts of my daggers, ready for trouble. At the back of the cave, I can see the outline of an opening, soft light shines from the lanterns on the walls. It takes my eyes no time at all to adjust to the change in light.

Jax holds up his hand and we all stop. He sniffs the air and motions to the left. The rest of the group follows behind him, but Achilles whispers words under his breath and a small pop sounds behind me, drawing my attention. The opening we just ventured through is now covered in a shimmer of black. A barrier to give the wolves no way out of the cave. They will all die here; we'll make sure of it.

The music I could hear is louder now, echoing off the stone walls. The bass reverberates through the floor and through the soles of my feet. I sense movement ahead and ready my daggers, but Jax beats me to it. A man walks out of a gap in the wall to the right of the hall, a can of beer clutched in his hand.

The man takes a swig as his gaze falls on our group. His mouth drops open, ready to shout a warning to his friends, but with a slash of his sword, Jax silences him. The man's head parts from his shoulders and falls to the floor with a thud, his body following close behind it.

Jax doesn't hesitate as he continues down the hallway, leaving the man's cooling body behind. A few of the arches in the rock have doors made from a mixture of wood and metal. As we pass a door, I can hear faint whimpers from within and the smell of blood. Tapping Achilles on the shoulder, I motion to the door and he nods.

Shifting my daggers into one hand, I place my other one on the door and open it as quietly as it will allow me. There's a woman on the bed, and a man with his pants down laid over the top, thrusting into her. He doesn't stop as I cross into the room.

"You'll have to wait. I'm not done with this one yet." The woman's whimpers fill the air and her eyes lock on me. She goes to open her mouth, but I lift a finger to my lips to silence her.

Moving closer to the two, I holster one dagger and stop to the side of them.

"I said you'll have to wait..." the man's head turns to me.

Before he can focus on me I grip his head, pulling it back and slice my dagger clean across his neck. His skin sizzles as the silver swipes across it. I drag him away from the woman, his dick still hanging from his pants as his blood pours from the open wound down his shirt. The scent of his blood flooding the air has my features shifting. I drop his body on the floor at the bottom of the bed.

"Wrong answer, fucker." I turn my red eyes to the woman, and she scrambles back on the bed. Pulling the flimsy dress she's wearing down to cover herself.

"Please... don't." Her words tumble out of her mouth as she raises her hands in front of her.

"I'm not going to hurt you." I sheathe the last dagger and hold my hands in front of me to placate her. "I'm looking for my mate Demi. How many of you are here?" I reach for the blanket on the floor and hold it out to her.

"I... I don't know... too many." She takes the blanket from me and wraps it around her shaking form. "Demi... she said you'd come." There's movement at the doorway and she pulls back again. Looking over my shoulder, I spot the others.

"It's okay. They're with me."

"We need to keep moving." Jax looks from me to the woman. "Achilles, stay with her. We'll bring anyone we find here."

Achilles nods and steps into the room. The woman eyes him cautiously but he gives her space and stays just inside the doorway.

I walk out of the room and rejoin Jax and Bane. We carry on down the hallway, following the scent of our mate. We pass more rooms but find them all empty. Each one contains a small cot-like bed and clothes strewn across the floor.

As we move further into the caves, the music gets louder, and Demi's scent gets stronger. We come to a junction, the pathway leading to the right is where the music is coming from with another corridor to the left, but there are no scents or sounds coming from that way. We follow the right path toward the music, Bane stops suddenly and tilts his head to the side, motioning to the door on the left. The need to get to my mate doesn't want me to stop, but as much as we want to get to Demi, I know she wouldn't forgive us if we didn't help any others being held here.

Jax and I pursue Bane as he shoves into a room with a closed door. Snarls and growls fill the room as we breach the doorway. Bane is already attacking, and one man inside is beginning the shift into his wolf form. There's a shriek as a naked woman scrambles off the bed and further into the room, but the men forget her. My daggers are forgotten as I jump on the half-shifted man and Bane tackles the two facing off against him.

As my body impacts with half fur and half skin, I rip my claws into the semi-transformed body, taking him to the ground. A growl escapes us both, his paws seeking purchase on my skin and his jaws snapping in my face. We tumble across the floor, and I find myself fighting with the now-shifted wolf. His claws rip across my skin, opening several wounds across my arms and chest.

The wolf's jaws close on my arm, and I grunt as his teeth sink deep. I reach for the dagger sheathed on my leg with my other arm and plunge it into the wolf's chest; the silver makes the skin sizzle. The smell of burning flesh nearly makes me gag, but the blade hits its mark as it sinks into the wolf's heart.

Ripping the dagger from the carcass, I wipe it on my pants and clamber to my feet. I swivel to help Bane, but he's already done. Two bodies lie at his feet. Jax's sword protrudes from one of their chests, the other is a bloody mess with a caved-in torso. Blood covers Bane's fists; it drips onto the floor and stains the dirt.

"Savage," I remark.

I turn my attention to the woman on the floor, repeating the same process as with the other female. I pick up the blanket and hand it to her. She doesn't take it as she curls up on herself and sobs. I move closer and lay it over her.

"We have to move her, the blood moon will start soon and we need to get to Demi."

With a nod, I crouch and lift the woman into my arms. She wails and cries, thumping her hands against my chest and shoulders, but I ignore her. I leave the room and head back to where we left Achilles. The female we left with him is sitting on the bed, the blanket pulled tightly around herself as Achilles crouches at her feet, inspecting marks I didn't notice before on her wrists. Magic shifts over and around each mark. When it fades away, the marks are also gone. Achilles leans back on his heels and gives the woman a small smile.

"Thea here is going to take me to where they keep the other women. I know of a safe place we can take them to."

The female in my arms squirms as she tries to get free of my hold. Slowly, I lower her to the ground until her feet are on the floor, but she stumbles. I help her over to the bed and she slumps down next to the first woman. Thea is what Achilles called her.

"Sasha." Thea wraps her arms around Sasha's shoulders and pulls her close. "I got you, but we have to move. These men are going to save us."

Thea rises to her feet and helps Sasha to hers. She wraps an arm around the other woman and makes her way to the door. Achilles follows closely behind them both.

"Go, I'll take care of them. Any wolves not in their own lairs will be with your mate for the ceremony."

With one last nod, we file out of the room and head back for the junction we found. This time we take the right with no other detours. When we reach the end of this hallway, there's one last door, and I know my mate is beyond it.

Chapter 31

Bane

Slamming my full weight into the door before me, the wood splinters as I take the entire thing off its hinges, frame and all. The heavy door slams into a man standing just beyond the threshold and the weight of it knocks him to the ground. Before anyone else in the room can react, I smash my booted foot on his head. It twists at an odd angle as I break his neck and shatter the bones in his face.

Howls echo through the large chamber and I glance around as some of the men begin their transformation into wolves. Jax and Diego flank me, our own snarls answering the howls. We may not transform into animals, but we are just as ruthless as them, and with our mate on the line we are a hundred times deadlier.

I take in the space quickly. There are two altars on the far side of the room, each has a naked figure lay upon them. Their limbs are tied down with rope and fabric across their mouths gagging them. One is unconscious, but the other is Demi. My eyes bleed red when I see her. Two naked men stand at the head of the altars, their appendages on full display. The snarl that reverberates through my chest has a man in front of me faltering. His eyes widen as he takes me in. Right now, I'm a feral beast, my fangs and claws on full display as my red eyes hone in on him.

With another snarl, I leap at the man before me. He's smaller in frame than me and an easy target. He's on his back before he can even think to defend himself. My claws slash at his face, ripping into his flesh as he howls in pain. One strike across his throat is enough to end him. My head whips up as I focus on the naked man standing close to Demi's head.

I'm about to leap up and head that way when a weight careens into my side, knocking me off my feet. A gray wolf poises over the top of me, his fangs dripping saliva on my face. He lunges his head forward, but I stop him from reaching my throat by slamming my arm into his open jaws. His fangs sink into my forearm with enough force to shatter the bone.

Ignoring the pain, a punch to the side of his head is enough to daze him and loosen his grip on my arm. I grab the gun from my holster - there's no need for stealth anymore. As he lunges for me again, I shove the muzzle of the firearm into his mouth and pull the trigger, spraying his brains out of the back of his skull.

His heavy body crashes down on me, but I shove him away. Taking a second to center myself, I look up at the sky through an opening at the top of the cave. The moon is nearly entirely red now. There is only a sliver of white left.

"Stop them! Kill them! They will not ruin this for me!" A voice bellows from across the room and my head shifts to look at the man by Demi.

The other naked man at his side shifts into a brown wolf. As soon as his paws hit the floor, he's on the move. Heading straight for Jax, who is already dealing with two wolves of his own. I flip myself up off the floor and intercept him. Leaning low, I shove my shoulder into the enormous wolf's body. The hit is enough to send him into the stone wall, his body going limp as he falls to the ground. I don't stop to check if he's alive or not.

Jax takes out one wolf that is circling him, his sword slicing through its neck like a knife through butter. The other tries to launch itself at his back, but I leap forward, my arms encircling its waist. I squeeze until I hear a crack. The wolf whimpers and slumps in my arms and I toss it to the ground, stomping down on its neck to break it.

The three of us work our way through man and beast. There is nothing but carnage in our wake. As I snap the neck of the last man attacking and drop his body in the pile of his friends on the floor, I glare at the leader of the pack. The only one left. He is standing at the head of the altar, a knife resting against Demi's neck.

"You can't have her! She's mine!" The leader screams. "She is promised to me, she is my mate." He sounds positively crazy.

I stalk closer to him, taking slow and measured steps as I palm my gun. His hand twitches, digging the knife into Demi's pale skin. A whimper pushes against the gag in her mouth, and a single drop of blood trickles down her neck. Demi pulls against her restraints, but it's no use.

"You cannot claim something that's not yours. Let her go now, and we'll consider letting you free." Jax keeps his tone calm, but I can see his hand tightening on his sword out of the corner of my eye. He has no plans to let the wolf go.

"I've hunted her for years. I've killed those who have gotten between me and my prey. I'll kill you next." The leader spits out, his hand shifts slightly, bringing the knife away from Demi's throat.

That's where he makes his mistake. As soon as the knife is far enough away, I raise my gun and pull the trigger. He tries to move, and I miss my intended target, but the bullet still hits him, ripping through his shoulder and knocking him off his feet. Diego is beside Demi in a second, his knife making quick work of her bindings, and she launches herself into his arms as soon as she's free.

"You came for me..." she whispers into his chest as he pulls her against him.

"We'll always come for you, Demi." Diego coos as he runs his fingers through her hair.

Speeding to the fallen wolf, I make quick work of binding him in the silver chain from around my chest. As the metal contacts with his bare skin, it burns into his flesh and he howls. His eyes glow amber as he tries to call on his wolf form, but the silver does its job and stops the transformation before it can take hold.

Jax moves up beside me, dragging the wolf by his hair. He slams him against the wall of the cavern by his throat. A menacing snarl rips from his lips as he bares his lethal fangs at his prey. That's what the wolf is now, our prey.

The wolf's amber eyes dart around the room, finally taking in his fallen pack. "You promised you'd let me go. Take her, she's not worth it."

"But you didn't let her go. We forced your hand. Even then, I was never planning on letting you free." The admission that he was never going to let the wolf go is so matter of fact, and the wolf's eyes widen in realization. With one hand still on the wolf's neck, Jax moves his other to the open wound in his shoulder. He digs a claw into the hole and the man howls in agony.

I move to the woman on the altar beside Demi. Unlike Demi, she was unconscious when we entered, a blessing no doubt. But now, with the wolf's screams and howls echoing through the cavern, she's starting to stir. I slice my dagger through the bindings on her wrists while Jax keeps the wolf pinned, and Diego helps Demi off the other altar. He quickly strips off his t-shirt and hands it to her. She pushes her arms and head through the holes, pulling it over her body as best she can.

When Demi reaches my side, she takes the dagger from me and cuts the last of the binding from the other woman's ankles.

"Come on, Lila. That's it, wake up." Demi rushes out as she moves back to the woman's head, brushing the matted blond hair away from her face.

Lila's eyes slowly open and they fall on me. I'm covered in blood from head to toe and I'm probably not the best thing to wake up to. A scream rushes through her lips, but Demi is there in an instant, pushing me out of the way and to take my place.

"Shush, Lila. You're okay. You're safe." Demi's voice is soft as she tries to soothe the woman.

Launching from the altar, Lila wraps her arms around Demi's waist and pulls her close. Demi moves her fingers over the top of Lila's head as they sob together. Diego reappears at my side, holding a ratty blanket in his hands. He passes it to Demi who wraps it around a shaking Lila's shoulders.

"You can't do this!" My attention pulls to the wolf leader, as he struggles in Jax's grasp. With a punch to the side of his head, Jax unceremoniously drops the wolf to the floor and he crumples. Demi's head whips round to glare at the wolf and stomps over to him. She sends a swift kick into his side, wincing as she does.

"You killed my parents, you fucking monster!" Demi screams as she drops down onto his legs, she plunges the silver dagger into his stomach and he howls. "You raped and murdered Ginny!" She yanks out the dagger and this time slams it into his crotch, the action making me wince. "You mutilated and killed countless women!" The knife withdraws again and she slices it into his torso once, then twice, then again. She keeps going, blood splattering all over her.

Even after his last breath leaves him, Demi keeps on stabbing him, screams of anger passing her lips as she does. It takes Jax placing a hand on her shoulder to still her movements. Demi turns on him, the dagger raised in her hand ready to take him on. Jax quickly removes his hand and holds them both in front of him.

A sigh of relief escapes her as she slumps down, the weapon clattering to the floor. Jax gathers Demi in his arms and pulls her to her feet. His arms wrap tightly around her, holding her close as tears start to fall. Diego continues to tend to Lila as I edge closer to the two. I never want to let her out of my sight again.

Chapter 32

Demi

Jax holds me in his arms, keeping me so close to him that I think he might smother me. Tears spill down my cheeks and soak into his t-shirt. I prayed they would come for me, but I was slowly losing hope that they would ever find where the wolves were hiding.

"I'm sorry... I'm so, so sorry." Jax whispers into my hair as he runs his fingers through it, trailing them slowly down my back.

We're both covered in blood, but I don't care. I just want him to hold me close and never let go. I should still be angry with him for everything, but right now I can't be. His lips brush across my forehead and down the side of my face, leaving wet kisses on my cheeks until he reaches my lips.

His lips connect with mine and the world explodes around me. The last time he kissed me, it was brutal and unforgiving. He left my lips bruised and my heart broken as he shoved me away from him. He had looked almost feral, and his cock was hard, but then he ran away from me.

Now though, his kiss is soft, yet demanding. His tongue sweeps across my upper lip and I open them for him. Thrusting his tongue into my mouth, he caresses mine with gentle strokes. His hands trail down my back and hold me flush against him.

A throat clearing behind us makes us pull apart, but he doesn't take his eyes off me as he takes me in. My eyes cut to Bane as he steps closer to me. His hands are covered in blood, but he opens his arms for me and I rush into them. They close around my back and he lifts me off the floor, holding me against his chest. His nose snakes up my neck, breathing me in as my legs wrap around his waist.

I plant my lips on his and his kiss is just as demanding as Jax's. Moving his hands to my bare ass, he holds me against him as he ravishes my mouth.

"Don't I get to hold our girl?" Diego's voice has me splitting apart from Bane as I look over my big guy's shoulder.

Sliding down Bane's body, I move to Diego and we clash together, his lips are on mine in the most dominating kiss. He tastes my mouth like he can't get enough of me, his arms wrap around me. When my lips are thoroughly swollen, he pulls away.

"Let's get out of here," Jax calls from his position next to Bane.

I glance over to Lila; she watches us with wide eyes. Rushing over to her, I take her hand in mine and lace our fingers together.

"We're free, Lila. This is Bane, Diego, and Capt... Jax." I point at each man as I say their names and they give her a nod. Her grip on my hand tightens. "Wait, there are more women here. We can't leave them." I shriek, dragging Lila toward the door.

"Shush, Demi. Achilles has already gone to free them, he knows a safe place we can take them to." Diego steps beside me.

Who the hell is Achilles?

Jax takes the lead as he walks us through the tunnels and away from the caves. When we get outside, my eyes take a second to adjust to the light. The sky above me has a vermillion hue, and the moon is entirely red. The sight sends a shiver running down my spine.

The other women are huddled together just outside the entrance wrapped in blankets. There is a man standing with them, with hair as white as snow. His purple eyes cut to me as he gives me a solemn nod. Jax makes his way over to the group, and the white-haired man steps to the side to speak to him.

"Oh my god, Lila, Demi. You're both okay." Thea rushes out, "I thought for sure when they took you both, we'd never see you again." A sob breaks from her and Lila moves towards her, wrapping her arms around Thea's shaking body.

"I told you they'd come for us," I say.

"I know. I heard you in the cave. I just didn't want to believe it. They've had us for so long, the only way to escape was death." Thea speaks, her voice thick with emotion.

Lila pulls back from Thea and takes her hands. Her face is stained with tears and blood.

"You're free now, all of you. The guys will help you." I gesture toward the men behind me and they all nod. Thea steps away from Lila and pulls me in for a hug.

"Thank you, Demi. Thank you so much."

"Achilles will make sure you are all healed and take you to a women's sanctuary." Jax steps forward as he speaks, followed by the white-haired man. I eye him curiously. "I know you're all scared, but all I ask is for you to trust us."

A few of the women look my way and nod, but some look like they want to run. They were brutalized while in captivity; the wolves had used and abused them just like they did with Ginny. Some had died in the same way and some just wished they had; their scars all ran deep.

"I trust you, Demi." Lila steps forward and Sasha follows her. A few more of the women move to join them, including Thea.

"Jax, I want to go with them. I need to make sure they're safe." I can see the look of disapproval on his face. He doesn't want me to go, but he gives a small nod.

"I'll make a portal. Stand back, ladies." Achilles steps away from the women and they shuffle closer to me and my men.

With his hands held out, black and purple mist appears from them, swirling around in front of him. It balls together at first, before circling wider and wider. There is no forest within the circle, but a light-colored room. When it's wide enough, Achilles drops his hands.

"Please don't dally. I won't be able to hold it for long."

Stepping close to Lila, I link my hand with hers. The women all follow suit, joining together in a chain. Their eyes are wide as they look at the portal before us. Diego and Bane step around our little group and walk straight through. When they get to the other side, Bane thrusts his hand back through the portal, holding it out to me.

Taking it, I let him pull me through the opening, and the others follow behind me. When I get to the other side, I gasp. The room we are in is huge and filled with what looks like hospital beds. The sheets are white and clean. It feels so long since I saw clean sheets and my shoulders relax.

The women stick to small groups, a few walk around the room, a few kneel on the floor crying as they take in everything around them. The compound was crude and unclean but where we were kept was even worse.

A rushing sound behind me has me turning, the portal is closing. Jax and Achilles are now on this side of it. Bane, Jax, and Diego surround me once more, and Achilles stays to one side away from the women exploring the room, but he watches them closely.

The huge double doors at the end of the room open, and a new group of women rushes inside. Most of them have the same white hair and purple eyes as Achilles. They're all wearing clothing in a variety of colors.

A woman, who looks like she's in charge, stops in front of our little group. She glances around the women in the room, a look of sympathy on her face. She doesn't need to be told what has happened, it's obvious to anyone they have been through hell.

"Jax," she nods towards him before pulling her gaze to Achilles. "Achilles, you made it."

"Were you worried about me, Ursa?" She scoffs at his comment.

"Never. You're too much of a pain in my ass to die." Achilles lets out a throaty chuckle, brushing a piece of invisible lint off his bloodstained clothing.

"Always." He grins at her, and she looks away.

"Ladies, please tend to our guests. My name is Ursa, I lead this sanctuary. You are all safe here, and welcome for as long as you need to stay. We'll get you healed and then cleaned up."

The women disperse around the room, leading the women we saved to the hospital beds. After helping them onto the beds, the traumatized group cling to the blankets around their shoulders, holding them close to their bodies. God only knew how long it had been since some of them had seen a setup like this.

"Now, gentlemen," Ursa looks at each man in turn. "I must ask you all to leave. I feel our new charges won't settle until you are all gone."

Achilles nods, The same magic he used for the portal swirls from his hands. I can see the apartment beyond the smoke, and I want to rush through. My guys move closer to it. I go to follow, but a hand grabs mine and I turn to Lila.

"Thank you." I can see tears in the corners of her eyes as she holds my hand in hers.

"It was all the guys. I'm just sorry I couldn't get us out of there myself." I can feel tears burning my own eyes.

"Because of you, they got us out, that's what matters." Lila pulls me into a quick hug before she lets me go again. Taking a step back, she hurries to one of the empty beds and sits on the edge, while another woman tends to her.

"Demetria, we should leave." I turn to look at Jax and nod.

When I get closer to the three guys, Bane wraps an arm around my shoulders, and Diego takes my hand in his. They drag me through the portal but this time when we get to the other side it doesn't snap shut. Instead, Achilles shifts his hands until the sanctuary disappears, and the portal displays another location.

"Gentlemen," he nods to Bane, Diego, and then Jax. "Miss Demi." He smiles at me and steps through the portal once more. It closes with a pop and I'm alone with them.

All three guys crowd around me, each one of them touching me. I want to melt into it. I don't know how long I've been gone, but it seems like forever ago since I watched Bane fall to the floor with a needle in his neck and then something heavy hitting the back of my head. When I woke up again, I was already in the compound.

Bane steps behind me, his arms wrapping around my waist as he holds me close. His lips ghost across my neck and I shiver. Placing my hands over his, I can feel the warmth of his skin beneath my fingers. He's alive, we're both alive. After seeing him fall to the wolves, I didn't know if he survived, but he's here with me now.

"I'm sorry I couldn't stop them," Bane whispers close to my ear.

Turning in the circle of his arms, I lay my head on his chest. I can hear his heart beating and I savor the sound. As the events of everything that happened hit me full force, I crumple in his arms, but he holds me up like my dead weight means nothing to him. Tears fall down my cheeks as sobs wrack through my body.

Heat encompasses my back as another body steps up behind me, the scent that hits my nostrils tells me it's Diego. His hands rest on my waist as he kisses my back and shoulders.

"We got you, Demi. Let it all out."

There's one person missing, Jax. Pulling my head from Bane's chest, I look over to him. He's standing close, almost within reaching distance, but he doesn't come any closer. The look of devastation on his face chips away at my heart.

"This is all my fault, Demetria. And for that, I am so, so sorry." Jax closes the space between us and kisses my forehead before he walks away.

The action and his apology confuse me. Before the wolves took me, he did nothing but push me away, even though I could tell he was attracted to me. My feelings for him are so conflicting. A part of me wants to curse him out, but the other part just wants him to love me. Wait, love? Is that what I feel for these three men?

Scrubbing a hand over my face, I wipe my tears away. Blood still stains my hands. I need to shower and wash it all off. It won't take away what I went through in the caves, but it will be a start.

"Shower?" I ask. Diego steps back and Bane lifts me from the ground, bridal style.

I snuggle into his chest as he walks through the apartment to my room. He carries me across the threshold and heads straight for the bathroom. I hear the bedroom door shut behind us, meaning Diego must have followed.

Walking into the bathroom, Bane sits me on the counter. The cold marble causes a small gasp as it touches my naked skin. He moves to the enormous shower that is more than big enough for all of us and turns on the water. Steam fills the room, misting the mirror behind me, I've never been so happy to see steam in a bathroom before.

Chapter 33

Diego

We have her back, and I for one never plan on letting her go again. Steam billows out from the shower, filling the room. We're all a mess, our clothes and bodies covered in blood. I take a step forward, settling myself between Demi's open thighs. I brush a hand through her matted hair, my eyes drinking her in as I take in the beauty before me. Even covered in dirt and blood, she is the most beautiful woman I've ever seen.

I hear the rustling of fabric behind me as Bane strips, letting his clothes fall to the floor, but I keep my focus on Demi. My hands rove over her body, touching every part of her like she could disappear before my eyes if I closed them.

"Never leave me again. I don't think my heart could take it." I've spent days pacing the apartment, working out my anger in the gym sparring with Bane, and ignoring Jax for the bullshit he pulled.

Demi doesn't speak, she just watches me with those turquoise orbs. Tears still stain her cheeks, and I wipe them away, taking some of the dirt with it. I hear the shower door open, then Bane is next to me again. I take a step back so I can remove my own clothing. Bane slots himself into my position, and Demi gasps as she looks up and down his body.

Something tells me she likes the sight of her giant with blood covering his skin, even if some of it is his own. Her hands trail up and down his thick arms, making sure she doesn't touch the open wounds from the wolves' claws and teeth. His fingers catch on the bottom of the t-shirt she is wearing and he pulls it from her body, throwing it into the same pile as his clothes.

Bane tugs her to the edge of the counter, his hands moving under her thighs as he pulls her against his body. Her long, pale legs wrap around his waist, and her arms loop around his neck as he steps into the shower with her. Popping the button on my jeans, I kick off my boots and socks and let them drop to the floor with a thud.

I join them both in the shower, closing the door behind me. The water hits some of the shallower wounds that haven't quite healed yet and it stings as it cleans the dirt from them. Bane holds Demi under the water, her legs still wrapped around him like she doesn't want to let him go. I step up behind them and mold my body to hers. Caressing the sides of her thighs, a gentle moan escapes her lips at my touch.

My cock twitches, but this isn't about what I want right now. It's about Demi's needs. The bond I now recognize as being that of true mates tugs at my very soul. It demands I claim what is mine, but I shove it away. There is a time and a place, and this isn't it.

Bane unwraps her thighs from around him and lowers her to the floor, her wet body sliding down his. Wrapping my arms around her, I run my hands over her skin. I lean close to her ear and kiss the top of it.

"Let us take care of you, Demi. Let us love you." Bane nods in agreement as Demi drops her head back onto my shoulder.

With her hair now wet, I reach for the shampoo while Bane reaches for the soap. Dropping a pea-sized amount into my hand, I massage the gel into her tresses. The foam steadily turns red as it mixes with the dried blood in her hair.

Bane, meanwhile, lathers up her skin, taking his time to wash away the blood and grime from every inch of her. He drops to his knees and works on her legs, from her feet all the way up to her thighs. When he reaches the apex, he taps the inside of her leg, and she opens for him. He reaches between them and washes her mound. Another of her moans echoes around the bathroom at his movements.

Rising to his feet, he runs the soap over his own body. I see the slight flinch as the soap hits his healing cuts, but Demi reaches out to him. Her hands shift across his skin, cataloging every single mark. When her hands reach for his hardening length, he swats them away and she huffs at him.

For someone who has been through so much, she is as receptive to us as we are to her. The bond is snapping at our heels, wanting us to claim her. Even though she is human, on some level, she must feel it too.

Giving Bane time to wash the grime from his own body, I place my hands on her shoulders and gently maneuver her under the spray, letting the water run through her hair until it turns clear. I take my place behind her and pull her body back against me. My own back hits the tiles behind me, the coolness of them quenching the heat taking over my very being.

When Bane finishes, he turns Demi so her chest is against mine and I tighten my arms around her waist. My hardness pushes against her stomach and I have to lecture my own body. I place a hand on her neck as Bane gets to work on her back. With my fingers under her chin, I tilt her head up and press my lips to hers in a gentle kiss.

Demi's hands grasp my shoulders as she rocks against me. Her nails bite into my skin and I can't stop my traitorous body from reacting. I moan against her lips, and she takes the opening, her tongue invading my mouth as she tastes me. Her hands move up the side of my neck, lacing through my hair and holding my mouth to hers.

As my lids close, my hands move over Demi's body. Touching every possible inch of her that I can. Our tongues move together at a steady pace, neither of us pushing to deepen the kiss any further.

When we split apart, she looks into my eyes. A small smile creeps across her lips and I offer her the same in return. I lace our fingers together, and she squeezes mine back. The door of the shower opens as Bane reaches outside for a fluffy towel off the rail. When he returns, I push Demi back towards him. He wraps the towel around her body and lifts her up into his arms.

A small giggle graces my ears as he steps out of the shower naked with her in his arms. Demi looks at me still standing under the spray of the water.

"Diego?" She murmurs, tiredness lacing her voice.

"I'll be through soon, *tesoro*."

"You better be." Bane takes that as his cue to leave and he carries her out of the bathroom.

I grab the shampoo and scrub it through my hair. The suds run down my back over the wounds inflicted by one of those nasty bastards and it stings like a bitch. I suck it up and carry on cleaning away the blood, mine and theirs. When the water is no longer a mixture of black and red, I turn off the shower and grab my own towel from the rack.

Scrubbing it over my head, I dry my hair as best as I can before I sling it low on my hips. When I walk out of the bathroom, Demi is lying in the middle of the bed, a silky robe wrapped around her body. Bane lies at her side, one arm slung under his head as he drinks from a blood sachet. There is another on my side. Jax must have brought them in while we were in the shower.

Bane's eyes track my movements as I walk across the room. Demi rolls over and curls herself up against his side, her head on his shoulder and her fingers resting against his chest.

Dropping the towel from around my waist as I near the bed, I climb in on the other side of Demi, grabbing the sheet to pull it over all three of us. As soon as I settle, Demi turns over and throws her leg over mine. I slip my arm under her head and pull her close. Her hand rests on my chest over my heart and I reach for the light next to the bed.

"Leave it on, please," Demi calls out, her voice panicked, as her hand on my chest fists. I withdraw my arm back into the bed and lay my hand over hers.

"Anything for you." I let my lips brush over her wet hair and rest my chin on top of her head.

Bane rolls over, his chest against Demi's back. He throws an arm over her side, resting his big hand on her hip.

"Thank you for coming for me." Demi's words are a little slurred as she speaks. Exhaustion is finally taking hold of her as she snuggles into my body.

"Always," Bane whispers behind her. Demi's breathing evens out and she drifts off to sleep surrounded by us both.

She doesn't hear the bedroom door open as Jax looks in on us. I can see the indecision on his face. He knows Demi is his true mate, but it's almost like he still doesn't want to act on it. But if that kiss in the cave is anything to go by, he wants her as much as Bane and I do. He just needs a good smack upside the head. Tomorrow though, it can wait until then.

For now, I'm going to savor having Demi back in my arms. Jax leaves the room without a word. I grab the blood sachet off the table, trying my hardest not to jostle Demi as I move. I pierce it with my fang before I drink the entire thing in just a few gulps. With my hunger satisfied, for now, I drop the empty sachet back onto the table and rest my head back on the pillows.

I don't want to sleep in case when I wake up, Demi is gone again, and this has all been a cruel dream. But with the gentle rhythm of her heart and her heat spreading over me, I soon lose the battle.

Chapter 34

Demi

Nightmares of fangs, claws, and fur shatter my sleep. Gasping for breath, I sit bolt upright in the bed, pressing a hand to my chest as I try to calm my racing heart. A soft snore sounds to my left and I rub at my eyes, trying to dislodge the sleep from the corners of them. Bane is still lying next to me, his arm slung over his face and the wounds I can see are just faint lines of red.

I glance to my right, and Diego is there as well. His body is turned towards mine as he murmurs in his sleep. I'm home, I'm safe, the monsters are dead, I made sure of that by killing Rufus. I only wish he'd been made to suffer as much as the other women he had kidnapped, but it's too late to think about that now.

I lie back on the bed between Diego and Bane. My body and mind are exhausted, but sleep evades me. I let out a huff and notice how dry my mouth is. Trying not to disturb the guys, I crawl to the end of the bed and sit on the edge as I pull my robe tight around my body, redoing the knot on the belt at my waist.

"Where are you going, *tesoro*?" I turn to look at Diego. He's alert now, resting back on his elbows in a half-seated position.

"I'm gonna get a glass of water."

"Would you like me to get it for you?" Diego moves to sit behind me. His thighs rest on either side of mine.

He brushes my hair away from my shoulder, kissing down the column of my neck to my shoulder and I rest back against him. Diego's tongue darts out, licking at the point where the two meet. With his arms snaking around my waist, he clasps his hands in front of me and I rest mine on top of his.

"It's okay, I'll go." He squeezes me gently before loosening his grip on me, planting one last kiss on my neck.

Standing, I smile down at him and make my way out of my bedroom and to the kitchen. The only lights on are those above the breakfast bar, which is where I find Jax sitting on a stool, a glass of dark liquid in his hand and a bottle of the same in front of him.

When I get closer, Jax lifts his head, his green eyes boring into mine. He's a mess. Although he's showered and changed his clothes since he found me with the others, the dark circles under his eyes tell an entirely different story. His usually styled hair hangs limply down across his forehead. I don't know what possesses me, but I raise my hand and give him a little wave. His lips lift into a small smile, but it's gone all too soon.

"Can I help you, Demetria?" He sounds annoyed, like I've interrupted him.

"I... thirsty... water." I stammer the words out. *Way to sound like a moron, Demi.*

Jax stands abruptly and moves to the cupboard behind him to grab a glass before he takes it to the sink and fills it. Then he's in front of me, so close he's getting in my personal space. He holds the glass between us, and I snatch it from his grasp, taking a few steps away from him. I lift it to my lips and take a sip. The cool liquid slips down my throat, lubricating the dryness.

Fidgeting as I drink the water, I eye Jax. He doesn't move a single step toward me as his eyes drift over me from head to toe, his gaze making me freeze on the spot. A hand suddenly reaches toward me before he withdraws it again. He lets out a sigh before he turns and walks back to the breakfast bar. He picks up his glass and downs the contents before he refills it again.

Shaking myself out of my stupor, I walk over to one of the other stools and sit, keeping one empty space between us. Jax makes my body react in so many ways, anger and lust being the main two. I want to keep my distance at the same time as wanting to crawl into his lap and have him kiss me like he did in the cave.

"Now the wolves are gone. I'll get out of your hair in the morning. I know my presence irritates you." I'm not sure if that's entirely true, but he is so hot and cold with me all the time. How am I meant to know how he really feels?

"They don't want you to leave. Diego and Bane, I mean." He lifts the glass to his lips and takes a sip. I watch him out of the corner of my eye, noting the scowl on his face. "I think they'd follow you to the ends of the world if you gave them half a chance."

"This was never a permanent thing, though, was it? You only kept me here until you could deal with the wolves, and now you have. I have a life to go back to, a job, one which I'll be surprised to still have when I get back there." Jax shifts uncomfortably in his seat. He sets his glass back down, but I can see his fingers flexing around it as his knuckles go white.

"So much has happened since you dropped into my life, our lives, Demetria." He takes another sip of his drink. "I thought I wouldn't see you again when the wolves took you and I regret every decision I made until that point. I'd burn the world to the ground for you."

I'm taken aback by his words, my mind struggling to grasp what he means. My lips part and I start to speak, but he doesn't give me a chance.

"I've been alive for a very long time. Much longer than both Diego and Bane. I've loved and lost, so I refused to let the same thing happen again. Things were different when I was first turned. My sire had his own nest, his own children, long before humans knew anything about us. He was the true meaning of the word monster. He kept humans as his slaves, fucking and draining their blood whenever he felt like it."

Jax has my full attention now, I sit quietly.

"There was a woman, a human woman, and I grew to care for her. Maybe I even loved her, but she wasn't mine. I approached my sire and asked for his permission to turn her. We planned to run away together. I didn't want to be alone, but I didn't want to remain in the nest either. Somehow he found out though. One evening when I retired to my room I found her fresh corpse in my bed. I didn't want to risk getting too close and having you ripped away from me like she was." I reach my hand across the space between us and place it on top of his, his eyes cut to me before he looks down at our hands.

"I'm sorry that happened to you."

"After that, I didn't want to get close to another human. You're too fragile, your lives are so easily snuffed out. Then you entered the club, and then I saw you across the dance floor. I couldn't stop myself from approaching you. When Diego found you in that alley I swore to myself that I wouldn't give in to my feelings. But you crawled under my skin, Demetria."

"I don't understand. Half the time I don't know if you hate me, or if you just want to fuck me. You're so frustrating." I pull my hand away from his and rest it in my lap.

"Likewise. You're very being drives me wild, Demetria. I've never hated you, and I should have never let you think I did. That's on me." The fact I drive him wild excites me.

"I don't know what it is about the three of you. It's like there's a connection that I just don't understand. I glimpsed Bane on the door, and at first, he scared me. Then I saw

Diego behind the bar, and I couldn't stop myself from wanting him, even though he is one of the monsters I swore to stay away from. But you hurt me, Jax. You've been nothing but an asshole to me since I ended up here like I was some sort of inconvenience to you."

"I don't know how I can ever make it up to you, Demetria. But I will spend the rest of eternity trying if you'll let me."

"Eternity is a long time, Jax. Some of us don't get to live forever."

"Whatever time you will give me, I'll take." There's more he isn't telling me, but I don't want to pry. It's the first time Jax has really opened up to me about anything, I don't want to ruin it.

I rise from the stool and sway a little. Jax jumps to his feet and rests his hand under my elbow so I can steady myself. My gaze shifts to where his fingers connect with my skin, and I feel it again, that confusing pull to him.

"Come, you need to sleep." Jax leads me down the hall and back to the bedroom.

Bane and Diego are both still sprawled out on the bed, with a space between them just for me. Jax stares at them both, and the look of longing on his face only adds to my confusion. With a barely noticeable shake of his head, he brushes his lips against my forehead.

"Good night, Demetria." And then he's gone, leaving me at the threshold of the room.

Crawling back into the bed, I nestle between Diego and Bane and close my eyes. As if sensing my presence, they both shift closer to me. I lay my head on Bane's chest, and Diego wraps an arm around my waist. It's not long before sleep takes me.

Chapter 35

Demi

When I wake the next morning, my hands drift to where Bane and Diego should be, but their spots are empty, the spaces cold to the touch. Pushing myself up, I glance around my room. It's completely empty. I slip out from between the sheets and adjust my robe.

As I get closer to the door, I can hear shouting from the direction of the living room. My hand stops just before the doorknob, which has thankfully been replaced since Bane destroyed it. I'm not sure if I even want to go out there, too much testosterone is flying around the place.

Diego's voice is clear, and I can hear the anger in it. "She's our true mate, she needs to know."

"We can't keep her if she doesn't want to be here, Diego." Jax cuts him off before he can say any more.

I open the door and step into the hallway. What does Diego mean, I'm their true mate? I try to remember back to the conversation I had with Jax. He told me about wolves having true mates, but he mentioned nothing about vampires having the same. This is the first I've heard of it.

"Jax, can you just get your head out of your ass for more than five minutes? We don't know what Demi wants. Have you ever thought to ask her?"

"She told me last night, Diego. She's leaving today." Jax doesn't sound pleased. I only told him what I thought he wanted to hear.

"But did you actually ask her what she wants? Without being an asshole at the same time?"

"I..."

A shadow falls over me where I stand outside my room. I look up to find Bane standing in front of me. He doesn't say a word and as I go to open my mouth he places a finger against my lips, halting anything I was about to say. Bane takes my hand in his and laces our fingers together. With a small tug, he jolts me into action, and I follow him toward the voices.

When I step out of the hallway, the other two men shift their eyes to me. Diego's eyebrows are knitted together. But Jax is the one that confuses me the most. His mouth is tipped down and the circles under his eyes look worse than yesterday. I want to go to him and hold him, to wipe his sadness away and make him smile.

Bane takes me to the dining room table and sits me down. I curl a leg underneath me and lean my elbows on the surface, watching all three of them.

"Tell her, or I will." Bane looks over to Jax and he looks like a deer in headlights waiting for the inevitable crash.

Diego makes his way over to where I'm sitting and leans on the back of the seat opposite me.

"We want to give you a choice, Demi. That's all I've ever wanted. But I want to make myself clear right now, all I've ever wanted is you." Diego runs a hand through his already messy hair. "From the moment I first saw you, you've been it for me. True mate or not, I don't want anyone else."

"I don't understand." I look towards Jax. I need him to explain it to me. "What do you mean, I'm your true mate?"

"You're ours, Demi. The other half of our souls." Jax doesn't move from where he's standing. "I knew before these two did, but as I told you last night, I didn't want to get close to someone again. I don't know if you feel the pull like we do, being human. When you said you were leaving, I assumed you didn't."

"Wait a minute. That's what this is? The feelings I've had this entire time are to do with this true mate thing." I glare at all three of them in turn. "I thought I was going crazy wanting three guys. Yeah, even you, Captain Asshole." My gaze falls on Jax. "But now you're telling me it's because we're mates?"

I look at each of them waiting for some sort of confirmation. My hormones have been hell since I met these three, constantly horny and begging for release. Even the times I've spent with Diego wasn't enough to tame them. There has always been another part of me wanting to claim them, all of them.

"You'd be ours forever, Demi, and we'd be yours. We'd love you, protect you." Diego leans forward over the back of the chair, and I swear that any second he's going to jump the table to get to me.

"Explain forever to me."

"When a vampire finds his or her true mate, they must join together through sex and blood." Jax talks like he's reading from a textbook. I didn't realize there was a Vampire 101 for these kinds of things. "At the moment of climax, we'd exchange blood. Then our souls would connect. As long as your true mate is alive, you'd share their immortality."

"So I'd be a vampire?"

"No, it's slightly different from siring another vampire. You won't need to drink blood, no fangs, no claws. You'd still be entirely you, but with the added perk of living as long as we do." Diego chimes in, the look on his face is hopeful.

"That's why you wanted to turn the woman your sire killed, isn't it?" I aim the question at Jax, and he drops his chin.

"Yes. I knew she wasn't my true mate, but I came to care for her, and I didn't want to be alone anymore. The only way for her to live forever was to turn her, it was what she wanted too though."

There's too much information to absorb. If I bond with them, I become immortal, but not a vampire. I'd get to live forever. But it's not just one of them that is my true mate, it's all three of them. I can feel my heart pounding in my chest now.

"I need some time to think." I rise from my chair and all three guys track my movements.

"Demi..." Bane speaks, but I ignore him and take off.

Spinning on my heel, I run down the hallway and into my room, slamming the door behind me. I lean against it and take a few calming breaths. None of the guys follow me, so that's a bonus.

Come on, Demi, think.

I move to the closet and spot the duffle bags I brought my things in are still on the floor.

Without thinking, I grab them and throw both onto the bed. Grabbing everything off the coat hangers, I stuff the clothes inside before I raid the drawers and empty those as well. It's too much. I can't stay here. I have to leave. As I pack, I change into some jeans and a hoodie and push my feet into my sneakers.

Glancing around the room, I make sure I haven't missed anything. Once I'm satisfied that I haven't, I sling both bags over my shoulders and head for the door. Diego is waiting on the other side, his hand poised to knock.

"Demi..." he stops when he spots the bags on my shoulders. "What are you doing?" There's concern in his voice.

"I'm leaving. I can't stay here." I shove past him and march down the hallway.

When I reach the main room, Jax and Bane both look up at me. Jax doesn't react, but I can see Bane's features drop as he looks from me to the bags I'm carrying. He lets out a sigh and turns his back to me. The action breaks my heart, but I guess I brought it on myself.

"You don't have to leave, Demetria." Jax's voice is calm and collected like it usually is.

"I do, I'm sorry. I just can't do this." I head for the door but sigh when I remember I still don't know the codes.

A hand reaches over my shoulder and keys it in. I look over my shoulder at Diego and he gives me a small nod with a sad smile. When we reach the bottom of the stairs and exit into the alley, there's an Uber already waiting for me. I turn to Diego.

"I thought you wouldn't let me go."

"I can't keep you here, if that's not what you want, *mi amor*. I love you enough to set you free." With that, he leans forward and kisses me. I close my eyes so I can savor the taste of him.

I feel him pull away, and when I open my eyes again, he's gone. My fingers brush over my lips as I turn back to the Uber. Throwing my things in the back, I climb in and confirm my address with the driver. As I look over my shoulder at the club behind me, my heart shatters into a thousand pieces.

It's been five days since I walked out of their lives, and five fitful nights plagued by nightmares of all the things that go bump in the night. At this point, I think I'm pretty much running on coffee that I wish came in an IV bag. When I got back to work, Michael told me I looked like crap and wanted to know if I needed more time off work. I told him a firm no; I had to get back to my life and my job.

Walking into my apartment that first day was surreal. The last time I'd seen my home it was trashed, but I realized as soon as I swung open the door that someone had taken care of the mess for me. Every item that had been destroyed was replaced, and the new items were more than I could afford on my salary, especially the furniture. Even though I hadn't picked out the items myself, they were perfect, each one something I would have chosen.

There was a new door, which was a lot sturdier than my old one, and new windows had been fitted with secure locking points. I stood in my living room and did a full circle, trying to take everything in. Jax had told me he'd had my apartment secured, but this was beyond that. He must have known that eventually, I'd be leaving his place above the club.

Ginny's parents had called me the same day and told me they'd been trying to contact me. It killed me that I couldn't tell them what had really happened. The police had notified them of Ginny's passing, but of course, I already knew. Rufus had taken not only my parents but one of my closest friends. I attended her funeral alone, staying just long enough for the service and to say a final goodbye to my friend.

Stepping through the double doors and into the parking lot at the hospital, the wind ruffles my hair. I didn't even bother to sort it when I got changed. All I want to do is get home and have a long hot shower before I call for takeout and veg in front of the TV watching some trashy reality show that I know I probably won't pay that much attention to.

I'll most likely fall asleep in front of it again, only to be woken by nightmares and covered in sweat. Then I'll have to drag my sorry ass for yet another shower. When I reach my car, I unlock the doors and jump in, throwing my small backpack on the seat beside me. I automatically lock the doors before pulling away. The wolves might be gone but I'm even less trusting of the world and the monsters within it.

But not those three. They will never be monsters to me. They were my saviors, my heroes, and God, I miss them. If I could turn back time I never would have walked out on them. I should have told them I needed time to think over everything they had told me, that I wasn't giving up on them. But it's too late now.

I drive home on autopilot and don't even notice until I'm already parked outside my apartment building. I grab my stuff and head inside, moving up the steps at a snail's pace, exhaustion weighing heavily at my limbs.

Locking up my car, I head inside and engage every lock that is now fitted to the inside of the door. I drop my things on the couch and head for my bedroom. After stripping off my clothes, I throw on my bathrobe and tie it at the waist before heading into my kitchen. I grab the already open bottle of wine from the fridge; I started it last night and I definitely plan on finishing it. Pouring myself a generous glass, I take a sip. It's sweet with undertones of honey, just like Diego's blood.

The thought of my tattooed vampire has my heart shattering all over again. I want him, and the others, more than anything. My heart and soul calls for them, but I don't know how to approach them again. I walked out of their lives, and I can't imagine they will ever want me back. Diego told me that he loves me, and I think I love him too. I love all of them in their own way.

There's a thud outside my apartment door, and I flinch. My heart rate increases as panic sets in. I've been on edge since I left them; the lack of sleep and the sheer amount of coffee I've consumed isn't helping matters. Slowly, I edge towards the door, my bare feet silent across the hardwood floor as I get closer to it.

Looking through the peephole, the hallway outside looks empty. Nothing seems amiss at all, but I have this sudden compulsion to open the door and investigate. Placing the glass of wine on the side table, my hand edges closer to the locks. With shaking hands, I undo them one by one, until all that is left for me to do is to turn the handle and open it.

Come on, Demi. Suck it up. The wolves are gone.

Shaking my head, I grasp the handle and pull the door open. I don't see him at first. It's not until my eyes drop that I notice legs sticking out to the left of my door. A familiar pair of baby blues look up at me.

"Bane? What are you doing here?" I squeak. Shifting on the floor, he stands slowly, his huge figure looming over me.

"I need to keep you safe." His words are simple and straightforward.

"You've been watching me since I left?" I thought I had felt someone watching me, but it wasn't in a creepy way.

"Yes." Bane takes a step forward and I take one back. I don't know what I'll do if he gets too close, probably jump him.

"Do you want to come in?" With a small nod from Bane, I step away from the door and give him room to cross the threshold. I pick up my glass of wine and down the contents as he shuts the door behind him.

Bane is in my apartment, and I don't know what to do. Has he been watching me because he wants to make sure I don't get into any more trouble, or is it something else? *Admit it, Demi, you want him to be here because he wants you.* Arms wrap around my waist and his body presses up against my back.

"I missed you."

"Missed you too, big guy."

Chapter 36

Bane

With my arms wrapped around her slender body, I finally feel like I'm home. I've spent the last five days following her, making sure she's safe. All she's done is work, but I followed her there, and then on to her apartment, where I sat outside inside Jax's car. Occasionally, I walked the edge of her property just to make sure everything was in order.

Things tonight were different, though. I watched from the shadows as she got home from work. She looked bone tired, dragging her feet up the steps until she shut the main door of the building, and something snapped. I approached the building and let myself inside with the spare key Jax had made. I could sense her inside her apartment as she moved around so I sat outside her door. My plan was only to stay here until the morning and I would leave before she realized I was even here.

Demi must have heard something though because the next minute she was on the other side of the wood and then she had opened it and stared down at me. She looked like a deer in headlights, shocked to find me outside her home.

"I couldn't stop myself." Demi twists herself around in my arms, her turquoise eyes looking up at me. "I needed to see you."

My lips slam down on hers, covering her mouth as I lift her. Her legs come around my waist and I settle my hands under her ass, supporting her weight with ease. Licking across the seam of her lips, she allows me entry and I take it. My tongue tangles with hers, and a rumble emits from my chest. Demi's hands fist in my hair as she tugs at the strands.

When I break the punishing kiss, her lips are swollen. Her tongue darts out and runs along her bottom lip. My cock hardens as I watch her. I want to devour her, but I need to know what she wants first. I slide her down my body until she is on her own two feet again.

"Demi, the bond." Her eyes widen and her eyebrows furrow. "I want you to be mine, to be ours."

"Bane... I..." She stutters before snapping her mouth closed again.

"If you don't want to be my mate, tell me now." I reach my hand up and lay it against her cheek, and she leans into my touch. "I'll leave if that's what you want."

"No." She snaps. "I want you, all of you. I just needed time to think. I've had that now. I'm yours, Bane. Your mate."

She wants to be mine. She's accepting me as her true mate. We're both moving at the same time as she slams her body into mine. I lift her bridal style and Demi's lips are on me in an instant. Her arms wrap around my neck as I carry her into the bedroom. I'm next to the bed in a second and I lower her to the edge.

Demi sits back on the mattress, leaning against her elbows as she looks up at me. I rip my t-shirt over my head and my hands reach for my belt. Undoing it, I pop the button on my jeans and pull the zip down over my throbbing cock. I hiss as the fabric slides over my sensitive head before dropping my jeans and boxers to the floor. I toe off my boots and kick them away before stepping out of my jeans.

Licking her lips, Demi's eyes focus on my erection, and I can't stop myself from groaning. I step closer to the bed as she shuffles up the mattress as I kneel over her. My body covers hers and my arms encase her on either side as I slide between her open thighs. My mouth is back on her lips as I shove my tongue inside her mouth and tangle it with hers again.

Demi's fingers move over my body, tracing up and down my skin, and I groan at the sensation. My cock brushes against her clothed mound and I swallow her moan. I break the kiss and lean back on my knees. I run my hands up the sides of her legs and feel her tremble beneath me. When I reach the knot of her robe, I undo it slowly before letting it drop open.

It slowly reveals her skin to me as the fabric parts. She still bears the faint scars from what the wolves did to her. I trace my fingers over the silvery skin on her neck and she shudders, taking in a deep breath. I dip down to her breasts and tweak her hardening nipples between my fingers. Leaning down again, I engulf one peak with my mouth, swirling my tongue around the point whilst my fingers play with the other.

Demi's panting now, her legs shifting against mine, and I can smell her arousal. I shift my mouth to her other breast and give it the same attention. With a pop I pull away, and take in her nipples as they glisten with my saliva. I start to kiss from her breasts down to her torso, moving closer to her intoxicating scent.

When I reach her panties, I kiss her just above the waistband. I hook my fingers into the top of the lace and pull them down her legs. Lifting the blue lacy fabric to my nose, I inhale deeply; the fabric is drenched in her arousal. It's only then I realize they are the panties she pushed in my face at the store. A chuckle escapes me as I drop them on the floor.

"What's so funny?" My gaze shifts to Demi, and she's staring up at me. Her turquoise eyes are now almost completely navy with lust.

"Nothing." Before she can ask any more questions, I part her legs further and drop my mouth to her pussy.

One lick is all it takes before Demi is moaning again. I delve my tongue inside her and I thrust it in and out. She's already dripping, but I need to get her ready for me. I withdraw my tongue and she mewls, but that stops when I push a finger inside her. I curl it up and must hit the right spot because her body nearly jumps off the bed.

I push another finger inside her, thrusting them in and out as I lick around her clit. Demi grabs onto my hair holding my head in place as I lap at her. I add another finger inside her, stretching her. My cock rubs against the bed and I groan. The vibrations must do something to Demi because the next minute her walls are clenching on my fingers as she comes all over them.

As I pull them from her, she whines and I grin. Demi's eyes are glazed and I move up the bed until I'm over her again. I grasp my cock and run it through her slickness, coating my entire length. I position myself at her entrance, lock my eyes with hers, seeking permission, and she gives me a small nod.

I push inside her tight, wet pussy inch by inch. Her walls are still clenching from her release, and I almost lose my load inside her. *Amateur.* Demi's body is gripping me so hard it takes a moment for her squeezing to stop as she stretches around my girth to accommodate my size. I bottom out within her and I need a second to calm myself. Demi grips my upper arms and squeezes, encouraging me to move.

Wrangling back my self-control, I draw out a few inches before I plunge back into her. Our moans fill the bedroom, and Demi keeps her eyes on me the entire time as I thrust. Her legs wrap around my waist and she urges me on. The feral part of me that's linked to the fact we're true mates rears its head and I know when she looks at me all she will see is red eyes, and my fangs digging into my lower lip. It pushes me to claim her fully.

With one hand still on the bed beside her head, I move the other to the back of her leg and pull it away from my waist so it lies against my chest. I leave my hand on her thigh and squeeze. My claws catch the soft skin. A yelp from Demi almost has me slowing, especially when I smell her blood, but it soon becomes a moan and I pick up my pace once more.

Demi grabs onto the back of my head and yanks me down. Her lips press against mine and as I groan, she pushes her tongue inside. It flickers over my fangs and my thrusts get quicker, my grip on her thigh tightening. Her back arches and her breasts rise as I push us both closer to our orgasms.

I know I'm close now. My fangs are aching to taste her blood and complete the bond. Our bodies are covered in a fine layer of sweat. The sounds of our skin slapping together, our moans and my heart thundering in my ears is all I can hear. I break the kiss and gaze down at her.

"Are you sure?" I ask. I need to know that I can complete the bond, that she's okay with it. Though even now, I'm not sure I can stop.

Demi doesn't answer, she just tilts her head to the side, exposing the slender column of her neck to me. I strike, my fangs puncturing the skin. Her blood explodes across my tongue, and I shudder. Each pull of her blood has her pussy tightening on my dick. Demi bites into my neck with her blunt human teeth but they aren't sharp enough. I take my hand from her thigh and slash it across my neck. My blood flows freely from the wound and Demi's lips cover it as she takes a gulp.

Lightning flashes down my spine and my balls draw up. With one last hard thrust, I spill my seed inside her as we continue to drink each other's blood. Her walls clench around my cock, milking my entire length. That's when I feel it, like a tether springing to life between me and Demi. It snaps together and I can feel her in my very soul. I experience her pleasure too as our bond is cemented.

My mouth pulls from her neck, and I roar. I continue with shallow thrusts as we both ride out our orgasms. Demi no longer drinks my blood, but her tongue laps over the closing wounds at my neck. I lick over the marks my teeth made as they heal as well.

I can feel her emotions and even get a glimpse of her thoughts as they tumble through her. For me, I feel whole, like a part of me that I didn't even know was missing has been reunited inside me. The grin that appears across my face makes my cheeks hurt, but I don't want to stop. I've never felt as comfortable with anyone as I do with Demi - she completes me.

We're both panting now and when I roll us onto our sides, my softening length still inside her, I can see the love in her sparkling eyes.

I've wanted this fragile human since I first saw her entering the club, her very being called to me from the start. When I found her in the alley with Diego, I thought I'd lost the chance, but the Fates brought us together and knew it wasn't her time to go yet. All I can hope now is she will accept my brothers as she has me.

"Mine," I growl.

"Yours, always."

I pull her in for another devastating kiss. Our bodies tangle together, and we beam in the afterglow of the true mate bond.

Chapter 37

Demi

I've never felt this way about anyone. There has been something pulling me towards Bane and the others since I first saw them. As a human, I don't think the true mate bond feels the same way as it does for the supernaturals, but there is something there drawing you to them. As the bond tethered Bane and I together, I could feel him everywhere.

Not just inside my body, but inside his mind. The sheer elation I could feel coming from him hit me like a wave, and it only increased my own happiness. It's like the missing part of my soul has been found, and I'm home. But even now I can still feel the tug towards the others.

Bane and I shower together, cleaning the sweat and blood from our bodies, only for us to come together more than once and have to shower all over again. When we're finally dressed again, I curl up beside him on the couch. He holds me close to his body as I finish my bottle of wine and we leave the television on in the background.

His hands trail over my body and I have to do everything in my power to not strip him down and let him take me all over again. The fresh bond is a potent thing, but it's still not complete. Crawling into Bane's lap, he curls his arms around my body as I lick up the side of his neck, where I drank his blood. Taking a path up to his ear, I lick around the lobe, and he shudders.

"Take me home, Bane." He pulls me back from him and stares into my eyes.

"Are you sure? We could stay here a little longer." I give him a nod.

"I need them as much as I need you. I don't feel complete without them." Placing his hands on my ass, he lifts me and stands, walking us into my bedroom.

Bane sets me down and heads for my closet, pulling my clothes from inside and throwing them on the bed. I grab my bags and fill them until I almost can't close the zips. There is more stuff I could take, but for now, I only need some clothes. At least, I'm hoping I'll not need them once I bond with the others.

I move to grab the bags but Bane takes them for me. I glance around my apartment; I've lived here since I left my parents' home and haven't known anywhere else. I spot the pictures of me with my family, as well as one of Ginny and me. I grab them both and hold them close to my chest. My family is all but gone now. My gaze shifts to Bane; I have a new family now.

"Let's go, big guy." I lace my fingers with his and we walk out of the apartment building.

"Demi. Good to see you." I spot Agnes as she walks up the steps loaded up with grocery bags.

"You too, Agnes. I just wanted to let you know I'll be moving out in the next few days. But if you ever need anything, please call me." The older woman smiles and looks at mine and Bane's joined hands.

"Ah, I see. I hope you plan on making an honest woman of my girl." My eyes widen at her words.

"We're not getting married, Agnes." I laugh. Bane squeezes my hand in his.

"Oh, hush now, dear. I can see the love this man has for you." Agnes shakes her head at me.

"I will protect her with my life, Agnes. We don't need a piece of paper to tell people that we love each other." Bane beams.

"That's all I need to know." Agnes gives Bane a nod. "But let me tell you right now, if you don't treat my girl right, I'll come after you with my broom." The thought of tiny Agnes going after Bane makes us all laugh.

I let go of Bane's hand and wrap my arms around Agnes, giving her a squeeze. She doesn't hug me back with the amount of bags she's carrying, but she leans into me. When we break apart, there is a huge smile on her face.

"Goodbye, Demi." She stares past me at Bane. "And you keep her out of trouble." If only she knew.

Shuffling inside the apartment, Agnes lets the door close behind her and we head for Jax's car. I'm surprised I didn't notice it when I got home earlier. I look at my tiny car down the street.

"I'll get Diego to come back and get it for you," Bane says before I can even utter a word.

We both get in, and I throw my seatbelt on. We hold hands for the entire drive across town to the club. The sun is setting, and the sky is painted with oranges and reds as it sinks beyond the horizon. Bane pulls up outside and helps me out. The anxiety is real now; the thought of seeing Jax and Diego again sets my nerves on edge.

Bane easily accepted me back, but what if they don't? Diego, probably would, but I'm still not sure about Jax. I'm in love with them both, but I'm not sure I can handle the rejection from either of them.

"Don't worry, they both still want you." Bane must pick up on how anxious I am, perhaps through the bond, but his words are comforting.

With my bags in his hand, he opens the bottom door and we head up the stairs. I want to run toward them now. I need to see them and complete the bond with them both. The door at the top of the stairs is flung open, and Diego stands in the doorway. I stop on the landing and take him in.

"Diego..." His name whispers through my lips as I fling myself at him and wrap my arms around his waist, burying my head into his chest.

"*Mi amor*." His words whisper against my ear and he nuzzles close to me. "Please say you will never leave me again?"

"Never again." The words tumble from my lips. Diego inhales, his nose pushed into my hair.

"You already bonded with Bane. I can smell him on you." Diego leans back from me. His hands trail up and down my arms and I shiver. "Does that mean?"

"It does. I want you, all of you." A huge grin appears on Diego's lips, and he lifts me into his arms as he spins on the spot.

Diego carries me inside the one place I've truly thought of as home since my parents died. Not a lot has changed since I left, apart from a few empty bottles of liquor on the coffee table. He takes me straight down the hallway, but we bypass the room I stayed in previously. He kicks open another door and carries me inside.

Lowering me back to the floor, I take in his room. It's a similar setup to the room I stayed in but with much darker furnishings. Diego reaches for the zip of my hoodie and lowers it slowly. He peels the fabric from my arms and lets the offending material fall to the floor.

I pull his t-shirt over his head and kiss down his chest, my tongue following the path of his tattoos to his waistband. I make quick work of the fastening on his jeans and peel the material down his legs. As always, he's commando underneath and his cock springs free, bobbing in front of my face. Pre-cum beads on the end and I can't stop myself from licking him clean. My tongue flickers over the ring through the head.

Diego moans as I lick the metal, and I swirl my tongue around his entire length. Before I can fully take him in my mouth, he grasps under my arms and pulls me to my feet. He works at the zip and button on my jeans as I kick off my shoes. He pulls them down my legs helping me to step out of my jeans. I stand in front him in just my underwear as a shiver runs through my body from the chill in the room.

He hooks his fingers in the sides of my panties, ready to rip them, but I place my hands on his to cease his movements. Diego glances at me, a smirk lifting the corner of my lips. Instead, I push his hands away and remove my own panties. I raise back to my full height once more, and undo my bra, letting it join the rest of my clothes on the floor.

Diego stalks around my body, his hands trailing over my skin leaving goosebumps in their wake. I clench my thighs together and I can feel my arousal dampening them. He stops at my back and presses his body up against me. His erection pushes against my ass and my legs quiver in anticipation of what is to come.

His featherlight touch skirts down my sides to my hips. Diego grasps one and pulls me so my back is completely against his front. His other hand moves across my stomach and down to the apex of my thighs. Using his foot, he nudges my feet apart, and his cock slides between my legs, slipping through my juices, but he doesn't enter me.

The fingers now between my legs brush against my clit and the only thing stopping me from falling from the jolt of pleasure that wracks through my body is the hand on my hip. After lubricating his fingers, he pushes one swiftly followed by another inside my tight pussy. A moan escapes my lips as I throw my head back to his shoulder. His chuckle echoes around the room.

"You're so responsive to me, Demi." His fingers continue their torturous rhythm.

Diego pushes me until I can't take any more. My orgasm is so close, but before he lets me finish, his fingers pull out and I whimper at the sudden emptiness.

"Get on the bed." He demands, withdrawing his hold entirely from my body. "No one will stop me claiming you this time."

On weak legs, I make my way to the edge of the bed. I lie down on my back and watch as Diego fists his already swollen cock. He pumps his length as he approaches. Letting go of his length, he takes hold of my legs and flips me onto my stomach, drawing my hips up so I'm on my knees with my elbows resting on the mattress.

The head of his cock breaches my entrance as my fingers grab at the sheets. Diego slowly pushes inside my body. When he reaches the hilt, we both sigh. My face turns to the side, resting my cheek on the bed as Diego begins at an agonizingly slow pace. His length slides in and out of me. The metal on the underside of his cock sends waves of pleasure through my body.

Picking up speed, Diego grabs onto my hips, holding me still as he pounds into me. My moans fill the room along with his grunts. I can feel the pull now, the bond demanding we complete it. Our hips clash together as we come together. Diego wraps a hand around my throat, his fingers caressing my skin as he pulls me up, so my back is against him.

I can feel my orgasm building. I'm so damn close to completion. His fingers trail around the side of my neck and I tilt my head to the side. He brushes my hair aside and bares my skin to him. My heart is pounding in my chest, and I know he must be able to hear it. Diego's lips sweep across my pulse, and his tongue darts out, lapping over the vein. He sucks on my skin hard enough to leave a bruise.

Fangs scrape across my neck, sending shudders through my body. But then they are gone again. Diego's arm wraps around my shoulder, and his bloody wrist stops in front of me. I watch in fascination as it gathers on his skin. My hands wrap around his wrist on either side of the puncture wounds his teeth have made and bring it closer to my lips.

"*Te amo, mi vida, mi alma.*" The words of love are whispered into my ear and then he strikes.

Diego's fangs sink into my vein as my mouth covers his wrist. The first draw of his blood tastes so much sweeter than when I've drunk from him before. He sucks my own blood into his mouth and shock waves flood their way through my system all the way to my core and I explode. My orgasm rushes through me, and my teeth dig into Diego's wrist. Wrapping a hand around my hip, he withdraws his cock until only the head remains before he slams back inside me, triggering his own orgasm.

His warm seed coats my insides as he growls against my neck. The bond detonates between us and the tether joins us together. Love cocoons me as his emotions flood me, and I bask in the sensation. Diego's hips don't stop, he continues to thrust inside me as he pulls at my blood, prolonging my orgasm until I collapse on the bed. His body drapes over me and he laps at my neck.

"I can't wait to spend forever with you, *mi amor*."

My body is weak from having bonded with two men in such a short amount of time, but I feel safe and content as my eyes close. Diego slips out of me, his cum dripping down my thighs as he rolls me onto my side and wraps an arm around me.

Chapter 38

Jax

The apartment smells of sex and her. Bane texted me ten minutes ago to tell me she had returned. I think I ran every red light to get here. Inhaling her scent, I glance around the living room expecting to find her but I only spot Bane sprawled across the couch, his head laid against the back of it and his feet crossed at the ankles on top of the coffee table. I clear my throat and he tilts his head in my direction.

"She's here?" I question.

"Yes." Bane pauses. "With Diego." He gestures down the hallway, where the smell of sex is the strongest.

"And I take it you completed the bond?" He nods in response and my teeth grind together at the thought of not being the first to complete the bond with our sweet Demetria.

"I did. Diego too." A smile plays on Bane's lips. "She claimed us both."

I have no idea if she will let me bond with her. Why would she when she has Bane and Diego already? I let her down the most; I pushed her away when I should have loved her like the others did. I wouldn't blame her if she rejected me now.

Storming down the hall, I head straight for Diego's room. I burst through the door and he jumps off the bed, glaring at me. He steps in front of the bathroom door where I can hear the shower running. Dried blood coats the inner wrist of his left arm and my gaze hones in on it, a growl rushing from between my gritted teeth.

"Get out and take Bane with you." I take a step closer to him.

Diego smirks at me and grabs his clothes off the floor, pulling them on. He swaggers towards me with a smirk on his face. Stopping just in front of me, he squares up to me.

"You better not hurt her brother, or you'll have me and Bane to deal with." Shoulder checking me as he walks out of the room, I listen as his footsteps grow quieter before I hear murmured voices and the apartment door opening and closing.

I strip off my clothes as I move toward the bathroom. I open the door and walk inside. The room is full of steam, but I can see Demetria through it. Her pale back faces me as she runs shampoo through her dark hair. I watch as the muscles in her back flex as she moves, and I bite my lower lip. My feet carry me closer to the shower until I step in behind her. Her movements falter for a brief second.

"Jax." She whispers my name but still doesn't turn to me.

When I'm directly behind her, I reach out my hands and run them down her waist to her hips. Demetria continues to run the soap across her skin. My fingers trace around her sides and up to her breasts and she sighs at my touch. Gathering the soap up, I move my hands over her body, washing every inch of her I can reach.

Demetria turns with closed eyes and steps back under the spray, leaning her head under the shower head and letting the water rinse the lather from her hair. Opening her eyes, she lowers her head so she can look at me. A small smile creases the corner of her mouth and she licks her lips.

"It's about time you got here, Captain Asshole." She chuckles, and I cringe at the use of the nickname she's given me. "I was beginning to think you didn't want me."

"I've always wanted you, Demetria. I just didn't want to admit it." She reaches her hands up and rests them on my shoulders.

"Then you better prove it." There's a glint in her eyes as she stares at me, challenging me.

Grabbing behind her legs, I lift her straight off the floor and slam her into the tiled wall. She's so wet already that she slides straight onto my cock as I lower her. We both groan and I kiss her, her fingers tangling with my hair. She thrusts her tongue inside my mouth and takes control of the kiss. My hips flex as I pump inside her, her body bouncing up and down from the sheer force of my thrusts.

My pace is brutal and Demetria thrashes against me as I conquer her body, pushing not only mine, but also her body to the limit. Her fingers claw at my skin, leaving crescent moon dents all over but my tongue continues to plunder her mouth. The bond pushes me to complete it, and as much as I wanted to take her in the comfort of my bed, I can't stop myself.

Demetria's walls clench at my cock, squeezing me tight, and the sensation sends electrical shocks through my entire system. Pumping wildly inside her, her moans fill the room. I grab her hands and push her wrists against the wall, holding them with one hand as the other drifts between us, flicking at her clit.

My mouth trails down her neck to the swell of her breast and I sink my fangs into her. Her blood explodes across my tongue and her pussy tightens its hold on me. When I pull my mouth away, I lick my way down to her nipple, dragging her blood in a trail as I go. I scrape my fangs over the sensitive bud.

"Fuck..." Demetria rasps out above me, her hands pulling at my grip on her wrists, but I don't let go. "Jax... please."

"Please what, Demetria?" I rasp as I lick at the blood now coating her breast.

"Make me yours..."

The claws on my free hand extend and I dash them across my neck. My blood spills from the wound. Demetria's gasp has my eyes moving to her face and she's staring at my blood as it falls down my neck and chest and her walls contract again as the motion of my hips never slowed.

My fangs extend fully as my gaze shifts to the column of her neck. I can practically see her pulse thrashing just below the surface. On pure instinct, I move closer to her, but before I can even sink them into her pale skin, she lunges forward. Her mouth latches onto the cuts on my neck and I follow suit.

Demetria's taste of honeysuckle floods my mouth and I take a long drag at her nectar. With my eyes closed my hips stutter as she sucks at my neck. My thrusts increase, and her body writhes against mine. Letting go of her wrists, I grab her hips, using them to lift and drop her onto my length as I pump inside her. Demetria's orgasm hits just seconds before my balls draw up, my cock pumping my seed deep inside her. Her body milks me for all I'm worth.

The bond snapping between us drives me to my knees and I do my best to protect Demetria as I fall. Her hands latch onto my shoulders and she continues to ride my cock, edging out her orgasm and taking the last of her own pleasure. Fireworks burst behind my closed lids and her emotions overwhelm me. Demetria is content now all three bonds are complete. I can even feel the tethers that splinter from her to Diego and Bane too.

Lowering myself to the ground, I lie on my back. Demetria lies against the front of me, my cock still deep inside her. Signs of our coupling leak from between her thighs as she nuzzles against my neck. I brush her hair from her face and look up at her. My mate, my love, she is the most precious thing to me now and I'll do anything to protect her.

Demetria's hands push into my chest, the movement sends twitches through my length and I harden within her.

"Round two, already?" Her hair forms a curtain on her face as she looks down at me and I chuckle.

"If that's what my mate wants, I won't tell her no." I smile up at her and she raises a few inches off me before she pushes back down my length. A moan escapes between her lips before she bites down on it. "God, you're beautiful."

Demetria sets a steady pace, her hands on my chest as she takes me within her. My hands lay on the floor of the shower as she has her way with me. Her breasts sway with each thrust, the blood lingering on her chest as the shower pours down over the two of us. She reaches her hands into her hair, pushing the strands away from her face as her back arches.

The tiled floor bites into my back, but I can't even think to care. Her supple body has my full attention, and I can no longer stop my urge to touch her. I wrap my hands around her hips and help guide her movements as she loses herself to the passion. My hips rise each time she drops down onto me and every time I reach the hilt, her walls clench as she moans.

Demetria's movements start to falter and I have to take over. I thrust up into her, my hands still on her hips.

"I need you to come for me, Demetria." I rasp between groans.

One of her hands drifts down her chest and abdomen until her fingers rest over her clit. My gaze drifts to where she touches herself as she circles the nub, speeding up her touch until she explodes over my cock. I hammer inside her, chasing my own release, and when it hits, I can feel it in every fiber of my being.

Demetria collapses on my chest as my cock still twitches inside her. One hand lies over my heart, her fingers ghosting over my skin. I gather her in my arms and stand, dipping us both under the still running water. I carefully place her down on the small bench at the back of the shower and reach for a cloth. Wetting it, I drop to my knees gently slide it over her mound, cleaning up any evidence of our lovemaking.

Once she's clean, I step back under the shower and soap up my own skin. When I'm done, I turn off the water and glance at Demetria. She looks ready to fall asleep where she's sitting. I step out of the shower and wrap a towel around my waist before I grab Diego's robe from the back of the door. I help her stand and wrap it around her wet body, tying it at the front.

Lifting her again, her head falls against my chest and I exit the bathroom. Diego is standing just inside the doorway, a smirk on his face as he looks from me to Demetria and back again.

"Why not just fuck her in my bathroom? Way to woo our mate." He shakes his head at me, but I can hear the laughter in his tone.

"Shut up, asshole." I stride past him and out into the hallway.

"Hey, don't let Demi hear you calling me that." He calls after me. "You're the designated Captain Asshole in this family." His laughter follows me as I kick open the door to Demetria's room.

Lying her down on one side of the bed, I slip in beside her and put the sheet over us both, the towel still around my hips. I shift the sheets so they cover us both, her head against my chest, and my arms wrapped around her.

"I love you, Jackson." She murmurs against my chest.

"And I you, angel."

Chapter 39

Demi

It's been three weeks since I bonded with all three of my men, and since then I've emptied my old apartment and moved in. I've claimed the room Jax gave me in the beginning as my own but I'm never alone. At least one of the guys sleeps with me every night, sometimes even all three of them. Jax is forever snarking about how little room there is. It doesn't help when Diego likes to push Jax as close as he can to the edge until he falls off, leaving Diego and I in fits of laughter. We even manage to pull a grin from Bane.

Heading out of the locker room at the hospital, I pass Michael on the way out and give him a little wave. He smiles at me from across the desk in the ER. I haven't told him about any of the guys yet, only that I've moved.

"See you tomorrow, Doctor Scott, Angela." I glance at the nurse sitting beside Michael. Angela gives me a smile before turning her attention back to the computer, but I don't miss the way she's watching Michael out of the corner of her eye. She's totally got the hots for him, but I don't think he even realizes it.

Stepping out of the double doors, I inhale a lungful of air, happy to be heading home after such a long shift. The sun is still low in the sky as it rises and a warm breeze brushes against me. I pull my phone out of my pocket and check the notifications. There are a few missed messages in our group chat. Diego telling me he will pick me up after my shift, Bane complaining that it's his turn to come get me, and Jax telling them to shut up before he smacks them both upside the head. A soft laugh peels out from my lips as I read through their antics.

`You can come to get me tomorrow, big guy.` I add a kissy face before hitting send.

`Promise?` Is the only response I get.

I'm about to send another text back when arms wrap around me from behind, hugging me against a hard body.

"I missed you, *mi amor*." Diego kisses the side of my neck, and I let out a small moan. "I can't wait to get you home and into my bed. But first," He slings an arm over my shoulder, "breakfast."

Diego leads me out to the car. He's taken to using mine because he's never had his own. Bane usually picks me up on his bike, and Jax in his BMW, but as they like to drive me to and from work, Diego just stole my keys one morning. I climb into the passenger seat, and Diego gets in next to me.

"So, how was work?" I ask.

"Dreadfully boring without you there." When I have days off or work earlier shifts, I like to spend a few hours helping behind the bar. Spending time with Diego and Harley is always fun, and I'm enjoying getting to know some of the other staff who work at the club.

"Which means you've spent the night winding up Harley. How many times has she smacked you this time?" I laugh.

"I have no idea what you mean." Diego starts the engine. I raise an eyebrow at him. "Fine, five times." He replies as he drives out of the parking lot and down the street.

"You're never going to learn, are you?" He has far too much fun messing with Harley. Diego loves nothing more than to comment on the way she shakes her ass to get better tips or tease her when she fills us in on her many conquests.

We drive for a few miles before Diego pulls up outside Mandy's. It's a cute little mom and pop diner we discovered last week on my lunch break when I was craving waffles and bacon. The food is amazing, but the prices are even better. I'm out of the car before Diego can even open the door. He appears at my side, takes my hand in his, and leads me to the door.

Holding it open, I scoot inside and drag him to my favorite booth. Diego sits with his back to the window, and I perch opposite him. The sun shining through heats my skin and I pick up the menu. I already know what I want but I like to check it out on the off chance something has been added.

When the server reaches our table with her pad in hand, I've already placed the menu back on the table.

"What can I get you guys?" She stands poised and ready to scribble down our order.

"Two coffees, and two of the waffle and bacon stack, please." Diego knows exactly what I want.

After noting down what we want and grabbing the menus, the server disappears again, leaving me and Diego alone.

"I'm so hungry. We were so busy earlier I only had time to grab an apple and an energy bar from the canteen." Diego looks a touch displeased, but he knows how it is in the ER sometimes. You don't always get a chance to eat much more than snacks.

Our coffees arrive and I add sugar and caramel creamer. Taking a sip, it's like ambrosia… well, almost. Ambrosia would be the guys' blood. We don't need to exchange blood anymore, but it makes my orgasms much more intense. Diego tastes sweet with hints of honey. Bane is like liquid heat, and Jax's blood is spicy and rich. Just the thought of letting me taste them again has me squeezing my thighs together and Diego inhales sharply, his gaze fixing on me from across the table.

"And what are you thinking about, *corazón*?" That devilish smile he's wearing has me rubbing my thighs together again. At that very moment, my stomach rumbles and Diego chuckles. "Breakfast first, then I'll feed you something else."

Our food arrives quickly after that and I practically inhale it, only stopping occasionally to add more maple syrup. When our plates are cleared, Diego throws cash, including a tip, onto the table and slides out of the booth. He takes my hand and pulls me out of my seat heading for the door. When we reach the car, he pushes my back against it and kisses me hard, thrusting his tongue between my lips and I moan. A wolf whistle comes from somewhere on the other side of the street and we break apart.

"Fuck, I need to get inside you." His voice is rough as he speaks.

"Take me home, Diego." He pushes away from me, and I clamber into the car, struggling with my seatbelt as I attempt to click it into place.

Diego gets in, starts the engine, and guns it down the street, heading for the apartment. We pull up outside and both dash out of the car for the door at the bottom of the stairs. I key in the code as he kisses the side of my neck, his hand squeezing my breast through my hoodie. It takes me three attempts to get it right before the locks disengage and we stumble through it.

Climbing to the top of the stairs seems to take forever, but this time Diego takes control of entering the code and we get in on the first try. Two doors down, and one to go. We reach the apartment door, and it opens before us. Jax stares at us both, noting my heated cheeks before his gaze drifts to Diego's growing erection.

"One job, Diego. Pick Demetria up from work and feed her so Bane and I have time to finish." Jax shakes his head at us and steps out of the doorway to let us both inside.

"Wait, finish what?" My brain suddenly realizes what he said.

"A surprise." Bane steps out of the hallway. He's wearing shorts and not much else, and I almost drool at his appearance. I turn my gaze to Jax, and he quirks a brow at me, a mischievous grin adorning his lips.

"I hate surprises."

"Oh, I'm sure you will love this one. I know I certainly will." Jax wraps his arms around my waist from behind and pushes me towards the hallway and past Bane.

He leads me to my bedroom, with Diego and Bane trailing behind us. When we're outside, Jax covers my eyes and I hear the door open. He slowly walks me inside before taking his hands away again. I gasp when I see what is in front of me. The queen bed that used to be in here is now gone. In its place is an enormous bed, big enough for all of us. The sheets are pale blue and navy, and there's a whole pile of pillows against the headboard.

"Oh my God, it's perfect." I squeal as I turn and throw my arms around Jax's neck.

"Yeah, no more of Jax whining when he falls out." Diego snickers.

"You mean when you push me out?" Jax retorts.

"Wanna test it out, *mi amor*? All of us?" My gaze shifts to Diego and I lick my lips. At some point, he removed his t-shirt and jacket, and his jeans are now undone, revealing the thin thatch of hair below his snail's trail.

"Definitely." I tear off my clothes, and I can hear the rustling of my guys dropping their own clothes to the floor behind me.

Without even waiting for them, I rush to the bed and jump on the mattress, sinking down into it. As comfy as my other bed was, this one is so much better. I roll onto my back and look at my guys. They are all standing at the end of the bed as naked as the day they were born, their cocks already hard and the ends glistening with pre-cum. Diego already has his hand on his length, pumping it with his fist.

"Get on the bed behind her, Bane. Make sure our mate is close to the edge," Jax orders.

Bane prowls closer to the bed. His blue eyes are almost inky pools as they rove over my naked body. He slides behind me, shuffling me forward so my ass is on the edge of the bed. He places a leg on either side of me, and his erection pushes into my back. His hands move up my stomach to my breasts, his fingers massaging them. When he pinches my nipples he has me moaning.

"Diego, get her ready for us."

Diego is the next to approach the bed, but Jax stands just inside the doorway, watching us all. Diego drops to the floor at my feet. He bends my legs so my feet are on the edge and pulls my knees open.

"You're so wet already, *corazón*." Diego runs a finger through my wetness and brings it to his mouth, licking the digit clean. "You taste delicious."

With my legs open for him, Diego devours my pussy. Like a man starved, he licks and sucks, nipping at my clit with his blunt teeth. My thighs clench around his head as Diego delves his tongue inside me. Bane massages my breasts still, his fingers tweaking my nipples, but Jax just watches us, his gaze flickering from Diego between my legs and Bane's movements on my breasts.

Diego pushes two fingers in and my back arches as he alternates between his tongue and his digits. My orgasm rushes through my body and I scream out as the sensations take over. Diego shifts back onto his knees, his lips and chin are glistening with my release.

Jax is before him in seconds, his hand curls around Diego's throat and pulls him to his feet. Their lips connect and Jax groans. He splits them apart and licks up Diego's chin before plundering his mouth once more.

They are a sight to behold, their naked bodies brushing together as they kiss. I clench my thighs again and let out a moan.

"Do you enjoy watching them, Demi?" Bane's hands work their way down my body, his fingers trailing through my leaking juices.

"Yes," I squeak.

My pussy is still tingling from my orgasm, but that doesn't stop Bane from pushing two thick fingers through my folds. My toes curl and I throw my head back against his shoulder, closing my eyes as he licks and bites up and down the column of my neck.

"Watch them, my love." My eyes snap open and I lift my head to do as Bane orders.

Bane continues his exquisite torture; his fingers thrust in and out of me at the same pace as my two men do the same with their tongues. Their bodies rock together before Jax slips a hand between them and grasps both of their cocks in his fist. They swallow each other's moans.

I can feel myself getting closer again, the sight of my men taking pleasure in each other driving me all the way to the edge, but Bane's thumb on my clit is what finally pushes me over. Who knew you could come twice so close together?

When my eyes open, Diego and Jax are standing at the end of the bed, staring down at Bane's fingers deep inside me. They look like the predators they really are; their eyes are fully red and their fangs peek out from between their lips.

"Is she ready for us?" Jax's eyes dart from my pussy to Bane behind me and I feel his nod against my shoulder. "Take what's yours, Demetria."

Bane removes his fingers and flips me over so my body is laid against his. His hard length is sandwiched between us as my thighs fall on either side of his. With my knees on the bed, I perch myself above Bane. Reaching a hand between us, I grasp his length and he groans as I run it through my juices.

With the head of his cock at my entrance, I lower myself down onto him. There's a sting of pain as my walls stretch around his girth. My gaze falls to him, and his eyes are already fully red. His lips are parted, and I can see his fangs glistening in the light. I take just a small portion of him inside me before rising back up to his tip and working my way down him further.

A moan leaves my lips when I am fully seated on him, and I place my hands against his chest to steady myself. There's movement behind me as Diego crawls up onto the bed. I gasp as Diego's tongue licks from where I'm joined with Bane and up between my cheeks, teasing my rosebud.

I've had anal once, and it wasn't the most pleasurable experience, but then I'm not even sure the guy knew what he was doing as he rammed inside me without much preparation. Diego however seems to know exactly what he's doing. His fingers mop up the wetness from around my pussy and he swirls it around my back hole as his tongue laps at me.

Bane starts to thrust slowly in and out of me as Diego plays with my rear entrance, Bane's fingers curling around my breasts and he squeezes my nipples. My breathing comes out in shallow pants as he works me into a frenzy. Diego removes his tongue and I whimper, but he soon replaces it with a finger, carefully working it inside me to the first knuckle.

Even then the small intrusion has my entire body shaking, Diego pushes in further, curling his finger as he does. Once he can enter without much resistance, his one finger becomes two and I can't help the shrieking sound I make. My fingers dig into Bane's chest as my hips jolt as he thrusts into me.

"Are you ready for me, *mi amor*?" Diego pushes his body against mine. I can feel his cock brushing against my ass and I nod.

Bane lets go of my breasts and grabs my arms, he pulls me high enough so his length is pulled out entirely, but another cock fills me as Diego thrusts himself into my waiting pussy. His fingers still pump inside my ass as he fills me over and over again. His piercings rub against my insides and Bane's length nudges against my clit.

With quick movements, Diego pulls out his fingers and cock, and he slams me back down onto Bane's waiting length. Diego runs his throbbing head against my rosebud and I can't stop my body from clenching.

"Relax, Demi." Diego's voice whispers against my ear, his tongue darting out and licking down the side of my neck.

Diego pushes the head of his cock through the tight ring of muscle and my pussy tightens around Bane's length as I come, all three of our moans echo around the room. Diego lays his hands on my hips as he rocks inside me, his length slipping further inside me as my orgasm still holds me in its grasp.

I'm so full right now, my body is being stretched to the max. Once Diego is fully seated within me, they stop moving, letting me get used to the sensation of them both inside me. When the slight pain turns to pleasure, I start to move, rocking against their length. They work in tandem, one plunging in while the other withdraws.

A shadow appears to my left. Jax is standing at the side of the bed, his cock in his hand as he strokes himself. The swollen head is weeping and I can't wait to get a taste of him, my tongue darts out and licks my lips and I hear his groan mixed in with those of the others. Jax climbs onto the bed and brings himself closer to me. His hand reaches out and his finger brushes across my lips.

I don't even wait for him to ask me to do anything, I take his cock in one hand and guide him to my waiting mouth. I lap at his head, licking up the pre-cum there and he shudders. My lips seal around him as I move up and down on his length. With Diego and Bane sliding in and out of me, it isn't long before the pace is set.

Jax starts pumping his hips, jerking his cock into me as I suck and lap at his silky, smooth length. He tangles his fingers in my hair, tugging gently on the strands. The push and pull of all three of my guys thrusting inside me makes me spiral out of control. Our moans, slapping flesh, and pants are all that can be heard around the room.

My orgasm hits like a tidal wave, my body contracting around Diego and Bane's members and they both start coming alongside me, their seed filling me. Jax tightens his grip on my hair, his cock hitting the back of my throat as he comes. His cum rushes down my throat and I struggle to swallow as my own release still seizes my body.

Jax slips from my mouth, brushing the leaking cum from my lips. He goes to move his hand away, but I pull his finger into my mouth and suck him clean, keeping my eyes on his as I do. Diego carefully removes his cock from my ass, his seed dripping down my thighs and helps me maneuver off Bane as Jax disappears into the bathroom. Diego pulls me into his arms and I collapse against him. His lips move to mine as he hums with pleasure.

"He tastes good on you, *tesoro*." I know he's referring to Jax, especially after that little display earlier.

I jump in shock as something warm and wet brushes between my thighs. I look and see Jax with a washcloth between my legs, cleaning up the mess the other two have made. He smiles at me as he works, before throwing the used cloth into the laundry hamper across the room.

Diego has already claimed the bed on one side, one arm under my head with me curled up against his chest. Jax crawls next to me on the other, his body wrapping around me with his chest against my back. Bane has already settled himself behind Diego, his arm over him and his hand now resting on my hip. It's like one great big puppy pile.

I never knew this was something that would happen to me. I never expected I'd have a real place to call home again with people who love me, who would die for me. So much tragedy led me to this very moment, but it gave me three guys who I have fallen irrevocably head over heels for. My heart is theirs and will be for eternity because we have all the time in the world now I'm vampire kissed.

Epilogue

Two months later

She never should have left me. She should have known I would always come for her. I spent weeks journeying to her location. I had first expected to be able to follow her through scent alone. They couldn't have taken her too far, but her scent disappeared just outside the cave entrance. What she didn't know is that we implanted trackers in all of our stock in case any of them escaped.

I'd hit Blackfoot only a few days ago, following the flashing marker on my tracker until it led me to this very building. The structure is immense; it looks like an old rundown church. Or at least that's what the magic born would have you think. The stone walls are crumbling, and the windows are all boarded up, but I bet once you step through the barrier, the appearance will change drastically.

I've been watching the comings and goings of those who live and work here for a couple of days. My plan was to capture one of them and force them to bring her to me. But that's no longer the case. I saw her a few hours ago when she met another woman at the edge of the barrier. They spoke in hushed tones, and the women hugged before they waved goodbye.

The same woman returns an hour later with an old, rundown car. Black smoke spews from the exhaust, and the engine stutters as she pulls up. The woman locks up the car and walks through the barrier, reappearing a few minutes later. She makes her way down the driveway as I follow behind her. Once she reaches the point where the drive meets the road, I jump from my hiding place. My weight takes her to the ground.

Closing my mouth over her neck, my teeth puncture her jugular and throat before she can scream. Her blood gurgles as she takes her last breath. I release her throat, licking the warm liquid from my lips. Latching my teeth around her foot, I drag her to the edge of the trees and into the woods beyond. I take her far enough that she won't be seen from the driveway.

My woman's scent hits my nostrils and I inhale deeply. She must have stepped past the barrier. It's the first time I've caught her scent since the night of the blood moon. I take off, running back to my original position. She walks around the car and pops the trunk, throwing a small suitcase into the back before closing it.

She wears a black beanie over her long blond hair and far more clothes than I like to see her in. Once I get her back, I'll make her walk around naked all the time. And as her belly swells with my pup, I can watch as her body grows. If I were in my human body right now, just the thought would have my cock hardening.

Her eyes turn to the trees where I lie on my belly inside the shadows at the edge of the treeline. She can't see me though. With a shake of her head, she climbs into the car and shuts the door behind her, pushing the lock down. Not that it will stop me. The engine turns over, and she switches on the lights. They light up the driveway, but I hide in the shadows where the illumination doesn't quite reach.

Dropping the car into gear, she pulls away from the building, leaving the safety she's known for the last few months. I take off from my hiding spot and follow her along the driveway till she reaches the end, her blinker flashes, signaling she is going right, and I wait. The car shifts away from the stop line and out onto the main road.

As soon as she hits the highway heading East, I know exactly where she's going. Her current direction puts her aiming for the wolf sector. That's where I'll strike. That's my domain. She'll never see me coming, and when I have her, I will never let her go again. I'll let her think she's safe. I can follow her using the tracker.

For now, I'll head back to the room in the seedy motel that charges by the hour. Not that I paid for it myself. I took great pleasure taking out the occupier and the whore he was fucking, but not before I sated myself in her body.

Don't worry, little bitch. I'm coming for you.

Afterword & Thanks

You did it, you made it to the end. Let me tell you, this story really took a toll on me. Demi was an absolute pain in the behind. I told her she needed to be a little traumatised and she asked me to hold her beer and just went for it. Would you believe that I actually wrote some of the darker chapters while watching Chicago Med and not even paying much attention to what Demi was actually doing, bad idea folks! Even I was a little shocked when I read back through those bits!

Now, what can I say about this book other than the fact it was one hell of a ride. I couldn't have done it without the help of my amazing beta team; Hayley, Theodora, and Tori. They whipped my book into shape and spent hours going over some of the same bits, again and again, to make sure everything was perfect.

A huge thank you to Blue Crescent Book Covers, who just happened to have this cover and another as part of a duet. As soon as I saw them, the characters started appearing and I haven't looked back. Hajer spent so much time helping to tweak this cover, so it was just right and you will get to see some more of her amazing covers through the rest of this series.

To my editor Maxwell, from BBB Publishings. He's been with me from the start of my journey in the publishing world and I adore working with him. He goes above and beyond, and even though I freak out every time I send my stuff off for editing in case he hates it, he always leaves me a super encouraging message on the document, which really lifts my spirits. The whole team from BBB are absolutely amazing and not sure what I'd do without them.

My proofreader, Mich, she's one of my favourite people in the world. I've known Mich for a long time and she should be super proud of me that I didn't use the word 'channel' in relation to a woman's private area. She totally kicked my ass for that one last time.

And lastly to my readers, without you guys, authors would be out of a job. If you made it this far, I really appreciate the fact that you took the time to read my story and get to know these characters.

About Author

Powered by tea and sarcasm.
S Lucas is a self-published indie author, who lives in the UK with their significant other. When they are not writing they can be found either reading, blogging, or sitting behind a sewing machine making costumes for various events around the country.
After completing NaNoWriMo for the first time in 2020 with the completed story of Against the Odds, they were set on the track of publishing their very first book.
You can find S Lucas at:

Facebook Page: https://www.facebook.com/authorslucas
Facebook Readers Group: https://bit.ly/2VucxSE
Amazon Author Profile: https://amzn.to/3wuOEbJ
Bookbub: https://www.bookbub.com/profile/s-lucas
Goodreads: https://bit.ly/2VnBoHT
Instagram: https://www.instagram.com/slucasauthor/
TikTok: https://www.tiktok.com/@slucasauthor
Website: https://slucasauthor.wixsite.com/home

You can also join my newsletter if you want to hear the inner ramblings of my mind: http://eepurl.com/hqyy8P

Also By

Odds and Expectations

Against the Odds
Defying the Odds

Printed in Great Britain
by Amazon